Soul Hunters
The Collectors of Fear

BENJAMIN MOLLENHOUR

Burning Bulb
PUBLISHING

Soul Hunters – The Collectors of Fear
By **Benjamin Mollenhour**

Burning Bulb Publishing
P.O. Box 4721
Bridgeport, WV 26330-4721
United States of America
www.BurningBulbPublishing.com

Cover photo by Dimart Graphics, used under license through Shutterstock.

First Edition.

Paperback Edition ISBN: 978-1-948278-35-5

Printed in the United States of America

PART ONE

CHAPTER 1

Finals week for thousands of college students in Central Florida stressed out not only the students, but all the teachers that would have to rush to grade many exams, papers, and final projects. Summer was coming but with one week to go, most students were cramming for their finals preparation. Jackie was one of them. She sat at her wooden desk in front of her desktop computer in her dorm room. She stared at the screen, watching the mouse icon blink repeatedly in the same location for a couple of minutes. She finally removed her eyes from the screen and looked out the window to her right, forcing herself to blink. She shut her eyes for a moment while her face remained directed outside. She reopened her eyes and looked towards the sky. Her dorm was on the third and top floor of her building. If she stood by the window, she could look down at a small yard where there was a picnic table where often students studied or barbequed. She was too busy now sitting at her desk to know what was happening there today. She continued to look at the blue sky with a randomly shaped white cloud slowly gliding by on the clear summer day. She sighed, disappointed that she was stuck in her dorm while the weather was so nice. She wasn't motivated and had been studying for three hours already that morning. Jackie had a roommate but she was away at the library studying. She turned back towards her monitor and placed her hand on the mouse and scrolled down to read more notes. She began reading when suddenly she was startled when her phone rang. She looked over towards her phone next to her bed and stood up from her plastic rolling chair and walked over to it. She sat on the edge of her bed and picked up the phone.

"Hello?" Jackie said, putting her other hand in between the phone cord to play with it by twisting it around, waiting for a response.

"Did I wake you up?" A familiar voice asked.

"Hey, Preston. No, been studying a few hours already."

"Wow, really?" Preston asked. He wasn't actually surprised since he had known Jackie for three years and knew she was a good student and studied often to ensure she got good grades. Preston, on the other hand, had just awoken and lied in bed. He could see through his curtains that the sun was bright and the day was nice. Preston was a 'B' student and he didn't mind while Jackie thrived to get straight A's.

"You just waking up?" Jackie asked. She could hear in his voice that he was still a bit groggy. "It's almost ten o'clock, you should be studying!"

"Eh, I'm fine. I'll study later. So, what are you doing? Studying?"

Jackie laughed, "Of course. I have a test in four days on Wednesday. Algebra has never been my best subject so I need to study a lot for that one."

"Yeah, mine either. I hate math but what else do you have planned today?" By now Preston had gotten out of bed and held his cordless phone between his shoulder and cheek and started to get dressed.

"Just study," Jackie said and pulled back on the phone cord and let go of it like a slingshot.

"That's it? Such a nice day," Preston replied as he moved his curtain to the edges and revealed the bright sky. "I have the weekend off and the day is too great to waste. What do you think I get you out for a few hours and we do something?"

Jackie thought for a few seconds, knowing she had to study and focus on her upcoming math final but she was already having a hard time concentrating on her notes having studied three hours. "Yeah, I guess a break would be nice," she finally said.

Barely finishing her sentence, Preston blurted out, "Remember that old abandoned drive-in theater across town?"

"Ah, yes, of course I do. We planned on going there and sneaking in on our next day off. Wait…"

"Are you thinking what I'm thinking, Jackie?"

"Let's go!" She said excitingly. Both her and Preston loved history and even though there weren't many abandoned places or historical areas in Central Florida where they lived, they often dreamed of traveling the world and seeing the historical ruins from Greece, Rome, and even the ghost towns of the American West.

Preston and Jackie met three years prior as freshmen at the University. They both attended an Ancient sports class together which taught the Olympics, Ancient Roman sporting events and the evolution of ancient sports. They sat next to each other from day one and formed a friendship and studied together. Finding out they were both going for a history degree, they often had the same courses and spent a lot of time with one another but remained only friends.

"I'll pick you up in an hour," Preston said, giving time for him to finish getting ready and to drive to her dorm. Preston lived in his own studio apartment, fifteen minutes away from Jackie.

"Sounds good, don't forget your camera," Jackie said. Preston enjoyed photography but in the past had forgotten his camera at the most inopportune times.

"You know me well!" He chuckled and replied. "It's sitting on the stand by the door."

CHAPTER 2

Fifty-five minutes had gone by and Jackie had finished getting ready and read through more notes on her computer. She was again startled when she heard a knocking on her door. She walked towards the door and looked through the peephole and saw Preston standing there. Preston wore a cotton muscle shirt since it was going to be hot and had a baseball cap on. He was skinnier than the average weight and not overly tall. His demeanor showed those that saw him to be a kind and caring young man. He was always smiling and made sure those around him were all doing fine. Jackie saw him going through some papers he was holding in front of him when she then opened the door.

Preston put his papers in his hand and saw Jackie and smiled. "You all ready?" He asked.

Jackie had her hair done in a ponytail and jeans on with a regular cotton t-shirt. She hadn't showered since the previous night but knowing that it would be hot and she would sweat again, she didn't shower before Preston got there. She was comfortable around Preston and never felt the need to dress up or put on makeup or be self-conscious.

"Looking good as always," Preston said which made Jackie blush – he was being honest. She could feel her face begin to blush and turned away. Preston had always had a bit of a crush on Jackie but they knew that friendship was the best option for both of them for now, anyway. That didn't stop Preston from seeing the true beauty in Jackie and he loved her brown hair and how her hair matched her brown eyes.

"Come in," she said. "I got two bottles of water ready." Jackie went towards her bed and sat down and put on her canvas shoes. She tied them and stood and was ready to go. They each grabbed a bottle of water on the foot of her bed, left her room and walked down the hall to go downstairs. While walking, Preston told Jackie what he had found out.

"So, this place is a bit hard to find and the old entrance is really overgrown," Preston said.

"How do you know where the entrance is?" Jackie asked.

"There isn't a whole lot of information on it because of what happened. The town let the trees and brush and other overgrowth take over the site since no one dares to build on the land. Just the nearby residents of the retirement home are all that there is. On the opposite side of the block though is a small opening, and walking a bit further back into the trees, the old road is supposedly visible."

"How do you know this?" Jackie asked as Preston opened the passenger side of the door for her to get in. She had heard a little before about the theater's past. He closed her door and went to get in the driver's side and started his car. Once the car started and he turned on the air condition, he reached into the backseat and grabbed a few pieces of paper and handed them to Jackie.

"Here, the first one is an aerial map I printed off. It's not very clear but you can still see the two roads where the theater sits on the corner. The entrance, which is the same as the exit, is barely seen in the photo. There are little remnants you can see through the trees, which should lead to the actual site of the old theater."

"Okay, yes, I do see it a little," she said and looked up at Preston. Preston looked serious with his eyes staring at the paper as he continued to point at the map until he noticed Jackie looking at him. He turned his head and saw her gazing at him, smiling, which made him quickly smile also. Jackie turned back towards the map and said, "Looks like we'll have to park a little down on the side street so we're out of view, too." Preston nodded. "At least it's a quiet area."

"That's what I was thinking too," Preston said as he backed out of the parking space he had parked in. He put the car into drive and made the first turn, having about twenty minutes of driving until they got to the site of the theater.

"So, tell me more about the fire," Jackie said.

"There isn't much history on it since the town seemed to want to forget the event. But, finding old newspaper articles on microfiche in the library, I did some research on the event." "What did you find?" Jackie asked impatiently in anticipation as they drove down the highway.

"Well, thirty years ago in 1964 there was a big fire in this theater, as you know. The fire was due to arson. There was a premiere of a big film and the theater was sold to capacity, nearly 80 or so cars. The newspaper reported that 178 people were killed and only two survived. The premier was so large that there were some cars still waiting to get in when the movie began to play."

In town, there was only one drive-in theater and a single screen cinema down main street. The drive-in was always popular since in Florida, the weather was nice year-round except for the summer humidity and mosquitos. Besides weather elements with rain and storms and heat that interrupted business once and a while, the theater was usually sold out – especially on weekends.

"How did the fire start though?" Jackie eagerly asked and fidgeted in her seat, looking at the second sheet in the papers Preston had - a bad black and white copy of a photograph someone took at the theater itself back in the early 1960s. She had already forgotten about her final and was excited to get out of her dorm a while to relax and rest her mind.

"Well, the main problem was with so many cars waiting to get in and having to turn around due to the theater being maxed to capacity when the fire began, the cars couldn't leave. Since the exit was where the entrance was, cars entering couldn't turn around fast enough to let the cars out that were attempting to leave. The traffic jam caused so much pandemonium to the point that no cars could leave with so much congestion. Sadly, as well, the fire began at the entrance and exit of the theater. The cars that could leave at first were stuck due to the other cars waiting in line attempting to turn around and leave when the fire got so bad, people tried to flee by foot."

"But how could there only be two survivors?" Jackie asked.

"I read that before the fire got too bad and overwhelming, the man at the ticket booth left his small booth to help direct traffic when a car trying to leave hit him and ran him over. The car then ran into the ticket booth when they were t-boned by another car, blocking the entrance and exit. Then the fire spread so fast with the trees nearby the fence that blocked the roads and outside from people peeking in and watching the movie. The fire also became so large due to the cars catching on fire and the gas which caused much combustion and the fire to spread to other cars. Smoke overtook the atmosphere and people couldn't see nor knew which direction to run. Two were lucky enough to be close to the entrance before the fire became worse while everyone else burned to death. One man who was there by himself pulled out quickly in his red truck. I remember reading it was a red truck because it was a little higher up so he was able to drive off the street and avoid other cars to get out alive."

"Wow. I can't imagine the horror. The saddened and sickening screams of everyone trapped," Jackie said and looked down in sadness and shook her head. She looked back up at Preston as they approached a stoplight. His eyes remained focused on the road, glancing every so often at the blue sky ahead of them and being ready to enjoy the nice day. "Did they ever catch who did it?" Jackie asked.

"No, they never did from what I read. There were only the two survivors that were in the theater from whom both said very minimal since everything happened so quickly. One man I remember did mention that the fire began by the entrance and exit and caught fire so fast and spread throughout, he got into his truck, left, and never looked back. The other witness and survivor never mentioned what he saw. Even when questioned by police, he only responded with, 'the horror…the horror…' and never spoke of anything else." Preston paused for a few seconds before he continued, "The others who were in the cars outside and fled by foot said they remember seeing big flames start at the entrance and everyone in line leaving. Explosions started happening with so much gasoline everywhere. Most of the outside survivors survived but no one witnessed what truly happened inside besides the two that escaped."

"Wow," Jackie said and paused for a moment, looking around at some farms near the road. They had just turned off the highway and were approaching closer. "It's amazing that the town kept something so tragic so quiet. I can understand why they would want to forget it."

"Me too," Preston agreed. "Keep your eyes out for the retirement home soon. It's not very big I guess but it was built next to where the drive-in theater used to be.

Another minute went by as they both continued to look around. "Wait, I think I see it," Jackie said once Preston turned another corner.

"You're right, that has to be it," Preston said. "I think we're here. Let's pull up around the corner straight ahead and as you said, we should park a little further down the road."

They proceeded around the corner of the retirement home and parked about a half a block down near the heavily forested area. There was rarely any traffic down this street since there was nothing around besides the retirement home so there wasn't any need for people to come to this area. The street was old and cracks lined the pavement. They parked on the dusty side just off the street. They both looked around, making sure that there wasn't anyone else nearby but they couldn't see anyone.

CHAPTER 3

"Pretty quiet and spooky out here," Preston said.

"Seems to be. Much quieter than my dorm," Jackie replied, thinking about how noisy everyone was in the hall and surrounding rooms. They both got out of the car and Preston stretched before shutting his door and walking around to go to Jackie's side.

"Don't forget your camera!" Jackie yelled at him as he shut his door. They both remembered the previous year when they went into an abandoned hospital to take photographs and walk around the eerie building but Preston had forgotten his camera.

Preston returned to his side of the car, used his key to unlock the door and opened it. He reached into the middle console and picked up the camera. "Got it!" He yelled before locking and shutting his door again.

They started walking slowly down the street, looking around at all the surrounding trees. Preston held onto his camera and had his aerial photo folded up in his pocket. He wore a small backpack that held both of their bottles of water since it was hot and humid. They looked around at the tall pine trees and palm trees dispersed within the forests that surrounded the land.

"Such a beautiful day," Jackie said, interrupting the still in the air. The area was so quiet that not even the breeze could be heard. Preston nodded in agreement.

"Here, Jackie," Preston said and pointed at the map he had unfolded and was looking at. He then pointed straight ahead as they walked in the direction of the corner that they had turned at. "I think this is it, through the trees over there." He glanced back down at the map and was sure they had found the entrance.

"Let's check it out!" Jackie said excitedly and started to jog to the area Preston pointed at.

"Wait for me," Preston said and followed behind her. They both stopped after jogging a couple of hundred yards once they got near what looked to be the entrance. They stopped on the side of the street and looked around once again for any people or traffic but didn't see anyone yet. They turned to the old entrance of the drive-in and looked straight ahead. The drive-in theater used to be a large space where cars could drive in and park but the area was surrounded by trees for one primary reason, to keep people from parking on the street and peeking in to watch the movie without paying. The large trees were banished during the fire but the land now had been overwhelmed by thirty years of foliage and trees. The entrance was hard to define due to the overgrowth but ahead, they could see signs of the drive-in.

"Look straight ahead, you can see part of the old asphalt leading through those trees," Preston started. "Wait, look over there to the right," he then said and pointed.

Jackie looked to the right where Preston was pointing and saw a part of the retirement home building. The building was built about a year after the fire next to the theater. After some criticism from locals, the owner who wanted to build the retirement home said it was prime land that was quiet, surrounded by forests to bring tranquility to the retirees. Also, the land was rather cheap after what had happened.

"You can see the retirement home from here," Preston said quietly.

"Oh yeah, wait!" Jackie blurted loudly. "There's an old man looking at us," she said quieter. "We're not supposed to be here."

Preston looked closer and saw the man standing on the end unit outside on his porch. They couldn't see if the man saw them but they noticed he was older after seeing a white beard and a bit of white hair on top of his head. He was tall and lanky, wearing jeans and a flannel shirt.

"Keep walking, Jackie," Preston said. They both immediately walked and looked straight ahead, not acknowledging the man they saw, hoping he wouldn't tell anyone or call the police. They got into the trees and out of plain sight and what they saw made them forget about the man.

"We made it, Preston," Jackie said.

"Yeah, look down at that asphalt, though." Preston pointed ahead of them and took a few steps each direction, looking at a couple of different pieces of the road that was filled with cracks, roots and trees coming from the weakened road. The dark, ash-colored asphalt instantly reminded them what had happened in that area thirty years earlier. Preston had his camera in his hand and started taking pictures of the road and the trees, waiting a couple of seconds between each picture to let the film process. "Stand there, Jackie," Preston said. Jackie turned around and saw Preston pointing the camera at her. She tilted one knee and stood at an angle with her arms in the air and posed while he took the picture. "Beautiful as always," he muttered under his breath while taking her picture.

Jackie heard Preston mutter the word 'beautiful' and asked, "How do I look?" She smiled upon asking him. She knew that Preston was attracted to her but with herself so focused on school, she didn't want a relationship at that time and wouldn't think it fair to whoever she dated since her main focus was on school.

Preston nervously stumbled his words and didn't know how to answer her but finally said, "You look great!" He smiled as they both kept walking. They walked down the dark road, watching where they stepped to not trip on a root or crack and looked straight ahead and saw them coming into a large opening. They walked in silence for a moment and looked around until they reached the large opening.

"Wow," Jackie said, enamored at the area she was looking at.

"I can't believe how this area was once a drive-in theater. The screen is long gone after being burned and seeing the dark pavement is eerie," Preston said and got his camera ready to take a few more photographs.

Jackie leaned down and touched the asphalt, turning her fingertip black. "It's almost like this ash is still fresh. Look at my finger."

Preston looked over and saw the black on her finger. He gently grabbed her hand and brought it closer to him to look at it. He then reached down and touched the asphalt for himself which released ash onto his finger also. He looked at it curiously for a few seconds before he wiped it on his shirt and began to walk around. He looked around, seeing numerous trees and a variety of aged flora spread throughout the area. The fence that was in-between the theater and trees was gone after it burnt in the original fire with even more trees growing throughout. The theater held a maximum of eighty cars within four rows of parking in front of where the screen once stood. The cars would park on the pavement with metal poles on the side of each one that held the speaker. There were a handful of poles still coming up from the ground and intact while a couple of others had been knocked down and bent from the chaos of traffic once the fire had started.

"Come here," Preston yelled to Jackie. Jackie was still wondering how the black ash had survived so many decades of Florida rains and storms and still came off with the slightest touch. She looked up and saw Preston standing and taking a photograph of the corner. Jackie walked over to him, looking down and noticing the edges of her semi-clean white shoes were getting dirty due to the ash.

"Is this where the screen once stood?" Jackie asked.

"It is," Preston said after taking the photograph. He walked around the grassy area to see if anything remained from the screen. There were a few burnt metal pieces strewn around the area from the old screen. "Now, I can see why so many people were trapped here," he said and looked at all directions of the opened area. "The fences were so high and nowhere to go but the entrance and exit. The road is so narrow and with so many cars in this vast area, if the fire started there, everyone would be trapped for sure."

"I agree," Jackie said when looking around the land. "Wait, do you hear that?" Faint sounds began to be heard as the sound of cars surrounded the area but they couldn't see anything.

"I hope that old man didn't call the cops," Preston said when he remembered that man and thought the cops were there. He looked through narrow openings between the trees to see if he noticed any flashing of police cars.

"Oh, no, you think so?" Jackie asked as they both fidgeted by looking both ways to find a possible way to hide or escape without being caught. Suddenly, the engine noises got louder and the sound of honking began. Jackie and Preston were unsure where the noises were coming from but stood still and looked towards the entrance, waiting to see if they can see a glimpse of cars driving by.

"What's going on?" Preston asked as they continued to hear the roar of engines but stood still – listening where the cars were coming from.

"I have no idea, maybe there's an event going on nearby?"

"Like, an antique car show? The engines sound really strong and loud," Preston said.

As they stood still, continuing to wait to see what happened, the noises began to get closer. Suddenly, a light was emitted from behind them as Jackie was the first to turn around and look. She turned and what she saw made her stumble and fall. Preston saw her fall on her side and seeing she was okay, he noticed a bright light on her face and out of the corner of his eye so he turned around and saw what Jackie saw.

"What? What is the screen doing here? Jackie! What is the screen doing here?" Preston asked nervously, his voice quivering in shock.

"I…I don't know. I mean, it wasn't here a minute ago. You said it had burnt down in the fire." When they turned around, the screen came out of nowhere and stood while projecting light as it did thirty years ago. Suddenly, as Preston continued watching in amazement, frozen, the screen began playing a cartoon of a dancing box of popcorn. Jackie slowly stood up and watched the screen alongside Preston when the noises of cars began to approach closer. Preston turned around and saw cars entering the area.

"Jackie, are you seeing this?" Preston asked and Jackie turned around. "Look, there are cars; actual cars that are visible. I can see through them, is this my imagination? Do you see them too?" Preston asked worriedly since he didn't know what was happening.

"Um, yeah, I see them too," Jackie said in a slow, loud voice since the cars were getting louder and it became harder to hear.

CHAPTER 4

Cars slowly came down the road into the theater and began parking. Jackie and Preston could hear the sound of chatter, people laughing, and children playing but could not see anyone.

"How, I mean, how are these cars here? This can't be real." Preston said to Jackie. "What is happening?"

"I don't know. Where are all the people?" Jackie asked. They both stood in the same spot and continued to watch as driver-less cars entered and parked in the area.

Suddenly, the sunlight from above which lit up most the area beside where trees provided shade became darker. The sky was overtaken by dark clouds and the wind began to blow. The wind became so powerful that Preston and Jackie clenched and held on to one another and closed their eyes. They walked together, holding each other tightly until they got to a large tree nearby. They knelt down at the base of the tree for a few moments until the wind stopped abruptly.

"Is it done?" Jackie asked as she slowly opened her eyes and looked at Preston. Preston opened his eyes and looked back at Jackie. He saw her eyes looking at his which made him smile – especially thinking that the storm was over.

"I think so," he answered back. They both helped each other stand up and looked at the area and saw all the cars parked in the parking spaces.

"Look at all these cars, this can't be happening. All these classic cars crammed in here," Preston started to say after realizing all the cars were from the 1960s and earlier. "Look at the screen, Jackie, there's a movie that looks to be starting," he said and Jackie looked over at it.

They slowly walked towards the cars as they remained standing near the area of the screen. The sounds of cars running, people talking, laughing, and children playing all remained but yet no people were seen. Preston and Jackie held each other's hands as they slowly walked and looked into the cars.

Where are all the people at?" Jackie asked.

"I don't know. I have no idea what's happening." Suddenly, after Preston spoke, the wind began picking up again. With the winds increasing in speed and power within seconds, screams started to be heard as flames started to rise near the area. Preston looked towards the entrance where the flames started and saw a man.

"Jackie!" Preston yelled to get her attention over the noises of the screams and cars as the cars began to start their engines. "Look! There's a man running from the fire holding a gas can."

Preston continued to watch the man from a distance and saw the man throw a can into the fire near the entrance. The can combusted and the fire spread increasingly to the cars nearby. Jackie could barely hear Preston and crouched down, unsure of what to do. "That's the man who started the fire! Look at him, Jackie." Jackie still could barely hear Preston and looked towards the flame anyway to see the commotion happening. "Jackie!" Preston said again and she looked up at him from a hunched position. "Do you see him? He just got into a big red truck."

Jackie stood up to hold onto Preston. There were no other people around and Jackie saw the man get into the truck. "I see him, he is the man," she said loudly to overcome the noise. "The big red truck, like you had mentioned. Now, look!" She said to get Preston's attention as he looked around at the chaos. He glanced back towards the entrance and saw him drive through the exit, hitting another car that ran into the ticket booth that was now there. The flames got larger and blocked the entire exit as the engines combusted nearby, making the pass impossible

"What is happening? Preston, I can feel the heat from the fire!" Jackie said, grabbing Preston's arm tight since she had become very scared. Preston could feel the heat too.

"We need to get out of here! Now!" He replied. "This fire is real." Preston looked around and saw that a large fence had somehow appeared around them, blocking them and everyone else in the theater area. "How do we get out?" He asked.

Jackie looked around, released her arm from Preston and pointed at the entrance. "There, the entrance is the only way, there's a fence everywhere else. We have to get out of here!" Smoke engulfed the area and made their sight obstructed but they could see all the cars trying to leave and honking with people continuing to scream and yell.

"There is no other way, we have to go that way!" Jackie reached for Preston but couldn't find him. "Preston?" She asked louder. The smoke had blinded them both and they couldn't see in front of them any longer. "Preston, where are you?" Jackie yelled.

"Jackie?" She heard Preston say back but from where she couldn't tell. Jackie began walking towards where she thought was the entrance but couldn't see where she was going. She held her hands out in front of her to feel where she was walking when she put her hand on one of the cars and the hot metal body of the car burned her hand.

"Ahh!" Preston heard Jackie scream.

"Jackie? Where are you?" Preston yelled after hearing Jackie scream. "I can't see you," he yelled again but with all the noise and paranoia happening, she couldn't hear him. Preston stood blindly, reaching around and hoping to find Jackie near him. The gray smoke blinded him but he could see the large, orange flames towards the entrance. He walked towards the flames, touching hot cars along the way that were parked and stagnant since no one could drive out and attempted to escape on foot. Walking a couple of dozen feet, he heard a loud, terrifying scream that he knew was Jackie.

"Jackie!" he yelled. Preston became paranoid and walked around faster, attempting to find Jackie but he was blinded and forced to now close his eyes with so much smoke burning his retinas. "Jackie!" He continued to yell until he heard cars crashing into each other as he heard the metal colliding. Preston kept walking with his arms in front of him when he kicked something with his foot. He looked down and saw he kicked the side of Jackie's body. He opened his eyes, the smoke burning but he looked down and saw Jackie's lifeless body. She lied between two cars that had collided, crushing her organs and her body collapsing onto the ash-filled pavement.

Preston knelt next to her body. "Jackie? Please…" he said but she didn't move. "Jackie?" He asked again and began crying uncontrollably. He picked her head up and sat beside her, holding her in his arms. Crying and cradling her body, he put his head on top of her head and shut his eyes. His lungs filled with smoke and he began to cough, not able to breathe until he suffocated with the lack of oxygen. His body fell gently next to Jackie's with his arm under her head, his tears drying quickly in the heat until the fire mysteriously vanished. Jackie and Preston's dead bodies lied on the ash coated pavement.

CHAPTER 5

The sun filled the horizon with the few hours of daylight that remained in the day. A large, ruby red colored trucked entered the former area of the drive-in theater, driving through the wooded area to get to the old parking spaces. He drove slowly over the cracks and roots in the road and parked. A tall, lanky man with short white hair and a short white beard, wearing jeans and a flannel shirt came out of the truck. He lowered the truck latch, allowing the empty truck bed to be accessed. He walked over to the two burnt, lifeless bodies and picked up each corpse, one at a time and rolled them into the bed of his truck. He lifted the hatch back up and locked it into place before slowly exiting the drive-in theater once again.

1788, down a dirt road in the outskirts of the town of Augusta, Georgia, Annie and Robert lived with their young child, Frederick. They were a prominent family and Robert was successful after the Revolutionary War as a lawyer. There weren't many lawyers around the area and Robert's services were highly sought after. Annie helped raise seven-year old Frederick while Robert worked daily and provided a good life for his family. They owned a two-story brick home with four bedrooms. Each bedroom was elaborate with ornate carvings on the ceiling boards, wood floors and multiple fireplaces. They were a highly respected family not only in Augusta but the surrounding towns and communities. Robert had a large office and library in their home and he was visited often by clients. He also received requests often by letter and traveled around to different towns and communities on horseback and carriage. Annie and Robert were very religious and raised Frederick to be the same.

Annie was raised in a religious faction that outlawed anything to do with the stories of death or violence. She met Robert when she was amongst a group of teenagers traveling to other churches and spreading the word of their religion. Robert liked the beliefs that were taught to him when he was living in Atlanta by himself when he was in church one Sunday. While Annie's group leader was speaking, he noticed her eyes looking at him. Robert was three years older at age twenty and afterward, they started to get to know one another. She instilled her beliefs into him and was very strict in raising Frederick to ban all horror stories, violence or anything having to do with macabre. Growing up, Frederick was only told positive and happy stories of heroic figures and religious tales.

One cool evening during the springtime, Robert was away a couple of towns over visiting a client in regards to a will and was going to be returning home late that evening. Annie fed Frederick and went to tuck him in.

"Read me a bedtime story, Mommy?" Frederick asked as he lied flat on his back with a wool blanket brought up to his neck. Annie sat beside him on the edge of his straw-filled bed. She reached up to Frederick's face and pushed the hair away from his forehead.

"You look tired, Frederick. Plus, I have to get the house ready for Daddy to come home soon. Tomorrow night?" Annie asked. She hadn't washed the dishes yet since she and Frederick worked on some writing practices until eight-thirty when it was then time for him to go to bed.

"Okay, Mommy," he said and nodded his head. "Can you leave the candle on for a while?" He asked. Frederick was scared of the dark and Annie often left the candle on for a while until she and Robert went to bed before blowing it out. She left the candle on that sat on the corner of Frederick's desk, next to his bed. She closed the door slightly and went back downstairs to the kitchen to clean the pans she used while making porridge for dinner. Robert and Annie's bedroom was also upstairs and down the hall next to Frederick's room. There was an additional room upstairs used for guests. Robert used the downstairs den for his office that was next to their parlor. The kitchen was built off the house a bit but Annie could hear Frederick if he yelled for her or needed anything.

She finished drying the pans and dishes that were used that night for dinner and with the candle near their large eight-pane window in the kitchen, she looked out for any lights or signs for Robert but could not yet see him. She was expecting him home any minute. While she waited, she wanted to go check on Frederick and make sure he was sleeping. She walked up the wood stairs, the wood steps creaking every two or three steps until she reached the top. She walked down the hall to the first room and could see the faint light emitting from the room. She got to the door and peeked inside to see if Frederick was sleeping.

She peeked in, the candle still lighting up the corner of the room, and saw Frederick sitting at his wooden desk reading a book. She was surprised and not sure what he was doing since he was supposed to be sleeping. "Frederick?" She asked as she walked into his room, pushing his door the rest of the way open.

Startled, Frederick jumped back in his oak chair and turned around. "I'm reading, Mommy."

"You're supposed to be sleeping," she responded and walked over to him to bring him back to his bed. She got to the desk and put her hand on his shoulder as he slowly stood up and backed away from the desk. She glanced down at the desk to see what he was reading. Robert had a vast library of over two-hundred books ranging from encyclopedias to law knowledge – all resources he used in his job. She put her fingers on the front of the book to close it. When she closed the book as Frederick walked back to bed, she read the cover. "Tales of Horror?" She yelled loudly.

Frederick turned back around to see what his mom was yelling about since her loud voice startled him. "Yes, Mommy," he responded quietly, scared because of how loudly his mom yelled. He stood still next to his bed and his hands fidgeted as his arms lied stiff beside his body.

"Where did you get such a book?" She asked.

"I got it from school," he said, remaining quiet and next to his bed. He put his head down to look towards the floor. Annie picked up the book and heard the front door shut.

"Your father is here, lay down now," Annie demanded and walked downstairs quickly to show Robert what Frederick brought into their home. "Robert!" She yelled, having walked halfway down the steps when she saw him hanging up his overcoat on the coat rack.

"Dear, is everything okay?" He asked, hearing the anger in her voice and her waving a book at him. He knew he was a little later than usual but there was additional paperwork that had to be filled out. He didn't think she was mad at him.

"No, look what Frederick was reading."

Robert ran his fingers through his hair to move the strands off of his face and went over to meet Annie halfway at the base of the steps.

He took the book from her and read the front cover. "Where did this come from?" He asked as his voice became deeper as anger set in since their household did not allow such stories to be brought in or spoken about.

"I'm scared," Annie said with her eyes beginning to turn red and watery.

"It'll be okay," Robert said while reaching his arms around her to hug Annie.

"But, what if it's not?" She asked, her head pressed firmly into his shoulder. Her religious belief since she was young and in the religious fact, hearing multiple stories and being told of true tales, once a horror story or book was brought into a house and either told or read, the action allowed evil spirits to come into that household since the home was no longer pure. This belief was passed down from previous generations and Annie's ancestors all believed that fact – as did she.

"I'll go check on him," Robert said. He released Annie and held the book in his hand and walked up the steps. He started down the hall and saw Frederick's door halfway opened. He took a couple of steps towards his room when suddenly the door slammed shut. The loud thud echoed through the hall before dispersing. He figured Frederick was scared he was going to be yelled at or punished for what he had done. Robert got to the door and knocked, allowing a few seconds for Frederick to open it. Annie stood silently behind him. He knocked on the door again. "Frederick!" He yelled. A few seconds of silence went by. "Frederick! Open the door!"

"I can't," Frederick said just loud enough to be heard from just beyond the other side. Robert tried turning the knob again but couldn't push it open.

"Frederick! Open the door! Right this moment!"

"Daddy, I can't!" Frederick said back a little louder. Robert stepped back and could see the doorknob turning as if Frederick was trying to open it but couldn't.

Suddenly, a loud knocking was heard on the door. Frederick thought his dad was knocking on the door while Robert thought Frederick was pleading for help.

"Maybe it's stuck," Robert murmured under his breath for Annie to hear. He went and tried the knob, this time pushing harder to open the door but couldn't budge it.

"Daddy! I'm scared!" Frederick pleaded, urging Robert to work quicker. The loud knocking continued.

"Step back, Son," Robert said and waited a couple of seconds for Frederick to move back. Robert was a tall, lanky man but didn't have much muscle. He whipped his head to his side to get his hair from his face and lowered his shoulder. He turned the doorknob and leveled his shoulder into the door. He then did it a second time, grimacing and holding his arm in slight pain. The door remained shut and he looked around the door frame to see if anything was jammed.

"Please, Daddy!"

"Hold on, Frederick!" Robert said as Annie stood behind them both holding the book under her armpit as she held her hands to her face, worried with what was going to happen. Fears of Frederick reading the book raced through her mind and she figured the worst had happened and that there was no turning back.

"No! Please, Daddy! Don't open the door!" Frederick then pleaded, confusing Robert. Robert then figured Frederick was scared he was going to be punished and may have locked the door.

"Step back!" He yelled and kicked the door, breaking the lock from the frame as the brass plate swung alongside the door. The door flew violently open and whipped around before crashing onto the wall. They saw Frederick in the back of his room, standing by his desk. Annie was the first to rush in to make sure he was okay, followed by an upset Robert. Annie hugged Frederick, glad that he was okay.

"Frederick," Robert started to say while walking towards him, staring at him with every step. He saw Frederick's eyes looking past him as his head slowly started shaking side to side when he then started crying again as Annie continued to kneel and hug him. Robert kneeled beside him to make sure he was okay and saw him looking past him towards the door again.

"Frederick," Robert said again, attempting to get his attention but he never made eye contact.

"Daddy," Frederick finally said and sniffled while he stared ahead towards the door. "He's here…"

CHAPTER 6

Frederick collapsed forward while facing his father. His eyes flipped to the back of his head and his body weakened and went limp. Robert caught him and twisted his body around and held his face up towards him. Annie had taken a couple of steps back and put her hand over her mouth and watched in fear. She was crying and continued staring at Frederick as Robert picked him up and held him in his arms. Frederick started shaking and Robert held onto his body tighter. Frederick's mouth began to foam and his eyelids opened, showing the whites of his eyes as the foam continued and dropped on the wood floor.

"Annie, we need to go to Doc Bedford's. We need to get in the carriage," he said sternly and stood up, holding on to Frederick as he turned around. He went down the steps while holding on to his son and Annie followed behind them.

"Why? Frederick, why?" Annie yelled while turning the corner from the last step to go to the front door. On the way, she blew out the candle in the kitchen and followed outside. She closed the door and got into the carriage parked on the side of their house. Annie stepped up onto the seat and Robert handed her Frederick. She realized she was still carrying the horror book and looked down at the cover and felt disgusted and sick in her stomach for what happened to Frederick and what she believed he brought into the home. She threw the book as far as she could as it landed in a pile of dirt near the side of the house so she could hold onto Frederick. Robert ran to the barn to get their horse and hurried to the front of the carriage to tie the reigns. They quickly rode the five-mile trip to the town doctor.

"He's burning up," Doc Bedford said once Robert lied Frederick down onto the doctor's examination table. Bedford was in his sixties and had been the town's most popular doctor for the last thirty years. He and Robert had been friends for many years and had brought Frederick to him before.

"What does he have?" Annie asked worriedly. She sat on a bench in the examination room while Robert and Bedford stood beside Frederick. She was too weak to stand anymore. Bedford had his practice on the first floor of his small, two-story home.

"I'm really not sure yet," Bedford said and looked inside Frederick's mouth. "There's a lot of blood, but he must have bit his tongue or something," he said. Annie sat terrified, thinking back to a story she had heard from her family and friends about a time when a teenage boy wrote a horror story and evil entered into the boy. She kept thinking back to how the boy instantly got sick and while he stayed in the house and was cared for by his parents, the house suddenly burned and all three were trapped and burned alive. No matter how much they tried to escape and break the windows, the flames surrounded the three of them. Never questioning whether the story was a façade to instill fear in everyone, Annie's remembrance of the story brought instant fear and paranoia to her. Robert, who wasn't raised with the same religious beliefs as Annie, understood her feelings and was taught by her since they had met fifteen years prior. Robert stood beside Frederick and constantly looked back at Annie and saw the fear in her face as she looked towards the base of the wall ahead of her. He knew exactly what Annie was thinking and knew she was scared of what was going to happen to Frederick as well as themselves.

"Will he be okay?" Robert asked when he turned back around to face the doctor from looking at Annie. Bedford wiped a little foam that came from Frederick's mouth and looked into his white eyes, moving the eyelids up as high as they could. His body had since stopped trembling.

"Yes, I'm sure he will be," Bedford replied even though he couldn't figure out what was wrong except for maybe a bad flu. He had never seen someone foam from the mouth with the symptoms that Frederick was having but got a wet washcloth and placed it upon his forehead to help cool the fever. "We must keep Frederick cool until the fever reduces."

"I will hold the cloth," Robert said and took the cloth.

"You two can stay here if you'd like. I have a sofa in the next room. One of you can sleep on that and there's a cot in here if you'd like. Sorry, I don't have an extra room or bed but I hope that will subdue."

"Thank you," Robert said and looked towards Annie who had her eyes shut and head tilted as if she was already sleeping but instead, overthinking the worst of what was going to happen to Frederick. He rotated the cloth and set it back on Frederick's forehead and walked over towards Annie. He put his hand on the back of Annie's head and she jumped up. Feeling startled from her deep thoughts, she looked up at Robert. "Does that sound okay to you, Annie? Do you want to stay here overnight?" Annie nodded instantly, wanting to make sure Frederick would be okay as well as she no longer felt safe in her own home.

CHAPTER 7

The following morning, Annie woke up from the couch in Doctor Bedford's home and could hear Robert and the doctor talking in the next room. She sat up slowly from the couch, letting her senses awaken from the sleep. She listened to them speak.

"I don't know what's wrong, I truly don't understand," she could recognize Bedford's voice say.

"What are we going to do next?" Robert asked. Annie slowly stood from the couch and quietly walked towards the entryway and stayed out of sight. She peeked around the corner and could see Frederick lying on the table, covered by a wool blanket which he wore last night to attempt to break the fever. She saw Robert standing by Frederick and the doctor on the other side, holding up Frederick's wrist and checking his pulse. Robert started to walk towards the bench in the room to have a seat and rest, revealing Frederick's face.

"Ah!" Annie screamed and gasped once Robert moved and she saw Frederick's face. She immediately screamed after seeing Frederick's opened eyes looking directly at her. Robert heard the scream and walked quickly over to Annie and hugged her.

"Are you okay?" He asked while wrapping his arms around her.

"How is Frederick?" She asked him, having turned away from looking at Frederick.

"Not good," Robert said as they began walking towards Frederick. "I mean, his fever broke last night and his mouth stopped foaming and the main thing is he's alert. But, he's not talking or responsive."

"Frederick?" Annie asked while she stood beside her son and his head faced towards her. "Frederick?" She asked again. Frederick blinked before moving his eyes away from Annie to look towards the ceiling.

"What's going to happen with him?" Annie asked.

Bedford looked over at her and said, "I think he needs rest. He broke the fever by morning and was sleeping very well. He needs to continue to sleep and stay hydrated. Make sure he eats to keep his strength up so soup or porridge if his stomach can handle it."

"Is there anything else we should know?" Robert asked.

"Just, if you need anything else, please ask," Bedford said and Robert nodded.

"We'll be taking Frederick home this morning," Robert told Annie. Annie looked up towards Robert and had a distinct look on her face with the way her head tilted and eyes squinted. "It'll be okay, Honey," Robert confirmed. He didn't realize at the time the fear and paranoia that Annie continued to think about and that she was uncomfortable returning home. Remembering the fire that occurred with the story that stuck in her memory, she wanted to go talk with an elder of the religious group she was part of as a child.

"Robert, if he doesn't get better, can I go speak with Ulmer?" Annie asked.

Robert paused and stood still for a few seconds, trying to remember Ulmer since he hadn't heard that name in quite a few years. "Ulmer?" He finally asked once remembering who he was.

"Yes, I want to ask him a few questions."

"Why?" Robert asked and right after asking, he remembered how Frederick was reading a book of horror tales and knew what was going through Annie's mind. "It's going to be okay, Annie," Robert said to reassure her. He put his hands on her shoulders and looked directly at her. "Frederick just got sick and will get better. Just…coincidence," he said.

"I'll feel better, though, if I speak with him," Annie said.

"Okay, okay. If he doesn't get better soon, we can go and see Ulmer. Is he still way outside of town in that dilapidated old farmhouse?"

"I, I believe so. I haven't seen him for years but for my comfort, I need to speak with him," Annie said. "I'll need to see him by myself."

"Okay, if it'll help," he said to Annie before turning back to Doctor Bedford.

"Thanks, Doctor Bedford," Robert said while the doctor took the blanket off of Frederick. "Bill us for your troubles and thanks for your help."

"Yes, thanks, Doctor Bedford," Annie said, helping Robert set Frederick up from the bed. Frederick's eyes were shut again and Robert picked him up in his arms to carry him back out to the carriage.

CHAPTER 8

After returning home, Frederick remained in bed for two days and slept constantly. His fever never returned but he never spoke or showed emotions. The third morning since Frederick had been home, with no improvement, Annie picked up a few pieces of fruit from the kitchen for a quick breakfast and got onto their horse to ride the couple of hour ride to see Ulmer. She waved to Robert who insisted to go with her but Annie told him to stay with Frederick. Annie knew Ulmer since her childhood and the man she once looked up to in her religious group. He was originally from East Germany and migrated to New York as a youth. His family was forced to emigrate from Germany. His parents were alcoholics and one night, Ulmer's dad burned down three buildings in their German village in rage. No one died but his punishment was either life in prison doing hard labor in Germany, or to leave to the United States in a small German settlement in New York. Ultimately, his parents chose to move to America. Once arriving, their drinking continued as did the lack of a good living with many people stuck in tiny, overcrowded houses and apartments and a lack of good-paying steady jobs.

About a year after being in New York, Ulmer joined a group of other children who one day came up with the idea they should run away from home and start their own life – they were tired of the lifestyle and poverty. They were a group of eleven children, ranging in age from nine to eighteen and most of them had broken homes that one or both parents were violent and uncaring. Ulmer's parents would both be enraged often while drinking and beat him, forcing him to run away with the rest of the children.

An evening in 1710, fifteen year old Ulmer, alongside the other ten children in his group, fled in the dark of night. Unsure as to where they would end up, they used an old map of the country one child had stolen from a local man and used that to travel south. Some of the children brought knapsacks while others carried what belongings they had such as stuffed animals and even crackers or any kind of food they could find or steal. On the first night of travel, they traveled for a few slow hours until coming across hilly farmland. As they walked the dirt road through the farms, they saw an incoming storm from behind them. They picked up their pace and quickly walked by moonlight but the clouds began to cover their light. Seeing the storm quickly overtake the sky, they rushed to the first dark building they could find. They found an old abandoned two-story barn and went inside and closed the wooden door behind them and latched the inside.

Five of them hovered behind an old haystack that had remained while the others went into a wood stall that once housed a horse. Suddenly, the thunder got louder and the storm increased in speed and velocity, the wind hitting the wood boards of the farm forcing them to rattle. Whistling spread throughout the barn within the holes and cracks in the boards creating an eerie, distorted sound.

"Everyone, in the stall!" one boy called when the rattling of the wood boards flapping on the sides of the building increased. The rest of the five by the hay rushed into the wood stall since the area looked the safest. One child had the candle lit in the center of the stall so everyone could see and feel safer within the storm.

"When will the storm be over?" One of the youngest children asked, scared and curled up near the wall in the small stall. The other children looked around at the darkness surrounding them in the barn. One young girl took her knapsack from behind them to move in front of them but a book fell out. Ulmer sat beside the child when Reginald, the eldest of the group, saw the book and reached for it. He picked it up and held it by the light to read through it and see what it was about. He read a passage:

The man erupted in rage and with a piece of lumber in hand, began attacking the soon to be victims. He battered the surrounding people, uncontrolled with anger and violence with bloodshed soon to be evolving as red lined the once light wood floor...

Reginald closed the book loudly, grabbing the attention of the children near him. He stood up quickly and held the book out in front of him, enraged as his arm shook while holding the book.

"What is this ideological nightmarish texts I read?" Reginald asked and continued to hold out the book. At that moment, a loud cracking was heard from the thunder with the incoming storm. A large lightning bolt emitted a bright light from a small window high on the wall of the barn.

"That's my book," the young girl said quietly and started crying.

"It's heathenness!" He demanded and threw the book harshly towards the hay by the barn's door. Reginald stood tall and more muscular than anyone else in the group. He looked to be in good health with his clean skin and muscular physique. His overalls and flannel shirt were clean and his leather shoes recently polished. His stature and being the oldest in the group gave him a powerful look and feel – especially when he raised his voice which bellowed throughout the stall within the barn. Once seeing the book, he blamed the storm on the violent readings.

"The storms! All because of this book!"

"I'm sorry," the girl said, remaining crying. Another loud thunder cracking was heard when lightning came inside through a broken window near the top of the barn and struck the book. The book instantly ignited and caught fire for a few moments before turning to ash. After the last flame burned the book before going out, the storm dispersed and a dark blue hue spread throughout the sky and was seen through the window. From that moment on, the rest of the children were drawn to Reginald and his beliefs. He realized that they hung on his every word and throughout the next few days, he taught and gained the respect of the group. He would soon team with Ulmer to begin their own religious fact, Heathenness Ideology.

CHAPTER 9

Annie parked her horse in front of the old barn on Ulmer's land and glanced around as she looked for any signs of life. She saw blooming flowers on the porch of the white-painted farmhouse and figured that was a good sign someone was still living there and she hoped it was Ulmer. The farmhouse looked peaceful with a wraparound porch on the two-story wood-framed house. There was an outhouse in the back along with a shed on the side. The grass around the house was about knee high but a path to the outhouse was outlined with flattened grass. There were large oak trees scattered scarcely around the house with brush growing up around where the farmland used to grow crops. Ulmer, who hadn't grown crops in over a decade due to his deteriorating health and inability to move after he suffered a stroke in his late seventies, had lived a lonely but peaceful life on his farmland. He would be visited by his followers once and a while but as time progressed, his followers had their own families and some went away from their original beliefs. Many others moved and formed their own groups while others, like Annie, still followed and believed in the Heathenness Ideology ways and stayed true to Ulmer's traditional beliefs. Ulmer didn't mind the more subtle and quiet life since when he came into town for supplies and food, couples were talking to one another and pointing at him and Ulmer knew people talked about him. He didn't care since he followed his beliefs and lived his own life. Ulmer never married even though many of the women in the groups glorified him. He didn't see the need to get married and he wanted to live life with his group and focus on his group instead of a family. As he aged, though, Ulmer had regretted ever finding anyone and after he had his stroke, he debated the fact even more. As he thought about finding a woman to marry, he felt bad that he was getting old and would need a lot of care so he didn't want to put the burden on anyone so he remained single – especially the more he aged.

Annie got off of her horse and stepped down when she heard a dog barking in the distance towards the house. She looked around to make sure she was safe when she saw a medium-sized hound dog run from the porch towards her. Annie took a quick step back, unsure whether the dog was going to attack her but as the dog got closer, Annie had her hand on her horse's mane to keep it calm and saw the dog wagging its tail erratically. The dog got close to her, his tongue flopping to the side when he jumped before reaching her and landed by her feet. The dog began smelling her leather shoes and looked up at her as his tail continued to wag – happy to have a visitor and someone new to meet.

"Hi, what's your name?" Annie asked playfully and reached down to attempt to pet the dog. The dog was pacing back and forth and Annie had a hard time calming down the dog's excitement. "Let's go inside," she told the dog. She walked up the dirt path up to the house and the dog followed behind her, periodically stopping to sniff around the grass on the way up to the house. She approached the house, walking slowly and looking around at the porch and house hoping Ulmer still lived there.

"Who's there?" She heard a man's voice ask. The voice was weak and she couldn't hear any forceful demand behind his words. Annie looked around but didn't see anyone. She slowly stepped onto the first step up to the porch when ahead of her, she saw the front door slowly open.

"Who is that?" The same voice asked. Annie stood cautiously at the front step, looking at the doorway and saw a man's figure peeking from behind the door.

"Ulmer?" She asked loudly enough for him to hear her.

"Yes, who are you?" He asked while remaining mostly behind the door. He stood with his head peeking from around the door while he held onto a wood cane.

"Ulmer, it's Annie. Emmie was my grandmother," she said, hoping Ulmer would remember her. She hadn't seen him for a long time and now that he was older, she wondered if he would even remember.

"Oh, yes, Annie. What's it been? Ten years?" Ulmer asked and walked out from behind the door. He walked through the doorway and onto the porch, using his cane with every cautious step. Annie was saddened by his appearance from the last time she saw him. She had always wondered how he had such a youthful and vibrant complexion and mobility as he aged. Now, though, he looked at every step as he walked on the wood slats of the porch. He was hunched over and had long, white hair down to his shoulders since he hadn't had a haircut in years. He had a small white mustache and beard but he kept that trimmed. He wore canvas pants and a wool flannel shirt with overalls holding his pants up. He was barefoot and walked on the porch a few steps over to a bench that was by the door.

"Ulmer, it's so nice to see you again," Annie said and walked up the remainder of the steps to the porch.

"Please, have a seat, Dear," Ulmer said and patted his hand on the bench to the left of him. Annie sat and looked at Ulmer who looked at her back. The dog went and sat beside Ulmer's feet and rested his head on the wood slats.

"So, how long has it been?" He asked her as they looked at one another while Ulmer didn't show much expression.

"Too long," Annie answered. "Over ten years I'm sure."

"Do I look older?" Ulmer asked and chuckled.

"Yes," Annie answered and smiled back. "We both look older," she said but noticed how much older Ulmer had gotten the past over ten years since she had seen him last. She remembered before when they saw each other more how it seemed that Ulmer never aged. Now, she figured, that time had finally caught up to him.

"You're looking like a nice young woman, Annie. You're looking more and more like your grandmother and mother. How is your mother anyway? She and your father doing well?"

"Yes, thank you for asking. I didn't have time to tell my mother that I was coming to see you but I'm sure she will be glad to hear you're doing well." Annie's parents lived in New York City and her father worked as a businessman. "But, I am here to ask for your help," Annie said and started to tremble. She had her hand on Ulmer's thigh and he could feel her hand shaking. He looked down at her hand and placed his on top of it and looked at her face and saw tears coming from her eyes.

"Are you okay?" Ulmer asked and remained looking at her.

"No. I'm sorry to come here to ask for your help but I don't know who else to turn to at a time like this. My, my son," Annie started to say but started crying more and had difficulty speaking.

"It's fine, Dear. Take your time," Ulmer said and sat patiently next to Annie while she wiped her tears with a rag she kept in the small bag she brought with her. He hadn't seen her in quite some time and didn't realize she had a son but knew this wasn't the time to ask but instead, let her tell him the situation.

"I caught him four days ago," Annie said and paused. "He brought a violent and terrible book into our house and was reading it in his bedroom." She continued to say before she looked up at Ulmer for his advice. Her tears had stopped while she anticipated his response.

"Hmm..." Ulmer started. He grabbed the wood cane that was nearby him and clenched it tightly before moving it so it wouldn't fall over. "This isn't a good thing. I know your grandmother and mother raised you well under the teachings of Heathenness Ideology and to know not to read anything like that nor nonetheless bring it into a house." Ulmer looked ahead at his farmland and pondered what to say next.

"Will he be okay? Will we be okay?" She asked while he thought of a response.

"Firstly, Annie, how old is your son? I didn't know you had a son since we hadn't seen each other in many years." Ulmer continued thinking when the last time Annie saw him and he was pretty baffled that why someone whose family was so close to him no longer went and visited him, especially living not overly far away. He wondered in his mind why she hadn't visited him. Even now that Annie and Robert had a child, he would imagine they would want him to meet their son.

"Frederick is his name. He is seven years old and a really good young boy. He's well behaved and we're raising him well. I'm just really worried that since this happened, I found him," Annie started to say and stopped. She hesitated to say more because she was getting more worried inside and cried again.

"Tell me more," Ulmer said.

"Well, I found him with the book. Robert had come home and had a hard time opening the door since it was stuck. When it finally opened, Frederick said something strange, as if we let something evil in. Ever since then, he got sick and he's been sick."

"What's wrong with him? Did you see a doctor?"

"Yes, we went and saw Dr. Bedford but he couldn't find anything wrong or a reason as to why Frederick is no longer speaking or showing emotions."

"Bedford is a good doctor," Ulmer said. "So, Frederick isn't sick in the sense of an illness per se but something else?"

"Yes, that what it seems. He hasn't talked since uttering the words of something evil. He looks distant as if he's no longer our child. He's not responsive nor has any emotions."

Ulmer sat and removed his hand from the top of Annie's. He scratched his head, understanding what was happening but didn't know what exactly to say to Annie with how worried she was. He knew that evil had possessed Frederick and that her son was no longer the young boy she once knew but he had an idea. He remained upset inside that he hadn't even met her son or seen Annie and her family in years so he contemplated an idea that would satisfy the teachings of Heathenness Ideology for those who go against the religion.

"A child with a wonderful name but a soul so young. His mind is weakened at such a young age and soul unaware of the dangers lurking around – the dangers praying on a young soul such as his."

"Will he be okay?" Annie blurted out.

"Time will tell. You will have to be patient and stay strong. I want you to see another doctor, though. I know this doctor well and he's seen your situation many times and can get children, and even adults, through such evil troubles."

"Who is he? Where might I be able to find him?" Annie quickly asked and sat up towards the edge of the bench and looked at Ulmer.

"He is a very trusted companion and friend. I have known him since he was a young man. His parents entered our church and I watched him grow up into becoming a successful doctor," Ulmer said and lied. "He saw what you are seeing now as he grew up and wanted to help those in similar situations and became a doctor. He is working at an asylum in Southern Georgia, about a day's ride from here."

"Okay, yes. I will go to him immediately and bring Frederick. Do you think he will be able to help us out?"

"Oh, yes, indeed," Ulmer said and gave a gentle smile to Annie.

"I thank you for your time and help, Ulmer."

"No worries, it's my pleasure to help you out since I remember your mother and grandmother so well. I miss your grandmother and how she would visit so often to check up on me. I wish she hadn't passed away so many years ago," Ulmer said. He and Annie's grandmother, Emmie, became close friends and confided in one another until Ulmer became violently ill one evening while she was with him. They were both alone and Ulmer could feel his heart begin beating quickly. He hadn't killed in a while and knew that if he didn't again, he might die at that time. He knelt on the ground, cringing in pain while he nearly collapsed over while his knee knocked on the wood floor loudly. Emmie drove to a nearby doctor and after the doctor rushed over, he made Ulmer remain in bed and eat a strict diet to help his heart. Emmie stopped by often to check on him and to help him out. One afternoon, she walked into Ulmer's house and saw him lying on the ground and holding his chest, fearing a heart attack while a tightness overwhelmed his chest. Emmie rushed over to him and put her arm on his back and knelt on the floor beside him.

"What's wrong?" She said in a panic and raised her voice. She could see him holding his chest. He looked over at her and in as much pain as he was in, he took his hand off his chest and used both hands to reach over to Emmie and put them around her throat. He squeezed hard and violently as his heart was getting ready to erupt. The pain he was enduring forced his hands to clench even tighter and as Emmie's legs began kicking and hands hitting him, Ulmer remained squeezing her throat until her body fell still and cold. He released his hands while looking at her face. He shook his head at what he had to do but stood up and reached down to dust off his pants. Throwing Emmie's body in a nearby stream that night, when questioned by Emmie's husband, Ulmer claimed that she never made it to his house. Everyone who knew Ulmer believed and respected him – even though they didn't know his true life.

CHAPTER 10

"It was nice seeing you again, Annie," Ulmer said while Annie was ready to go back home to get Frederick to bring to the doctor.

"Nice seeing you, too, and thank you for your help. I'm so scared and worried about Frederick and all of us," Annie said while forcing a slight grin.

"Trust me, everything will be all right," Ulmer said, attempting to stand up but realizing the struggle, he remained seated. "You will want to go to the hospital in Macon. You will meet a doctor named Reginald Wiley. Tell him that I sent you and he will take care of you and Frederick."

"Thanks again, Ulmer. I'm beginning to feel better and more relieved already," Annie said. She bent down and hugged Ulmer and in as much pain as Ulmer was in, not only was he too weak to attempt to kill again, he was tired of living.

Annie left Ulmer's house and held the reigns on her horse as she hurried back home. The ride was about two hours and she wanted to get back before it got dark but she figured she had plenty of time. As she left, Ulmer sat on his bench and shook his head, knowing that his time was coming soon. He held no guilt for killing Annie's grandmother, nor the few others through his life but he was ready to move on as he was tired of the pain of being sick and wanted to die. Through the past few years, he got tired of thinking about killing and more than one time he wanted to end life due to the pains of being sick. As Annie left, he said to himself, "never again, he often thought when remembering his past, never again will I kill and put myself through this miserable world and I can only imagine the torture I'll inflict on someone if anyone were to make me live longer in this agony called life."

CHAPTER 11

Annie arrived back home and was greeted by Robert who was outside getting water from their well. He set the bucket down and ran over towards her once he saw her coming down the road to their house.

"How is he?" Annie immediately asked when Robert held his hand out to help her down off the horse.

"Same," he answered. Annie landed on the dusty path and gave Robert the reigns to take the horse to the pasture while she went and checked on Frederick. He took the horse while Annie rushed into the house. She opened the door and looked quickly around the living room and dining room but didn't see Frederick and figured he was in his room. She went quickly upstairs and saw his door was nearly shut. She pressed it gently to not wake him if he was sleeping and peeked around the door to his bed. He lied on his back with his head facing the door and his eyes looking at Annie as she peeked in. She was startled by the look on his face but continued inside and sat beside him.

"How are you feeling, Frederick?" She asked and put her hand on his forehead. His body temperature felt normal and the temperature tepid so she moved the blanket to cover the bottom half of his body so he would stay warm but not get too hot. Frederick never answered. "Do you need anything?" She asked and smiled at him while she remained next to him on his bed. He continued to stare at her, blinking every few seconds but not showing any emotions. "Make sure you continue to rest, okay? We will be going to another doctor tomorrow morning early so make sure you get plenty of sleep for the ride. I love you, Frederick," Annie finished saying and kissed him on the forehead before leaving. She went downstairs and saw Robert coming into the house with the bucket of water.

"How did the visit go?" Robert asked and set the bucket down by the kitchen sink.

"It went really well. Ulmer is having me take Frederick to a great doctor he knows very well in Macon."

"Macon? That's a long trip," Robert said.

"Yes, it is. We will have to leave early tomorrow."

"Okay, let me get the horses and carriage ready for the trip. We need to get clothes ready, and food."

"You don't have to go, Robert. You have work to do," Annie said, not wanting to interrupt Robert's work and making money.

"No worries. You and Frederick's safety is more important. So, tell me more about this doctor."

"Ulmer said he's really good and has helped people in this same situation before, so he has experience at least."

"Great, I'm glad to hear that," Robert answered with a smile and gently pat Annie's arm before he went to begin washing dishes in the sink.

Annie sat at the table beside him, tired after the traveling and not looking forward to the long trip the following day but knew they had to go. "The doctor's name is Doctor Wiley and we need to tell him that Ulmer sent us."

"Sounds fine. Let's make sure we go to bed early to get enough rest. After I clean the pans, we need to pack and go to bed. I can pack our stuff if you want to pack Frederick's," Robert said.

"Did Frederick say or show any emotions or do anything like he used to while I was gone?"

"He just lied in bed and the only time he moved was when he went to use the pot by his bed to go to the bathroom."

"Hmm…I just wish I knew what was wrong. It was all that awful book he brought into this house and read," Annie said. "It has to be!" She yelled loudly.

"Yes, that has to be why. Or else this is just a coincidence but did Ulmer agree that the book likely caused this?"

"He agreed."

Robert finished the dishes and got the trunk for their essentials. They weren't sure how long they would be gone so they packed enough to last four days just to be sure. Annie went into Frederick's bedroom and grabbed clothes. The entire time he stared at her and showed no emotions or made any noise. Robert got their essentials ready and packed in order to get up early the following morning. It was getting dark in their house as nighttime began to appear. Annie lit a couple of candles in their bedroom and went to tuck Frederick in.

"Frederick, we are leaving early in the morning to go to another doctor. Get plenty of rest tonight so you're strong for the trip," Annie said and kissed his face before leaving his room and getting ready for bed herself. She and Robert went to bed soon after when the sky had just turned completely dark and lied down on their firm straw-filled bed.

CHAPTER 12

Morning came and Robert and Annie hardly got any sleep thinking about Frederick. They lied in bed most the night and whispered to one another with regards to Frederick and what would happen. Finally, the sun was nearly ready to peek above the horizon when they got out of bed. They readied their trunk and essentials and loaded the wagon to leave to the hospital in Macon with what was estimated to be about a half-day ride. Robert got the wagon ready and put the reigns around the horse while Annie went and got Frederick. She slowly opened his door which was slightly open to begin with. They had kept it open in case they had heard any noise from him throughout the night. She slowly walked inside and upon seeing Frederick in bed, a slight crease of sunlight from the window in his room appeared on his face as his face was directed towards the door and his eyes looking at Annie. She was startled again and wondered why he wasn't sleeping since she had been quiet to not make any noise and scare him. She wondered if he had slept at all that night.

"Frederick, good morning," Annie said while she walked over to him and sat on the edge of the bed. "Did you sleep any last night?" She asked, not expecting an answer. He continued to look at her with no emotions on his face.

"We need to get ready to go to the hospital so let me get you out of bed and dressed so help me out here," she said and slowly sat him up in bed. His body was loose and easy to maneuver which made it easy for Annie to change his clothes. When it came time to stand, he helped move his legs to put his pants on and then his socks and boots. They walked downstairs with Annie holding his hand and went to the wagon where Robert was sitting on the driver's box to drive them. Annie sat in the back with the trunk and held Frederick next to her. As they started with the sun beginning to light up the horizon, she looked down at Frederick's face while she had her arm around him and saw him looking at their house as they drove away. She noticed a tear come down his face, possibly him inside knowing that this might be the last time he would see their house.

They continued down the dirt path and drove through town to go south to Macon where the hospital was. Robert was hoping this long day of travel would be worth it and help Frederick. He wasn't as close to Ulmer as Annie so he wasn't sure if this doctor would be any more help than anyone else. With the way Annie described the doctor to Robert, he held some hope that it would help their only child. Annie slept partway on the way to Macon and every time she looked at Frederick, he would look blankly at the surrounding farmlands, grassy areas and trees throughout the areas they passed. Annie slept most of the way and woke hours later and looked around and saw numerous brick buildings – reminiscent of a decent-sized town. She looked over her shoulder to make sure Robert was doing okay.

"Robert, you feeling fine?"

"Yes, did you get any sleep?"

"I did. Frederick is still awake, not sure if he slept any," Annie said back after glancing at Frederick while continuing to hold him. "Where are we?"

"We are almost to the hospital, I believe. We're in Macon. Just need to find directions," Robert said while he came to a stop down the street next to a pub. "Let me ask inside for directions."

"Okay, I'll see if Frederick needs to use the bathroom and we will stretch a bit," Annie said while she went off the side of the wagon. She picked up Frederick and brought him to the ground and he stood.

"Let's go use the outhouse, Frederick," she said after she noticed an outhouse to the side of a building across the street. They walked over, stretching their legs while she held his hand and had him use the outhouse. He came out with his pants back on and buttoned and walked slowly to Annie. "Wait out here for me, okay Frederick?" She said so she could go to the outhouse next. Frederick just stood and didn't answer. Annie went and used the restroom for no longer than a minute and came back outside.

"Frederick!" She yelled when she didn't see him anywhere. "Frederick?" She yelled again and ran towards the wagon to find Robert. She saw Frederick sitting in the back of the wagon while Robert walked out of the pub and saw Annie and nodded with a slight grin.

Annie walked over to the wagon, relieved Frederick was there. "You scared me, Frederick," Annie said while Annie crawled up the wagon to sit next to him. "Don't do that again, okay? You really scared me," she said again while looking at Frederick. Frederick smiled. Annie continued to look at him, making sure that he had finally shown some expression but the smile didn't last but a slight second. She wondered why he would smile knowing he had scared her – unless he smiled knowing how much Annie cared about him. That wasn't the case. Annie was still very worried.

"Did you get directions?" She asked Robert.

"Sure did," he said while he situated himself on the bench. "Not much further. Just down the road another half-mile or so and by then, we'll see the large wood hospital to the right. They continued to ride for almost a half-mile when Robert saw the two-story hospital off the road to the right. The building was large and easy to see. He drove the wagon towards the turnoff and saw trees surrounding the large building. He could see multiple wagons and horses outside the building and on the opposite side, a gazebo, swing set, slide, and picnic area.

"It's up ahead," Robert told Annie who was facing the opposite direction. "Looks like a nice one."

Annie turned around and looked at the building and surrounding area. The grass was green and the trees were tall and provided much shade and the building was painted a bright white color.

"Indeed, the hospital is very nice," Annie agreed. Frederick remained facing the opposite direction, watching the dust come up from behind them with their wheels going over the road. Robert turned the wagon down the path to the hospital which was about a block away from the main road coming from town. Robert stopped the wagon as he approached the large flat area where others had parked and tied his horse up to the stall. Annie got out of the wagon and reached for Frederick. She picked him up and brought him out and placed him on the ground. She re-adjusted his suspenders and used her hand to comb his hair over to the side. She patted the clothing on his arms and back to remove the dust that had settled on them while they rode in the back of the wagon. Robert walked towards them after tying up the horse and made sure they were both okay.

"Frederick, son, how are you doing?" He asked while he knelt next to him. Frederick looked at his father with no emotions. "Everything will be fine. We are here to make sure you get better, okay?" He said. Frederick remained still.

"Annie, let's go ahead and go inside. The sooner the better."

"Yes," Annie agreed. "Frederick, hold on to mommy's hand and let's go inside," She said while she reached for Frederick's hand and they all walked up to the building.

Robert and Annie were impressed at the hospital and how everything looked. There were about a dozen horses and trailers parked so they were expecting the hospital to be busy and full of people and they were right. They opened the right side of a large double door with ornate designs carved into it and walked inside. Robert closed the door behind them while Annie looked at the room with wood chairs situated alongside three walls with people sitting in most of them. There was a pine wood slat floor and walls that matched the exterior of the building. There were men, women and children that sat quietly and looked at the three of them. Even though there was rarely any speaking amongst the people seeing three more strangers enter the room, children and adults were coughing, moaning in pain, and everyone was hoping to get helped next.

"Hello, Sir, Madam," a female voice said once Robert turned around from closing the door. They looked over to a desk and saw an elderly woman sitting behind it. She had gray curls coming from below a white nurse's hat she was wearing. She wore a matching white uniform sitting at a large wooden desk. "How can I help you?" The nurse asked and held a pencil in her hand with papers scattered amongst the desk.

"Hi, Nurse," Annie started to say. "I was sent here to see Doctor Wiley."

"Is he expecting you?" The nurse asked.

"No, not unless he received notice from someone that we were coming here but I am sure we got here before any notice or telegram could get here," Annie said.

"Please, Nurse," Robert stepped in. "Our son is sick and needs help. We traveled half the day to come here and were sent here since we were told the doctor could help."

"Yes, Sir, Madam," the nurse responded. "Who sent you here if I may ask?"

"A man named Ulmer," Annie said. "Ulmer wanted me to tell the doctor that he had sent us here."

"I see," the nurse said and tilted her head, looking first at Annie, then Robert and finally Frederick. She leaned forward in her chair and looked at Frederick's face while he stood behind his dad. She could see half of Frederick's face while he peeked around his father's hip and stared at the nurse. "I see," she repeated. "Please, have a seat and I will let Doctor Wiley know that you are here to see him and that Ulmer sent you."

"Thank you, Nurse," Annie said and smiled. Robert smiled and nodded, hoping the doctor would have time to see their son soon. Robert and Annie turned around and saw two open chairs near the corner of the room while Frederick remained looking at and watching the nurse. The nurse remained glaring back at him while smiling.

"Honey, why don't you and Frederick have a seat in the corner and I will go outside and give our horse some water. I saw a well near the back of the building. Call for me when the doctor gets here, okay?"

"Yes, Dear," Annie said. "Frederick?" Annie said, turning around and seeing Frederick facing the other direction. She turned around to lean down next to him and interrupted the nurse from looking at him as she looked back down quickly at her papers and continued writing on a sheet of paper. "Frederick, we're going to sit over here and wait for the doctor," she said and grabbed his shoulders and turned him around to walk towards the corner. They walked to the seat and the other people inside remained quiet. A few whispers were heard but no one was speaking loudly. Some of the children there were asking their parents questions, while others were talking to one another but all remained discreet. A few of the people inside the room were bored and watched the new people to the room and pondered what was wrong with them. Robert left the room and went to their wagon and made sure their horse was doing okay. Their horse was standing and whipped his tail when Robert petted his mane.

"Let me get you some water," he said to his horse and went to get a bucket near the well and put the bucket on the rope. He lowered the bucket into the well until he felt it hit the water. He waited for the bucket to fill and rotated the handle to pull the bucket back up. He looked into the bucket and saw the water was clear. *Must be a spring nearby since patients need clean water*, he thought to himself, impressed, and brought the bucket over to their horse. He poured the water into a trough next to his horse. The horse quickly drank the water and brought its mouth out and blew the water off his nose and looked around. Robert knew he had enough and went to put the bucket back next to the well. He then walked back to the entrance where there were two benches and had a seat. He looked around at the vast area that was very quiet. The hospital was built outside of town so townspeople wouldn't be worried and scared that sickness would escape and expose itself to the town. He brought a pipe out from inside his jacket pocket and took a bag of tobacco out and poured it slightly inside the pipe. He brought out a match as he crossed one leg over the other leg and looked around a bit more. While holding his pipe and match, he lowered his head and shut his eyes to rest them a few seconds when he unintentionally fell asleep – resting finally after a long drive. What felt like no less than a minute while Robert rested, he heard Annie's voice.

"Robert, he's ready for us," she shouted from the front door. Robert suddenly opened his eyes and looked around, familiarizing and reminding himself where he was when he turned around and saw Annie. He quickly stood, putting away his pipe as tobacco poured inside his coat pocket as he ran to the door and went inside. Frederick was standing behind Annie and Robert looked behind them in the hallway and saw another nurse standing. Annie grabbed Frederick's hand and they all walked towards the nurse.

CHAPTER 13

"Please, follow me," the younger nurse said and started down the hallway. They walked passed many closed doors, some with grunts and painful sounding noises coming from them while a few other doors remained opened. Annie focused on the hallway and wondered where they were going while Robert glanced quickly inside the open doors as he walked by. He saw there were wooden chairs in them as well as a counter covered with varieties of medical equipment and a wooden table with a thin cover for the patient. Each open room that they passed made him wonder more about where they were going. They walked to the end of the hallway and saw the direction turned left. The nurse continued to turn the corner as they continued to walk. The hallway was dimly lit with small windows spread minimally throughout as well as candles hanging on the walls that made the area bright enough to see. They kept walking and now Annie was beginning to look around, amazed at how large the building seemed. They approached the end of another hallway and saw a staircase.

"Here, follow me. Doctor Wiley's room is upstairs. Please, follow me," the nurse said while proceeded upstairs, holding onto the handrail. Annie walked up first while reaching back to keep her hand on Frederick's and Robert followed behind them. They walked up the steps and reached the top and turned to the left and saw two different hallways. One hallway had many candles for light just as the ones downstairs while the other hallway was very dark and hard to see where the hallway went. There were only a few dim candles lighting up a small portion down the very end of it. Annie and Robert became a bit worried momentarily hoping they wouldn't be going down the dark hallway but instead the nurse led them down the lit-up hallway. They began walking and as they walked, Robert noticed each of the doors were shut and had signs on them that said: "Do Not Enter." He didn't notice signs on the other doors downstairs but they continued walking when suddenly they reached the end of yet another hallway. The nurse turned to the right and said, "We're almost there." They followed the candlelight when suddenly, after walking past each candle, the flame would flicker before turning off for no more than a second until it suddenly ignited back on. After the first candle flickered, went out and lit back up, they all continued walking. Robert and Annie had no idea what was happening when they looked up at the nurse and saw her glancing at them while she continued to walk. She smiled and looked down at Frederick and nodded before turning back around to face down the hallway. Annie turned to look at Robert and both had a concerned look on their face with the ways their eyes squinted at one another and lips pouted. Suddenly, reaching the second candle, it happened again. The flame flickered before going out for no more than a second and ignited back up. The nurse continued to walk as if there was nothing wrong.

"What's happening?" Annie finally turned to look at Robert and asked as they kept walking.

"I have no idea," he said when it happened yet again.

"Nurse, are the candles okay? What is happening?" Robert finally asked since the candle flames seemed more than just a coincidence. The nurse continued walking when it happened for the fourth time and she stopped walking.

"Yes, perfectly fine," she said, turning her head towards Robert and smiling. She then looked down at Frederick. Continuing to smile, she repeated in a more hollow tone, "perfectly fine."

Robert and Annie looked at one another and Robert continued to stand behind Frederick. Annie, who stood beside Frederick, then looked down and saw the same smile on his face that she had seen in the wagon when she told him he had scared her.

"We're finally here," the nurse said while facing them and pointed to her left to an open room while holding papers in her other arm. The room was lit up and Robert entered first, cautiously. He looked around as he first entered, making sure the room was safe for Annie and Frederick to enter. He took an additional few steps inside just to be sure and noticed the table for the patient, a couple of wooden chairs and counter just as the other rooms had. He wondered, though, why they had to walk so far when there were numerous other rooms just like this down on the first floor. Annie and Frederick slowly walked in and Annie looked around also.

"The doctor will be with you soon," the nurse said and as Annie and Robert turned around she quickly shut the door.

"What just happened?" Annie asked Robert, referring to the candles flickering and an odd sensation each were feeling. They both were curious why the doctor's room was so far in the back of the hospital and why the nurse acted the way she did when staring at them as well as Frederick.

"I am not sure," Robert answered. "I really don't know but let's wait here and hope the doctor can at least help us out."

"Have a seat, Frederick," Robert then said and pointed at the table. He took Frederick by his shoulder and directed him towards the table. There was a thin cushion on top and Robert grabbed Frederick under his arms and brought him and sat him on top of the table. Frederick looked directly at Robert and seemed uninterested with what was going on or where he was by the way he constantly stared at either Robert or Annie.

Robert walked to the door while Annie watched Frederick as he sat on the table. He looked at Robert while he walked away. Suddenly, as Annie sat by the door and Robert stood near her, there was a loud knocking on the door. They both quickly glanced over and saw the door slowly open up. They saw a man outside the door who was about to enter when he stepped back. Robert, who stood closer to the door, saw the nurse walk up to the man and whisper something in his ear. She told him something for a few seconds when the man grinned and continued to grin until she finished whispering to him.

"The candles flickered," she had whispered to him, unbeknownst to Annie or Robert.

The nurse moved her head back and the doctor nodded while smiling and turned back to the door. He pushed the door open all the way and the man appeared wearing a white uniform with gray pants on underneath. He dressed very professionally wearing his black leather shoes. His hair was slicked back and glowed near the light from the window down the hallway. He smiled upon seeing Robert and Annie when he first walked in.

"Hi, I'm Doctor Reginald Wiley, it's a pleasure to meet you," Wiley said and shook Robert's hand and smiled and nodded at Annie. Wiley seemed to be very young for a doctor but Annie thought that he must be good if Ulmer recommended him and gotten through school so quick. She always knew doctors to be men with gray hair and gray beards so when she first saw Wiley, with a smooth face and full black hair, she was caught off guard. "So, who do we have sitting on the table?" He proceeded to ask when he looked over at Frederick.

"This is our son, Frederick," Robert said.

"Hi, Frederick. My name is Doctor Wiley and there's nothing to be afraid of," he said as he walked towards Frederick. As he approached, he smiled and brought his face close to Frederick's. He looked into Frederick's eyes and then moved Frederick's head to the left and right while continuing to look into his eyes.

"He's very sick and has been sick for a few days. We don't know what's wrong and our local doctor in Athens couldn't help," Robert said.

"And, Ulmer told you to come to see me? One of my nurses told me."

"Correct. He said you have dealt with this before and have helped people with similar conditions," Annie said.

"How do you know Ulmer, if you don't mind me asking?" Wiley asked while he brought his hand down and placed it on Frederick's chest to feel his heartbeat. He then brought his ear down and placed it on Frederick's chest to listen to his breathing.

"My grandmother knew him well and was part of the same religion. So, I've known him my entire life and, well, I had to come to him for help with what Frederick did."

"What did the little man do?" Wiley asked in regards to Frederick.

"Well, my family and I believe that if anyone brings a book with violent or dark tales or tells of such a story, then they allow evil to come into the household. Frederick was reading a book a few nights ago about evil," Annie told Wiley.

"Yes, I have heard of similar stories to that," Wiley said. "You aren't the first parents to come in with a child who they believed was possessed with something like a demonic presence."

"Really? So you believe us? You think it is true?" Annie asked, surprised that there have been others but also a bit relieved. Robert continued to stand by Annie's side and put his hand on her back to support her.

"Not sure if believe is the correct word, but I've seen similar instances and I've helped numerous other children."

"So, you can help our Frederick?" Annie quickly asked.

"I will do my best, Ma'am. Sometimes the instances are beyond my control but I give you my word that I will do my best. I've done this quite a few times the past few hun…I mean, past few years after becoming a doctor and specializing in demonic studies."

"I am glad Ulmer recommended you," Robert said.

"Me too, you're our last resort," Annie said and began to cry knowing that if Wiley wasn't able to help, she wasn't sure what to do next.

"Can you help me with Frederick, please?" Wiley asked and Annie stood while Robert walked over.

"What do you need me to do?" Robert asked.

"I need to draw some blood for analyzing. I will need you to hold him down and keep him still. Robert, can you hold one side and Annie the other and keep him comfortable?"

Annie walked to the other side of the bed while Wiley went over to the cabinet and got a large syringe ready to draw the blood.

"How do you know Ulmer? If you don't mind me asking," Annie finally asked. She looked at Wiley as did Robert since they were both curious to hear his answer. Wiley waited a few seconds before answering while he looked at the syringe.

"Well, he and I go back quite a few years," Wiley started. "When I first started studying demonic creatures and evil presence during my schooling, I needed to learn about different religions and beliefs. I had heard of Ulmer and went to visit him and we started a friendship. It's been my honor to have gotten to know him and help out many people he has sent my way," Wiley said but lied – unknowing to Robert and Annie. "So, how is Ulmer these days?" Wiley asked as he walked back over to Frederick. "Is he still as youthful as ever?"

Annie was too busy watching and worrying about Frederick and only heard parts of Wiley's question. "He's aged a lot, not doing overly well," she said to quickly answer his question.

Wiley got back to Frederick and stood beside Robert. "Robert, can you please bring up Frederick's sleeve so I can take blood from his vein?" He asked and pointed to Frederick's forearm. Robert unbuttoned his son's sleeve and rolled it up to his bicep.

"Thank you," Wiley said. "Please, gently hold him down now."

Robert and Annie held their son's arms down to prevent too much moving as Wiley inserted the needle and spent fifteen seconds taking out blood. He only drew one vile since the test was simple. He took out the needle and placed a piece of wet cotton on the hole that began to pour out a little blood. He wrapped a piece of cloth around it to hold it in place and said, "Please, follow me." He began to walk to the counter and Robert and Annie followed behind him. "I'll place this vial of blood in front of this candle and the color will tell the level of contamination."

"What do you mean?" Robert asked when they got to the counter.

"The darker the blood, the more evil that has possessed the body. The lighter and more reddish the blood the better," Wiley said and took out a piece of paper from his desk with a row of color starting from a light red to a red color that looked more black than any other color. "We will compare his blood to our color chart here," he said and placed the paper on the counter. He then moved the candle closer on the counter to make the counter brighter. He brought out a white cloth from a drawer and put it on the countertop next to the paper with the color chart. He took the clear vile and placed it on the white cloth and the three of them looked at it. Wiley held back his smile when he first saw the results.

"What does the color mean?" Annie first asked.

"It looks dark," Robert followed up by saying.

"The blood is very dark, I'm sorry to say," Wiley said before being interrupted.

"What do you mean to say you're 'sorry'?" Annie shockingly asked and turned to look at the doctor.

"He's not well. We need to keep him here overnight and perform a few more tests but the results, I'm sorry, do not look good. Look at this chart," he said and pointed. "Look at the color of your son's blood, the color is dark just like the last color on this chart. His blood looks almost black instead of reddish. This color means he's possessed and his soul weak. It, it will be hard for him to overcome this."

"What will happen?" Robert asked while Annie stood still, not yet crying with the anticipation with what the doctor would say next. She then went next to Robert and put her arm around his back.

"Well, let me keep him overnight. We have a room across the hall with a bed and he'll have nurse care all night. I need to focus on him and I want you to trust that I will do my best but with the way his blood looks, the chances are slim."

Annie finally began crying hysterically and Robert walked her over to the chair and had her sit down.

"I'm so sorry," Wiley said again, knowing what Robert and Annie were going through since even though he was able to cure most that he had seen, there were a couple that were too forgone just as it seemed Frederick was. The light red colored infected were easy to cure and since evil wasn't as persistent in their souls, it wasn't worth Wiley's time to keep them. "There is a hotel here in town, a nice hotel. Tell them that your son is staying at the hospital and mention my name and they'll let you stay the night for no charge.

"Can we stay here? Next to Frederick?" Annie asked, wanting to be next to her son.

"Sorry, but I need to focus and have concentration and try my best. His soul is really dark and I will need all the focus to help him. With that in mind, time is ticking and I must begin immediately. The nurse will show you back down to the office. Come back tomorrow at seven in the morning and I'll meet you in the office for an update. Until then, I know you've traveled far so get some rest and know I will do my best."

Annie continued to cry and Robert consulted her by wrapping his arm around her as the doctor let them out of the office. As Wiley pushed them out of the room by placing his hand behind Robert's lower back and gently nudging him, Annie looked back at Frederick one last time before they left the room. She looked at her son and saw his face looking at her blankly while she continued to cry. Wiley closed the door as they got to the hallway.

"Nurse?" Wiley shouted down the hall. She came walking out of one of the nearby rooms. "Please, show Robert and Annie back to the waiting area. We will need to get the room ready for Frederick tonight for testing and observation."

"Yes, Doctor," she said. The same nurse that brought them upstairs showed them the way downstairs as they all walked in silence. Annie sobbed the entire way while Robert held her hand. They were both speechless and dumbfounded as to what was happening as the realism that Frederick might not be okay went through their minds.

CHAPTER 14

Doctor Wiley sat Frederick up at the table. "Frederick, we need to run a few more tests on you so please, come with me," he said to begin earning Frederick's trust, even though he knew Frederick wouldn't speak since he's seen this condition numerous times. Wiley had seen the darkness in young children's souls before and knew what to do and had a plan. He brought Frederick to the room across the hall where there was a window allowing a bit of light to come in on an overcast day. The nurse eventually returned and saw the door to the room across the hall opened and walked inside and saw Frederick lying in the bed.

"Well?" She asked Wiley, wondering what was going to happen next.

"Do we have a new soul hunter?" He said quietly to her as they both smiled.

"Are you sure?" She asked him as her eyes perked up in excitement.

"Yes," he reiterated.

"Who's the source?"

"Ulmer. I know, before you say anything, he hasn't had a lead for many decades but this boy seems like a strong soul," Wiley said. Reginald Wiley and his nurse, Clarice, had been married for over two hundred years and survived by killing. They are both soul hunters – just like Ulmer.

Reginald had first met Ulmer in New York when Reginald had just killed two teenagers to regain some youth. Teenagers and runaways were easy targets and easy for manipulation. When he would kill someone, depending on how strong souled the person was, he gained multiple years but if someone was weak, their life longevity was less whereas he wouldn't become as youthful. He had murdered the two teenagers before coming up with a plan to help his aging wife.

Reginald joined a group of runaways as he was again youthful and upon speaking with and befriending Ulmer, he decided to bring them to his wife since she hadn't killed in a decade and needed strong souls. Reginald showed his dominance and power and impressed Ulmer. His plan was to start a new religious faction with Ulmer as an eventual soul hunter as long as he became possessed himself. He saw the perfect opportunity to draw Ulmer and anyone else in when he saw the young girl in the group had a book that featured violence. Upon seeing that book, he shared his beliefs and drew fear into all the kids in the group. He conjured his strong spirit and brought evil into the barn to strike lightning to show and prove his dominance. Ulmer was impressed and when they were apart from the rest of the group, Reginald told Ulmer his true identity.

"You'll meet my wife soon," Reginald said as they both walked to a nearby small dilapidated shed and sat behind it on a fallen tree trunk. The rest of the group remained in another smaller barn for the night.

"You're married?" Ulmer asked surprisingly. "What are you doing out here then?"

"I hold all my confidence in you. I've noticed your strong will, your strong soul, and your strong beliefs and I'll tell you my true identity. With that in mind, are you willing to uphold the law in possession and evil in Heathenness Ideology?"

"What do you mean?" Ulmer asked and stared at Reginald. He was caught off guard since he thought they were fighting off evil as they did the previous day in the barn.

"Do you want to be invincible?" Reginald asked.

"Umm...I, I," Ulmer started and stuttered. "Yes, yes I would, I think," he said. Ulmer had always idolized the gods in Greek mythology and the thought of being invincible brought satisfaction into his mind.

"You hesitated, are you sure?" Reginald asked again after hearing Ulmer mess up his words while speaking. "You need to be one hundred percent engaged in this and you and only you."

"Yes, I want that," Ulmer stated a bit too loud.

"Quiet, the others might hear us," Reginald said while they remained outside the barn on the way to Georgia.

"Sorry," Ulmer said and looked around to be sure no one else was around. "What do I need to do?" He asked worriedly, hoping this wasn't some crazy idea or notion from a stranger he had just met. He had seen Reginald's power previously in the barn and was willing to listen.

"Pledge your life to the soul hunters to become one. There is evil around us and some of us accidentally fall into the life of a soul hunter, such as myself, but others can find a way as long as they're willing and their souls strong enough. A lot of people, mainly children, have weak souls and when their souls become possessed, their souls become strong but they're no longer who they once were. If whatever possesses them is strong enough, their souls can be manipulated to become a soul hunter and live forever. We started as a small fraction worldwide, thousands of years ago but now we're in the estimated thousands. You will need to have connections and know who you can truly trust and contact. I have numerous contacts worldwide."

"Wow," Ulmer murmured and sat silently, moving his head from looking at Reginald to looking straight ahead at the vast farmland under the darkness of night. He attempted to comprehend what Reginald was telling him. "So, how did you become a soul hunter?" An astonished Ulmer asked as he sat on the fallen wood tree behind the shed. Reginald sat next to him and put his hands on his knees and placed his head on the back of the shed.

"Mine was accidental. It happened almost three hundred years ago when I stayed at a friend's house and he told me a scary story. I was very young and my friend told the story which I was frightened. Then after, we heard knocking on his door in his room. He ran up and locked it and came down next to me when suddenly, the candle blew out and the room was pitch black. Within a couple of minutes of silence as we both sat scared, the candle flame came back and when the room lit up, the door was opened. I thought my friend had done it and he thought I had done it but when we both realized it was neither of us, we ran to his parent's room when I was tripped – by someone or something. When I woke up and what I remember next, I was in a house with a lady and man who said they were my mom and dad but I could not remember anything or even who I was. I later found out they weren't my real parents and that I had become possessed."

"What happened to your real mother and father?" Ulmer asked curiously.

"At the time, I didn't know. After I tripped, I didn't remember anything nor knew what happened. I asked my new parents numerous times why I couldn't remember anything about my past and what happened to me. They knew I couldn't remember what happened so they told me I had parents before but they were evil and wanted to put me up for adoption and my new parents adopted me. It hurt when I was younger but I got used to it. I didn't realize until I got older what really happened."

"What really happened?" Ulmer asked, remaining curious and wanting to hear the rest of the story.

"I was raised by my new parents and lived a normal life. I went to school a few more years before getting a job on a farm and as I got into my late teenager years, I realized that I was different."

"Different?"

"It's hard to explain but you'll feel it soon. I felt different in a way that I started to remember back to the night that I was tripped. I asked my parents, well, my new parents, now that eight years had gone by and I was remembering the night I was tripped, what had happened. I sat down with them and told them what I remembered. I remembered the door was opened in my friend's bedroom and when we ran, I felt a hand reach my leg and trip me. It was at that time something entered my spirit and took over my soul."

"Who would take it over? How?"

"I'll get to that soon. But, once my soul was overtaken, I went into the hospital and nobody could figure out what was wrong with me and my parents disowned me and saw me as too much of a challenge to raise so they put me up for adoption. A group of people who are also soul hunters scour the news and orphanages for troubled children such as myself and see if I'm curable or strong souled – strong enough to become the next soul hunter. My evil was too big but since I was still so young and so weak spiritually, it's the jobs of the parents to raise the child into adulthood or until the child realizes they're different."

"You mean your parents were soul hunters? Your new parents? Where are they now?"

"They not only raised me but dozens of other children, possibly even more, throughout their lifetime. I remember about a century ago was the last time I saw them. They were tired and wanted to cease existence so they stopped soul hunting and became aged before they died of illness. There are still many others out there throughout the world that raise troubled children which is why connections are so important to have."

"Your story sounds so surreal," Ulmer said in disbelief but continued watching Reginald to hear more.

"Trust me, it does for everyone. When I was told the story by my new parents, I didn't know what to expect until I saw a soul hunter kill and become younger."

After a few seconds of silence, Ulmer asked, "Do you know how all the soul hunters began or who the first soul hunter was?"

"Yes. Remember when I said my soul was taken over?" Ulmer nodded. "That's the master soul hunter. He finds the weakest and most vulnerable people and enters into their soul to take over and create internal evil."

"So it's not a real person?"

"He used to be. You'll find out soon. He's become so powerful that he's more than a man now."

"How can you prove this is all real to me?"

"Trust me for a couple of more days. You'll meet my wife soon and see her much older than I. Then, we'll do a ritual and she'll become younger. That, indeed, should be enough proof for you. Then, when it's your turn, you'll feel the power of the main soul hunter – the man himself. Just remember, Ulmer, don't kill too often or too much where you will become younger than when you became a soul hunter since your soul will be erased and banished into nothingness."

CHAPTER 15

A couple of days went by when they approached closer to Reginald's home. Nobody else in the group knew where they were going or that he was even married. While the group rested near a stream in the forest, Reginald pulled Ulmer aside.

"We're almost to my house," Reginald told Ulmer while they walked further down the stream and alone.

"What are we going to do with everyone? Are you going to kill them?" Ulmer asked with sad emotion in his voice after getting to know them so well while traveling together.

"No, not but a couple. Here's the plan I've been thinking of. As soul hunters, we need to also feed the master soul hunter."

"How do we do that?" Ulmer asked as they stopped walking and stood while Reginald stared into the stream.

"We need to create weakness in people. We help the master by making people weak and therefore, he can find them and conquer their souls. It's up to us all to work as teams around the world in order to feed him so we don't upset him."

"Where does he live?" Ulmer asked, wondering how someone could travel the world so often.

Reginald hesitated a few seconds, thinking of an answer but nobody really knew where he lived. "We don't find him, he finds us," he finally said.

"Oh, I see," Ulmer said and was continuing having difficulty grasping what Reginald was telling him since it all sounded strange. They both stood quietly for a moment while Reginald looked up towards the sky and around at all the bright stars through the trees surrounding the river.

"Have you heard of any old superstitions and wives' tales?" Reginald asked.

"Yes, I grew up with a few."

"What was one of them?"

"I do recall hearing a cat cry at night will bring death into a household," Ulmer answered after thinking for a few seconds.

"Believe it or not, soul hunters created most superstitions to instill fear. Having people be scared and be filled with weakness is what welcomes us into their lives as well as the master. Just as if someone reads a book featuring evil or horror, the superstition creates a void in their soul that they are questioning what will happen and instill fear within themselves. This way, we can fill the fear of violence in the household and for nobody to let violence into their homes. When parents become overly paranoid, they leave a void and entrance for evil to enter upon them and evil will overtake anyone who's weak – usually the child, one, or even both parents or whoever else might be in the household. I've seen three sisters become overtaken once at the same time."

"That's interesting," Ulmer said, dragging out the syllables of the last word. He was so overwhelmed with everything Reginald was telling him. He continued to think every so often that Reginald was lying or just telling a story until he remembered the lightning strike in the barn that caught the old book on fire. "I remember a few other old tales and each time I would think about them in the past, I would be a bit worried indeed."

"Exactly. Throughout the thousands of years we have been around as a collective people, we've created many superstitions and tales and passed them through many generations and many still survive today. Many more are being created as we speak."

"So, if I can ask, when did everything begin? I mean, when did the soul hunter first appear?"

"That's a very good question," Reginald responded. He walked next to the river, pacing back and forth a few yards each way. He looked over at Ulmer who was now sitting on a rock and watched Reginald's every move. Reginald then lied down on the dirt and put his hands together and interlocked his fingers and placed it behind his head. "I love watching the stars. I mean, they don't move or anything, but there's a slight twinkle often times."

Ulmer nodded and began thinking why Reginald enjoyed watching the stars so often and thought maybe it had something to do with his past or life. "What do you find so fascinating about the stars?" He finally asked.

Reginald chucked. "First, let me start about the soul hunters." Reginald sat up and brought up his knees and placed his arms behind him to lean back. He looked around, continuing to make sure nobody else was around them so he could carry on with his story. "Egypt, nearly 5,000 years ago, when Upper and Lower Egypt combined into one. Look up towards the North Star," Reginald said and pointed towards a section of the sky. Ulmer looked towards that direction and noticed one star brighter than the other in between the scattered tree tops. "Do you see it?"

"Yes, I think so," Ulmer said, knowing the brightest star was the North Star.

"Remember, if you ever feel lost or about to give up, look towards the North Star. Even in the brightest of lights, know in the sky where to look and you'll be noticed."

Reginald brought his head down and looked towards Ulmer who continued to look towards the sky, making a mental note on where its location was if it were daylight. Ulmer looked down and noticed Reginald looking at him.

"The North Star is where he lives," Reginald said.

"Who is 'he'?" Ulmer asked curiously.

"He, is the Master. So, back to the story. About 5,000 or so years ago, the Pharaoh of Egypt named Narmer united Upper and Lower Egypt. Remember that Lower is actually the north part of Egypt and Upper is the southern portion," Reginald said and saw Ulmer nod as if he understood. "So, Narmer made a deal with the Underworld to unite Upper and Lower and to do so, he made a deal with Anubis."

"Who is Anubis?" Ulmer asked. Ulmer knew about Greek mythology but not much about Ancient Egypt and Egyptology.

"Anubis, traditionally known as Anpu during the days of Narmer, was a jackal faced deity from Ancient Egypt who was the god of the dead and the Underworld."

"Wow, what did Narmer do?" Ulmer asked. He was really wanting to know what kind of deal was made. Reginald turned and looked at Ulmer and saw his eyes staring at him wanting an answer. Reginald smiled, knowing the story had Ulmer on edge and wanting more.

"So, do you want to know what Narmer did?" Reginald asked and continued to look at Ulmer. Ulmer shook his head immediately. "Well, Narmer had a priest transcribe his words in hieroglyphics onto a scroll. He and a priest sat inside the priest's temple on a hot night. Candles lit up the room and the priest wrote word by word what Narmer told him to write. As the priest was halfway done with what Narmer was telling him, he supposedly looked up to Narmer and said, 'why do you demand I write such terror?' Narmer looked at him with fierceness in his bulging eyes and with a deep demanding voice, he yelled, 'write what I tell you,' as his voice echoed through the large room. The priest was terrified and dared not go against his Pharaoh and continued to write. Nearly a half hour went by when the priest finished writing and looked up to Narmer. Narmer grabbed the pen from the priest and dipped it in ink and signed his name on the bottom. 'Roll it and bring it outside,' Narmer demanded the priest to do. The priest rolled up the scroll and walked past the door where Narmer had two guards standing outside the door. Narmer grabbed a nearby candle and followed the priest outside.

The priest stood outside in the dark sky, terrified as what would happen next. Narmer walked and stood directly behind the priest. The priest started to turn when Narmer demanded, 'look straight ahead!' Suddenly, there was a rumble in the sky that told Narmer that it was time. Narmer came from behind the priest and told the priest to hold out the scroll. Narmer tipped the candle slowly towards the scroll to drop melted wax onto it to seal it. A few moments went by when there were finally enough drops on the edge of the scroll to seal it. Narmer was careful to hold the candle away enough to not light the scroll on fire until it was sealed. Once the scroll was secure, when Narmer was ready to move the candle back, a flame jumped from the candle and pressed against the dry scroll and immediately brought it into a blaze. The priest jumped back and attempted to let go of the scroll but couldn't. He tried to move his hands but his hands were paralyzed and he did what he could and turned to find water but it was too late. The fire spread instantly onto the priest's hands, onto his arms and throughout his clothing to engulf his body in flames. He stood on fire for less than a minute until his lifeless body fell over onto the dirt ground. The guards by the door remained standing as Narmer pointed at them to remain. Narmer watched as the priest's body squirmed for a few additional seconds until the nerves stopped moving.

Narmer continued standing near the priest until he died and when life went away from the priest, the scroll continued to be ablaze and the ashes floated up into the air. Narmer watched, astonished at where the ashes were going as they continued to float into the night sky. He watched the flames and ash go into the dark sky until the fire stopped when the scroll was out of sight. He continued looking around and saw stars and a partial moon in his peripheral vision but could no longer see any remnants of the scroll. He looked back down and saw the burnt remains and ashes of the priest and told his two guards to get rid of the body. As they moved from the doorway and stood by the priest, Narmer took out a knife and stabbed both of his guards – there were to be no witnesses. Narmer stepped back and whispered, 'Burn them to death…' directed towards Anubis. He took a few steps back waiting for a blaze but nothing happened. Louder, he demanded, 'Burn them!' but again, nothing happened.

He didn't know why Anubis wouldn't burn their bodies or what happened and he then looked around at the darkness surrounding him. The only light was from the partial moon and candles coming from inside the priests' temple. Suddenly, something fell from the sky and hit him on the head. He looked down towards the ground and saw his scroll as if nothing had happened to it. Shocked, he hurried and picked it up and saw the seal had been broken so he unraveled it and it was indeed his scroll. He glanced through it and everything was how he remembered except by his name, there was a signature of Set. Set, also known as Seth, is another Egyptian deity. Set is known for his trickery and master of chaos and violence as well as the god of fire."

"Woah, what happened next?" Ulmer asked.

"Narmer was tricked."

"What do you mean? How was he tricked?"

"The whole time, Narmer thought he was dealing with Anubis but instead, Set had intervened and portrayed himself as Anubis to trick Narmer. In the document that was signed by Narmer, he agreed to give his soul to Anubis, but only if Anubis agreed with the document but by Set signing it, Narmer's soul now belonged to Set. When Narmer saw Set's signature beside his own on the scroll, he threw the scroll in not only disbelief but anger and as it landed, the scroll bounced onto one of his guards and immediately lit both guards on fire. Having made a deal with an evil deity and demon, Narmer was deemed to live an eternity under Set's reign."

"What happened to Narmer?" Ulmer then asked. It was beginning to get late and Reginald knew he had to finish the story before someone came down the river to check on them.

"Within history, nobody truly knows or agrees how Narmer died. What I know and other soul hunters know is that when he died, his soul was abolished to the dark sky in flames. Do you see the North Star, Ulmer?"

Ulmer looked back up and saw the bright star in the sky and looked back at Reginald and nodded.

"His soul was sent to the night sky in flames after he died and disappeared into the sky such as when his scroll vanished into the darkness. Instead, as the man who united Upper and Lower Egypt, his soul went into the sky and lit up what we now know as the North Star. The legend goes, that Anubis was so angered with Set that Set agreed to give Anubis the lost souls. The reason the ending is a legend is that when a soul hunter dies, they never come back – a lost soul."

"What happens when a soul hunter dies?" Ulmer asked, needing to know if he was going to become a soul hunter himself.

"As I said, nobody really knows besides that your soul is given to Anubis to be taken to the Underworld for the rest of eternity – whatever that is since no one has ever escaped the Underworld to tell."

"I'm sure living under Anubis' mercy for eternity would not be a good thing," Ulmer said, worried what would happen after death.

"I can't even imagine. I guess just another reason for a soul hunter to keep killing to survive and live," Reginald said.

"So, I'm curious to ask now," Ulmer said and hesitated to ask.

"What's that?" Reginald asked him back after waiting for a few seconds of silence.

"Is Narmer the master soul hunter?"

"Good question and that is an answer I do not know. Legend says yes, but legend also says no. With regards to those who say no, some believe the master is Set, while others do believe it to be Narmer. One thing that I do know is, you never want to meet the master. So, keep the master happy by living, killing and giving him power instead of dying and giving power to Anubis."

Wow, Ulmer thought to himself and looked again towards the sky and looked for the North Star which he found almost immediately.

At that time, Ulmer was in disbelief what he was hearing about the beginning of the soul hunters but was startled when he heard the noise of someone or something walking on the leaves in the forest. He and Reginald sat quietly and looked at that direction in the darkness and eventually saw one of the teenagers in their group come out.

"Oh, here you guys are. We were all wondering where you were and to make sure you were both safe," the boy asked.

"Just enjoying the fresh air and watching the stars," Reginald said.

The boy looked up at the sky and said, "Yes, there are many of them out today." He paused a few seconds while looking up until he spoke again, "Some of the kids are going to sleep since it's getting late, you both going to come back to the camp?" They had set up sleeping areas in the forest that night since there were no barns or buildings to sleep and the weather was nice.

Reginald sprung up from the ground and stretched his arms and back and looked at Ulmer. Ulmer still was confused and overwhelmed with what Reginald told him. He believed him but wasn't totally sure that everything he said was the truth but knew he would be finding out soon if Reginald was right or not. Inside, Ulmer was having second thoughts of what he was getting into and wanted to prevent those from bringing weakness into their souls by doing things such as bringing violent and horrific texts into their households but also felt the greed to live forever.

CHAPTER 16

The following morning the group left early at sunset and walked for a half a day when they saw a ranch house and barn down a dusty road.

"Everyone, let's stop at this house up here and see if they may have any food for us. When we get up there, you see there's a barn up there. You all hide behind the barn and I'll go up to the house and see if they have any food, water or anything else for us," Reginald said. The group all agreed by either shaking their heads or mumbling in agreement. When they reached the barn, the sun was at the highest peak in the sky and the kids were all hot and thirsty. There was no breeze and the corn stalks they had walked by through the day's journey stood still with the lack of wind. Sweat dripped down onto the wool shirts of everyone and seeing the barn up ahead was the first they had seen for hours.

"Actually, Ulmer, why don't you come with me just in case," Reginald then said before he turned around to begin walking down the road. They all got to the barn and Reginald had them stand behind it in the shade so they could rest and cool down. They looked around for water but couldn't find a well or trough that might have water in it. The two began to walk towards the house. Reginald walked casually towards the house while Ulmer looked cautiously around them.

"Reginald, walk slower, we don't know if the people here will have guns like before," Ulmer said, referencing back to two weeks prior where a man held a rifle at the group.

"Oh, don't worry, Ulmer. This is where I live."

Ulmer stopped walking and looked at Reginald. "What?" He blurted loudly but not quite loud enough for the others to hear.

"Keep it quiet. This is my house. I want you to meet my wife. Let's go inside and you can meet her and we can talk."

Ulmer started walking again but this time slower. A lot went through his mind including Reginald and his wife being soul hunters. He was worried they may try and kill him so he was very cautious as to what was around him while he walked – looking at every detail. He noticed a porch wrapping halfway around the front of the house as well as a shed in the back with the door shut. He looked up at a large tree providing shade for a large portion of the house and attempted to find any signs of threat or other people he didn't know.

"What are you going to do with me?" Ulmer quietly asked, not wanting to upset Reginald.

Reginald stopped walking and turned towards Ulmer and looked at him directly. "Out of everyone here, you're the one I trust and I see potential in and want you to join me as a soul hunter. Not just join me, but join us and I need your help."

"But, what if I said no?" Ulmer finally asked. He had a hard time falling asleep the night before thinking all that Reginald told him and what if he didn't want to become a soul hunter. He contemplated the idea numerous times before finally falling asleep due to such a long day walking.

"After all is said and done, I know you won't," Reginald said.

"How do you know?" A nervous Ulmer asked and stood a few feet away from Reginald.

"I saw the way you looked at the North Star and the twinkle it had when you looked at it."

"Oh," Ulmer said, knowing that he was indeed very interested in joining Reginald but was still on the cautious side.

They both silently continued up to the two story house with an attic. Ulmer looked at the attic window and was positive he had seen something but then the curtain fell, blocking the window. He looked around the rest of the house and saw curtains closed on all the other windows. The house needed to be painted as there was chipping and discoloration around what used to a white house. They proceeded closer when the door opened and a female voice was heard. "Reg!" the voice yelled.

"Shhh, not so loud," Reginald said back but not loud enough where the others could hear him.

Both he and Ulmer walked up to the front door and Ulmer could see a woman's head looking out from the slightly opened door. "Come on in, Ulmer," Reginald said as the woman opened the door. "Ulmer, this is my wife, Helen."

Ulmer was surprised seeing a woman that was old enough to be Reginald's mother, nonetheless his grandmother. The woman had long, curly black hair with numerous gray highlights that stood out even in the darkened home. There was a curtain letting in light from the kitchen in the room past the living room, lighting up the room enough for Ulmer to see a few wrinkles in the woman's face. Her long white gown draped to the grown as she walked barefoot on the wood slat floor. The kitchen window was open which let in a nice breeze that flew in and hit the front door and wall and stopped, bringing a coolness into the first floor of their home.

"Hi, Helen. It is my pleasure to meet you, my name is Ulmer."

"Ulmer, the pleasure is mine," Helen said and smiled towards him.

"I saw you hesitate there for a few seconds, Ulmer," Reginald started. "As I told you, Helen hasn't killed in a while and needs more life to become younger. Hence, why I brought the group this way."

"Who are you going to kill?" Ulmer asked. "I'm sorry, I don't mean to bring such violent talk within the presence of a woman."

Helen chuckled, "No worries, Dear."

"Not all of them. I wanted to bring you inside to not only meet Helen but to go over a plan I had been thinking about after all the hours walking the past weeks. I became the leader of the group and brought them here for a reason so please, come into the kitchen and have a seat at the table. Helen, would you mind getting us some water?"

Helen went to a large bucket next to the sink and Ulmer watched her reach in with a metal cup and pour the water from the cup into a pitcher. He watched out of the corner of his eyes while Reginald began speaking. He still wasn't in complete trust.

"So, Ulmer, my first question is do you want to become a soul hunter?"

Without hesitation, Ulmer nodded and said, "Yes, I do."

"How sure are you? Once you do, there's no turning back and remember the story I told you last night."

"I'm sure, Reginald. I want this."

Reginald smiled and nodded in satisfaction. "Okay, let's go over the plan. Let me know what you think," Reginald began while Helen brought over the pitcher and two glasses.

"Thanks, Ma'am," Ulmer said and immediately poured water into his glass and began to drink since he was thirsty.

"First, do not tell anyone Helen is in here nor anything else besides that the person who lives here let us stay in the barn for the night and gave us some bread and water," Reginald said while Ulmer nodded as he poured more water into his glass. "Second, we go over the plan with the group later tonight before bed. What I want you to do is take just over half the group and lead a congregation somewhere here in Georgia – let's say, Athens? Then, I'll take the others, the three eldest, and they will come with me and give Helen life."

"What do you want me to do with the congregation?" Ulmer asked after he set his glass down on top of the tablecloth on the small round table in the corner of the kitchen.

"Heathenness Ideology…become a teacher. Not just a teacher, but a leader. You need to instill fear into their minds as I did days ago in the barn when young Emmie was reading the book. Teach them superstition and instill the fears and make them weak so when they falter, the master can feed and even possibly find strong candidates for future soul hunters. "

"Should I set up a Church or something?"

Reginald took two swigs of water and set his glass down. "No need, just teach out of your house and be a mentor to them so when they become older, they can pass the ideas down to their children, their children's children, and others in their communities and wherever they go."

"Okay, is there anything else I need to know?"

"Yes, come find me if you need anything. I'll be your mentor and help when able. But, most importantly do not forget what I am about to tell you. Remember, if you get tired of living, a soul hunter who no longer wants to live can stop killing and indeed die of illness, old age, suicide, or whatever the case, but think of what awaits you in the Underworld for eternity. Also, continue instilling fear into people you come in contact with and the stronger souled the person is, the more life you will receive from their death. The elderly and children are weak. So, let me take the eldest and you the rest and we'll go our separate ways tomorrow morning."

"Athens, that's a couple of hours away, at most?" Ulmer asked, having remembered recently seeing a map and wanting to know how far Reginald would be if he needed to find him.

"If that, I believe. I'll be here if you need me or even ask Helen," Reginald said. By then, Helen had joined them at the table and listened to their conversation. She was excited that there were a few strong teenagers that would help her become young and strong again.

Ulmer sat silently as more questions rushed through his mind but he was too overwhelmed to ask except for one. "Reginald, how did you come up with the religion? Heathenness Ideology?"

"Well, I was initially raised Catholic since my mother and father were catholic for what I heard from my foster parents. After I was possessed and shown to be a strong leader, I wanted to create a group following not only so I can have contacts and people to trust, but also so we can spread the word of paranoia to help the master and keep him happy."

Ulmer nodded. "So, what's going to happen next? What will happen to me?" He asked worriedly since he didn't know how he would become a soul hunter.

"This is your final chance," Reginald said while Helen smiled with excitement. "Are you sure you want to become a soul hunter? There will be no turning back."

Ulmer nodded again. "I do."

"Hold out your right hand," Reginald said and stood from the chair. He walked over to the sink and got a sharp knife. He plunged it into a pale of water and walked over to the table with it. Ulmer was immediately terrified seeing Reginald holding a knife and didn't know what was going to happen next.

"Don't be scared. Don't be scared," Reginald whispered as he got closer to the table. "Stand up," he said. Reginald used the knife to cut the palm of his hand as blood began to gush from his palm. With his bloody hand, Reginald reached for Ulmer's and used the same knife to cut a gash into his right palm and immediately grasped hands and whispered, "ut infra caelum, nunc anima mae es tu venandi. Puer occisio et mors addendi," which translates to, 'to the heavens below, you are now a soul hunter. Killing and death adds to youth.' Reginald released Ulmer's shaking hand and Ulmer took a couple of steps back and stood silent. They both stared at one another for a long minute until Ulmer finally smiled. Reginald smiled immediately after. "Killing will make you younger. Try it for the first time and you shall see but wait until you are older as remember what I had said before, do not kill and become younger than this age from when you became a soul hunter."

Ulmer nodded and they went their separate ways. Since that day, Ulmer had felt different inside. He could feel more hatred towards people and felt the evil within him but Reginald knew Ulmer was strong and could handle the feelings in order to make the cause greater. Little did Ulmer know that Reginald had lied to him about his past and how he became possessed.

CHAPTER 17

The truth behind Reginald and the reason he lied to Ulmer was to make the story simpler. The truth of the matter is Reginald's father was head of a clan that came from England to the United States during the late eighteenth century that killed American Indians to gain youth. They then resorted to killing Africans and then even their fellow Europeans. Reginald was warry of his father's ways and ran away from home to start his own group once his father vanished. He felt the power within him and knew that he could start his own powerful religious group – so he thought.

Reginald was raised Catholic since his mother was Catholic and his father acted like he was. Instead, his father believed the satanic way and was a member of the group that had Reginald possessed. The evening when Reginald became seventeen years old, his father stood in front of him in their basement. Their mother was outside doing laundry when his father pulled a knife from a shelf in the basement. His father cut his hand such as Reginald did in front of Ulmer, and Reginald began crying.

"Stop crying, Son. Stop crying," his father said so he did. His father continued to whisper the same phrase to him that Reginald said to Ulmer. Reginald never told his mother who died ten years later but oddly, the following day his father vanished. It wouldn't be until nearly one hundred years later when they would come back in contact.

CHAPTER 18

In the 1860s, the American Civil War was booming where the Union and Confederacy fought numerous deadly battles. Death numbers were increasing daily and news of the War was featured all over newspapers throughout the country. Not soon after war began did Reginald read the headline, "Many Dead in War," and came up with an idea. He contacted many other soul hunters, including Ulmer and his friends, to get together and fight for the South. Firstly, they wanted to fight for the South to keep slavery and free labor but also, they found war to be an easy way to kill and get away with killing. Hundreds of them joined the Confederacy but it didn't take long for them to realize that being soul hunters didn't mean they were invincible. They found out their chances of survival became slimmer with the way they were outmanned and outmatched with weaponry and resources than the Union.

Quickly trained, Reginald, Ulmer and numerous other soul hunters from Georgia were fighting in what would later be known as the Battle of Shiloh in Tennessee. Outnumbered tremendously during the April 1862 battle, the soul hunters were on the wrong side of defeat. As guns blasted and cannons thundered through the fields, Ulmer and Reginald saw many of their friends killed. They attempted to fire their guns but with so much smoke and overwhelming of their senses, they struggled and ran behind a large wooded area to hide from incoming Union soldiers.

"Ulmer!" Reginald yelled in between the echoes of gunshots firing from all sides. Ulmer looked over towards the area where there were trees behind a small hill where he had barely heard his name. He saw Reginald squatting behind a large oak tree and ran immediately towards him. "Hurry!" Reginald yelled as a bullet whistled by him as he knelt lower and covered his head. He could hear Ulmer's footsteps come towards him as his head remained covered. Ulmer ran and jumped quickly to sit down next to Reginald.

"Reginald!" Ulmer yelled. "What are we going to do now?" He asked and looked around the tree to make sure the Union soldiers weren't coming their way.

Reginald looked back up and said, "I don't know." It was the only time Ulmer had heard the worry in Reginald's voice with the way he didn't have any idea on how to solve a problem. Reginald peeked around the tree again and saw another one of their soldiers coming their way. He didn't recognize him but turned and kept his back against the tree – thinking what to do next. After a few seconds, he turned back and looked again and the soldier had gotten close enough for Reginald to see the man's face. Ulmer looked in the distance for any oncoming soldiers. Reginald kept watching the man get close, wanting to bring him into safety. The man ran as fast as he could, his arms swinging from front to back as he stepped wildly on the uneven terrain with his worn boots. His head continued looking into the trees hoping for safety as his hat fell off but he continued running. As he came less than a few steps away, Reginald looked closely at the man's face.

"Dad?" He yelled and the man looked the direction of Reginald and stared blankly. Less than a step away from Reginald and Ulmer, a bullet splattered through his chest and blood exited the front with the bullet going in an unknown direction. "Dad!" Reginald yelled even louder with firepower echoing throughout. The man collapsed onto his knees and fell face first into the dirt. "Cover me," he told Ulmer. Ulmer held his rifle out from behind the tree while Reginald pulled the man towards him. He rolled him over and saw it was his dad but he no longer had a pulse, never truly knowing where his dad had gone or why he vanished.

After the battle and losing numerous friends and even family, many of the surviving soul hunters evaded further battle and went into hiding until after the war. What they figured as easy killing turned out to be a lot of being outnumbered by soldiers, weapons and resources. A few times after the war, Reginald and Ulmer got together to visit the graves in Confederate cemeteries of his father as well as some of their fallen friends and soul hunters from the battle – including some that stayed in the war but were eventually killed.

CHAPTER 19

Frederick remained lying in the bed with the sheets brought up under his chin to keep him warm in the cool room. The door to the corridor was open and Reginald and Helen spoke outside in the hall and Frederick could have heard them but he just stared into the ceiling as he lied flat on his back.

"The candles flickered as he walked down the hall," Helen told Reginald. "His soul is strong but weak…"

"I know, I feel it," Reginald said and interrupted her. "I must get to work on him immediately."

Helen went and sat at a chair near the far corner of the room Frederick was in. Reginald shut the door and walked over and sat on the side of the bed. Frederick continued looking blankly at the ceiling covered with thin wood slate while light lit up a shadow of a tree outside the window and placed a silhouette onto the wall. Reginald looked at Frederick's face and then from the side he looked into his eyes. He placed his hand on Frederick's neck to feel and count his pulse and kept his hand there for thirty seconds. He released his hand and looked back at Helen who had a pencil and paper to transcribe notes on what was going to happen. Reginald smiled and nodded and returned back to look at Frederick.

"Frederick," Reginald said while looking at him. Frederick slowly turned his face towards Reginald and looked at him.

"Is that me?" Frederick finally answered; the first words he had spoken in many days. His voice was weak and shallow but just loud enough for Helen to hear.

"Yes, your name is Frederick," Reginald said. When a young child was overtaken in their weakened soul, before transplanting into their new life, they must speak to a professional soul hunter as Reginald. Many times, though, weakened children would be mistaken for mentally ill or brain damaged and the parents often disgraced to have such a child. In this instance, Robert and Annie wanted to help

Frederick and get him better and put all their hope in Reginald, the man they know as Doctor Wiley.

"Frederick?" Frederick said slowly, emphasizing every letter to help him pronounce it.

"Yes, that is your name. How do you feel?"

After a moment of hesitation, Frederick looked around the room at Reginald and Helen and continued to look around at the empty space in the room with wood floors and white walls. "Are you my mom and dad?" He asked sorrowfully, having already forgotten about Robert and Annie. His bottom lip pouted and for the first time since he can remember, Frederick began feeling confused and unsure of what was happening. He had no remembrance of his past or even who his parents were. Reginald expected this and knew that Frederick was a great candidate to raise into a strong soul hunter.

"No, my name is Doctor Wiley and over in the corner is my nurse. We are here to help you out," Reginald said with a smile to affirm positivity in Frederick's mind which was forming many ideas and questions. He was very vulnerable in his state.

"What am I doing here? Where are my mom and dad?" Frederick was sad and confused where he was and continued to look back at Helen in the corner and then back up to Reginald.

"Don't worry, Frederick. Everything is okay. Let me tell you why you're here." Reginald had gone through this process numerous times with other gifted children so he knew what was going to happen and what to tell Frederick.

"Your parents are not doing well and had me help you out. We will be here to help you regain your life again," Reginald said. Frederick started to cry having heard his parents are not well since he was so young and emotional, even though he couldn't even remember Robert or Annie. "Don't worry, okay? Everything will be just fine and I assure you of that."

CHAPTER 20

The following morning at exactly seven o'clock, Robert and Annie returned to the hospital to get an update on their son.

"Welcome back, Mr. and Mrs. Gunley," Dr. Reginald Wiley said upon seeing Robert and Annie in the waiting room. "Please, come on back," he said, showing no emotion whatsoever with the stillness in his eyes and lips, not wanting to present hope. He held the large door open for them to come back. Both Robert and Annie looked closely at the doctor's face to see if there was any positive look upon how his eyes set and his smile but his face showed no emotion without the slightest grin. They believed they would be seeing Frederick again but to their surprise, they would not. The walk was silent as they strode the same hallway and up the steps to the second floor. Robert and Annie held hands the entire way and were both very nervous to hear the update but both remained hopeful. The hallway seemed darker this day and as they continued to the room they were in the day before, the candles didn't flicker as before but they didn't notice. All they wanted to do was see Frederick and get an update.

"Please, come in," Reginald said and directed them in the same room they were in the day before. Helen held the door open while she wore her white nurse's gown.

"Thank you, Nurse," Annie said and proceeded inside behind Robert, followed by the doctor. Reginald leaned against the counter while Robert and Annie had a seat. They stared at the doctor, anticipating an answer but they look on the doctor's face showed them a bit of dread. He looked at the ground knowing they were both looking at him and he showed no emotion. Finally, as Helen closed the door Reginald began to speak.

"Firstly, let me get to the point. You both brought in young Frederick, entrusting me and hoping I would be of some help," Reginald began speaking when he stood up from leaning against the counter. He walked a couple of steps from the counter but remained staring at the ground. He stopped and finally looked towards Robert and Annie. Annie held up a silk handkerchief to her mouth to hide her fear and nervousness. She put her other hand on top of Robert's thigh and he put his hand atop her hand. Robert began tapping his foot once Reginald leaned off the counter and Annie could feel he was nervous too. She patted her hand on his thigh to tell him everything would be okay but when Reginald looked at the both of them, his foot stopped tapping.

"I'm sorry," Reginald said when looking at Annie before dropping his head immediately after speaking. Annie began to sob and brought the handkerchief up to her eyes to wipe the tears. Her head tilted in sadness and her eyes shut. Robert moved his arm to embrace her and moved her closer into his arm and hugged her. He looked at her and saw her crying and he learned over to kiss her on the side of her forehead.

Robert looked back over at Reginald who had since looked back at Robert and Annie. "What happens next?" Robert said and was very nervous as his words trembled slightly.

"Well, let me tell you what I know. I've done this numerous times before. Usually, with good results but once and a while, a child is beyond a child anymore," Reginald said. He moved over and walked towards Helen who had been standing in the dark corner, out of the way of the conversation. She was holding the small stack of papers from the previous day and Reginald held out his hand in a way to tell her to hand him the papers. She did and he brought them back to the counter. He browsed through a couple of sheets, already knowing what he would say but wanting to put on an act. He moved one sheet to the top of the stack and brought the papers up to his chest. He leaned back against the counter. "Frederick shows signs of being possessed," Reginald started.

"Possessed?" Annie blurted angrily in surprise and moved the handkerchief from her face.

Reginald nodded slightly while they both watched his every moment and listened to every word. "Yes, I'm afraid so. He showed numerous signs of possession, evil possession, and beyond being reconciled with who he once was."

"I knew it!" Annie demanded loudly.

Robert patted Annie's back and said in a quieter tone, "What do you mean possessed?"

"I'm sorry to say, Frederick is no longer who he used to be," Reginald said. Immediately Annie began sobbing again and Robert, who continued holding her in his arm leaned over and whispered in her ear. He whispered loud enough she could hear over her crying.

"Annie, it'll all be okay," he whispered to reassure her while holding her in his arm.

"I assure the both of you that I did what I could to bring him back," Reginald said before being interrupted by Robert.

"Is Frederick dead?" Robert asked before his mouth fell open. His bottom lip quivered anticipating a response and even saying those words. Annie kept her head down, tears falling onto her dress while she thought the worst.

"No, but, for his soul is."

Robert shook his head in disbelief. "What are we going to do now?" He asked.

"Well, there's only one option for what I can see. Two, actually, but I only recommend one. The one option I don't recommend is he going back home to you and Mrs. Gunley and you can raise him but he's no longer the boy he used to be. He won't be responsive and would be bed ridden all day long. The option I do recommend is I'll send him to foster care that takes care of children in the same state as he is in. The home is in Chicago and there will be a handful of other children in the same situation as him. He wouldn't be alone and he'll be brought up by care workers who are trained to help children like Frederick."

"When can we see him?" A sobbing Annie asked. She brought down her handkerchief from her face and with her head tilted towards the ground, she raised her eyes towards Reginald.

"Unfortunately, you cannot," he answered.

"Why not?" Robert asked.

"It's for the best," Reginald said. He moved away from the counter and took a few steps towards Robert and Annie and knelt beside them. "Look, I'm sorry for what happened but we here have Frederick's best interest at heart," he said while looking up towards Annie and then Robert.

"Will we ever see him again?" Annie hesitantly asked and kept her eyes shut to wipe the tears under her eyelids.

"I'm sorry," is all Reginald said before he paused. He finally spoke again after Robert brought his other arm to hug Annie tightly. "Frederick needs to go to the foster home where there are other children like himself and he can live the most normal life possible. Trust me, they have great people there that want to help and will help and have great success."

After hearing the unfortunate news, Reginald brought them back to the front door as all three of them walked in quiet, not saying a word until they got to the front door.

Reginald opened the door inward to let Robert and Annie out and said, "Again, I'm sorry. Cases like this are our worst results but think about the good the foster home will be doing to let Frederick live a normal life again." Robert and Annie left in silence, disappointed not in the doctor but instead for what happened.

CHAPTER 21

The following year, Frederick lived in a large room with seven other boys – some younger than him and some older, each with their own bed. Down the hall was the room for the girls and there six of them. Each room was led by a married couple, both of whom were soul hunters that were trained to raise children who were in the beginning stages of possession. They had been trained for many decades, sometimes even over a century and knew the potential of each child. Frederick socialized with most of the children in the same foster home. None of the children knew anything of the soul hunter culture; they only knew they all were foster children. The home wasn't large, a single-story building but had a large corridor. Through the large double-door entrance there was a room with a high ceiling and glass Italian chandelier hanging from the center. There was a door straight ahead that led to the corridor with the boy's room down on the left and girl's room down on the right. At the end of each hallway was a master bedroom for the set of foster parents. Within the high ceiling room at the entrance, there was a fireplace with chairs around the fireplace on a large rug. That room was an area used for playing when the weather outside was bad or it was late but was also used to teach. The room to the right was the dining area and kitchen. There was a chef employed there that cooked for the children and a couple of assistants to help clean. They were all soul hunters and worked together. The chef and two assistants lived down the road in a nearby small village.

On a cold, winter night where snow settled outside the home, a chill spread throughout each room. The fireplace was on and children circled around it, reading books or working on puzzles before bed. The home was in an area by itself with no other buildings except for those a quarter mile away in the village. Being on the outskirts of Chicago, the foster home parents had access to supplies and everything as needed. Also, being outside of the city brought quiet and less interruption. White snow rested on the once green grass surrounding the home and the roof was the same. There were minimal footsteps leading from the fence post gate to the front door from the staff since not many people came to the foster home.

After warming up by the fireplace, the children all went to bed where each room had a stove to help warm up the area. The parents let the fire go out from the fireplace in the room by the entrance and had the iron fireplace on in each room to keep everyone warm. Everyone had gone to bed but one small spark recreated itself from the hot embers in the fireplace and jumped onto the rug nearby. The brittle edge of the rug, frail from children running over it throughout the day made for a quick fire starter. On the cold, chilly and windy night with threats of a blizzard blowing in, the fire spread quickly over the rug and onto the dry, wood furniture. The flames increased over each chair before jumping onto another nearby chair and finally onto the wallpaper on the walls. The fire continued to spread over the door frames and smoke entered into the corridor. One of the girls down the hall first smelled the smoke as it came over the open window above the door to their room. She sat up in her small bed and looked and noticed the smoke seeping in slowly. She woke up another girl that was in a bed two feet away from hers and being older she knew what to do and yelled, "Fire!"

All the girls were startled and most began to scream which woke up the boys down the hall and the foster parents in the room nearby. The parents got out of their bed and quickly threw on their robes. Their door was shut tight and the window above their door was sealed. They rushed out to see what was happening and opened the door when smoke came into their faces and caused them both to cough and eyes to burn. They brought their clothing up to their mouth and nose to help block out the smoke and quickly opened the door to the girl's room. They heard the screaming and demanded everyone get up and get outside. By then, the boys and the other set of parents had heard the commotion. The boys were just leaving the room and the other parents opening their door as the boys went into the hallway. Frederick was the first one out and saw all the smoke coming from the door to the room by the entrance. He rushed down to the doorway that led to the large room by the entrance – the only way in and out. As soon as he got to the doorway, he looked towards the front door and was nearly blinded with so much smoke and orange flames overwhelming his sight. He looked one way down the hallway and saw the girls starting to rush out of their room and looked behind him and saw the boys catching up to him. He looked straight ahead to the front door and ran as quickly as he could. He jumped over a flame on the wood floor in the center and felt the heat on his leg but kept pushing. His pajamas nearly caught fire but he went quickly enough over the flames to avoid being burnt. He reached out for the front door and the brass handle was extremely hot but he twisted it quickly and noticed it was locked. He reached up and pulled out the lock and twisted again and opened the door. He stepped on the brick steps outside the front door and looked back at the other boys and girls coming right behind him with some hesitating stepping over the fire. One of Frederick's best friends was running quickly and was halfway across the room.

Suddenly, while watching his friends get near the entrance, Frederick slammed the front door as hard as he could. With the weakened infrastructure from the fire, part of the ceiling collapsed, falling on some of his friends as well as blocking the front door. More ceiling collapsed after a few seconds and trapped a lot of the children in the room. Some girls and boys had made it to the hallway when the fire spread even quicker with the ceiling collapsing and flames spit out through the entrance to the corridor, bringing a large blaze amongst all their clothing and skin. Before being burnt, the parents from the girl's room that stood near the doorway to the large room yelled across at the other parents who stood next to their room by the boy's side.

"Frederick locked us in!" The man yelled. At that time, another blaze took over the confined area when the flames dispersed so quickly and took their lives and the remaining children.

As the ceiling collapsed, a piece of board by the front door had fallen and knocked Frederick unconscious. The two remaining parents had still been near the boy's room down the hall making sure all the children were out of their rooms so they survived the blaze. They quickly rushed back to their room, knowing it was the only other way out and closed the door behind them to help keep additional smoke and to slow the fire in case they needed more time. The man grabbed one of the books near their bed on the night stand and used it to break through the window. The book fell on its binding outside in the snow. He held his wife's arm as he let her out first. She was careful to avoid the glass shards still remaining on the window sill. He held her hand to ensure she avoided the glass and she jumped the three feet onto the ground and into the snow to a soft landing. He followed immediately after as they both then rushed away from the house towards the front when they saw Frederick's body by the front door. The man rushed over to pick up Frederick from the flames that were now blazing on the front walls of the house and ran back with him to the road up to the house. They watched as the house burnt to blackened remains and nothing was left besides the brick fireplace.

Frederick was the only child who survived and after the travesty occurred, the two parents decided to keep Frederick by himself and raise him. They had always figured that Frederick kept everyone inside for a reason but Frederick never could remember what had even happened since the board had knocked him unconscious. When he awoke hours later at a hotel room the following day, he asked the parents what happened. After they told him, he was astonished and extremely saddened and wept for a long time. They were careful though to not mention to him that he had shut the door on the other children attempting to escape. They had been soul hunters for half a century and knew the master soul hunter sometimes performed tests to see who are the strongest and who are the weakest and to get rid of the weak links- a test where only Frederick, the strongest, survived.

CHAPTER 22

The years went by when, eight years later from the day of the fire, Frederick was walking home from school. He was living a normal life being raised by the same foster parents that he now considered his only parents since he never could remember Robert or Annie or what happened at the foster home. He went to school daily and was excelling in every subject. His family lived a normal life and his new mom was a housewife and took care of the chores while his dad worked at a nearby law firm as an accountant – a façade but they still needed to make a living.

The exact day of the fire, Frederick at age sixteen walked by a park on his way home as he usually did. He carried his books in his hand that were wrapped by a piece of rope to keep them together. He looked at a merry-go-round at a park and saw children watching him. There were boys and girls sitting on the ride, not moving. He thought it was kind of peculiar that nobody was pushing it to make it go in circles but instead, everyone just sitting on it and watching him walk by. He didn't think anything of it except just children taking a break after playing. The following day, he walked to school and passed by a bookstore. He saw a book in the front window about science that drew interest. He walked inside to take a quick read of it since he always got to school a few minutes early, he knew he had a couple of minutes. He went inside and nodded to the clerk at the desk who had a duster in hand to clean shelves. He crept around towards the front window and gently picked up the book. He turned around to look at it as he was fascinated and opened to a random page when he felt like he was being watched. He looked up to the corner of the bookstore and saw a group of children looking at him. He pretended like he didn't see them and glanced back down at the book, minding his own business but he could still feel them looking at him. They were all standing still and had dark looking clothing on.

"Why are you looking at me?" He finally asked loudly and closed the book, keeping it between his hands. The store clerk looked around at the small bookstore and then looked back at Frederick.

"Are you okay, Son?" He asked, not sure who Frederick was talking to since he had been cleaning and wasn't looking at him.

Frederick turned and glanced at the clerk before looking back at the corner and the children were gone. Without saying another word, he put the book back in the window display and left the store quickly to go to school. He never mentioned the two events to his parents until the following day, Frederick's patience got to him when he was walking home from school. He walked on the side of the dusty road towards his home about a half mile away from the small school. He had to walk, whether rain or snow and often his mind wandered and thought about school and what he wanted to do for work. He knew he had to get a job soon but his dad made enough money for the family where he could keep going to school and hopefully graduate. He wanted to become a scientist and loved learning chemistry and his dream job was to become a chemist.

This particular day he was halfway home, walking by a few homes on the side of the road when he heard noises behind him of feet shuffling. He continued to walk and turned his head to glance behind him when he noticed the same kids walking towards him. He turned straight ahead and walked faster and a block later he looked behind him again and saw the kids still following him. He stopped and turned around and began walking backwards, watching the children. He didn't count but saw there were ten or so of them and they looked ragged. All of the boy's hair was not combed and the girl's hair was scraggly. Their clothing was dark and looked like they had just come out of a coal mine. He became very paranoid as each of them stared directly at him with no expressions when out of the corner of his eye, he saw two adults standing near a picket fence on a house to the left of him.

He stopped and turned to the adults and said, "These kids keep following me. It's been three days." He continued looking at the man and woman who stood, standing by the fence with their backs towards Frederick. They didn't move but from what Frederick could see, their skin was as dirty as their clothes. Frederick began backing up again and kept his eyes on the children who had encroached closer while he spoke to the man and woman. He kept his eyes on them also as they all stared at Frederick. He decided to run the rest of the way home.

Frederick got home and rushed inside and slammed the door behind him and found his mom in the kitchen getting dinner prepped. She saw the look on Frederick's face once she turned around after hearing the door slam. His face drooped and his eyes were wide and looked in shock.

"What's the matter, Frederick?" She asked and walked over towards him. He was shivering and shaking minimally and was speechless. "Come here," she said and she sat on a chair at the table. He walked with her and stood by her side. "Frederick, tell me what happened?"

Finally, after a few seconds of his lips trembling, Frederick answered. "There are kids following me."

"Kids? Kids from school?" She asked. She knew that Frederick had a few friends from school but wasn't aware of any issues with any of the other children.

"No, no…" he said and hesitated, not knowing how to answer since he didn't know who they were.

"Then, who are they?" His mom asked.

"I don't know. There's a lot of them, and they're dirty. They show up and stare at me and don't talk. I've seen them for three days in a row now."

"Oh," His mom replied, thinking that she might know why.

"How many of them are there?" She asked.

"Um, like ten, maybe more?" He said, guessing the amount that he had seen but knowing there were at least ten of them. "And two grown-ups too."

"Everything is okay now," she said, running her hand through Frederick's long and dusty hair, thinking of a way to stall until her husband came home. "Frederick, why don't you go to your room and get some rest before you start your homework. Everything will be just fine, okay? You're safe now," she said and smiled to reassure that everything would be fine. Frederick walked casually upstairs to his room, trusting his mom that everything would be fine.

As soon as her husband came home two hours later, Frederick was doing homework. She pulled her husband aside in the pantry, listening closely if Frederick was coming out of his room.

"Are you okay, Honey?" He asked since she was acting differently. He was curious by the way she stopped him and pulled him close to her and looked down at the kitchen that goes to Frederick's room.

"No, it's time to tell Frederick the truth," she whispered into his ear. She stepped back and saw a grin on her husband's face.

"It's about time," he said and continued to smile. "I've been looking forward to this day for a while."

They both knew that Frederick was seeing the children of the past that he had killed in the fire and that he was ready to be taught. When someone was in the beginning stages of becoming a soul hunter but was not yet prepared to become a soul hunter, if they did collect souls, the souls didn't show up until the child became old enough. Nobody knew though when the child was old enough until the souls appeared – a sacrifice as the souls were released for the master.

Frederick's foster parents took the next two years teaching Frederick the ways of a soul hunter. They told him the truth about his past including his original parents, from the information they acquired from Reginald, as well as what happened at the fire in the foster home. Once Frederick reached the age of eighteen, he was ready to be on his own and set out on his own path, leaving his foster parents.

CHAPTER 23

Decades later... Groups of soul hunters have begun to settle in Florida due to the increasing number of senior citizens beginning to move into the state. It's the 1960's and there are many elderly who moved to Florida due to the warmer weather year round. Groups of soul hunters settled and would prey on the elderly since they were easy targets. As a few years went by, there were enough people to hunt but one particular group of soul hunters in DeLand looked for other ways. When soul hunting, the strongest souls that were killed would provide the most life to the soul hunter. When killing an elderly person, their lives and souls were weak whereas with not much life to live nor much extra life was given to the hunter. Though the targets were easy and plenty but with the higher number of murders needed, the risk was higher. With chances of being caught higher and life needed, one group found a new way to give them extra life in one night of mass killing. The group consisted of fifteen men and women that lived in a golf resort community nearby in multiple houses throughout the neighborhood. The golf course was built within the last five years and they sought the area the best place to move since there were many families and elderly that lived there. The group had to be close knit to one another since they could only trust each other. They had to keep their secret and when they killed to become more youthful, they could only rely on one another. At times, if someone became too youthful, they would have to move and start a new life so they wouldn't have to figure out a way to explain to their neighbors or people around them and risk being caught.

A few miles down the road from the golf course community was a drive-in movie theater that was built in the mid-1940s. The theater was the only one within a few town radii and always busy when they were open on Friday and weekend nights. One man was in charge of the group of the fourteen other soul hunters. He wasn't the eldest of the group, not in age or birth date but he was the strongest of them all. He sat on the back of his porch, aging and once again in his mid-sixties. He opened the DeLand News Reporter, a daily newspaper, and read over the front page. He set the paper down as he watched a twosome tee off from down the right. One of the golfers duffed his drive and it dribbled barely across the women's tee box. He heard the man yell something but what he yelled was inaudible. One of the golfers got in the cart while the other grabbed a club and walked over to his ball, visibly embarrassed. He watched as the man, walking a bit hunched over, got to his ball and took half a practice swing before hurrying as fast as he could to hit his ball again before more people would see him. He hit the ball but topped it now and it went a bit in the air before bouncing to the left and landed in the soul hunter's yard. He leaned back in the chair he had in his porch and awaited the man to walk nervously up to his ball. The ball was barely in his yard but often times, golfers were worried about going onto someone yard so the ball would be left. The man walked to his ball again since it was faster to walk rather than go to the golf cart and ride up since the ball didn't go very far. The man, carrying the same golf club he had just used, came walking up to his ball and looked around. He hurried and picked it up and threw it a few yards to his right. It was bad etiquette to hit the ball off of someone's yard so most people if they didn't leave the ball, would pick it up. The soul hunter remained in his porch, watching the man and thinking of how easy it would be to take this man's life except for the fact he was with another golfer who waited across the fairway in the golf cart watching.

The two golfers passed and the soul hunter kept browsing the newspaper, not really interested in much that was going around. He read the crimes in the area and then flipped through to the obituary – wondering how many of those who have died were killed by soul hunters. Elderly people often filled the obituary and when a soul hunter would take their life, the killing didn't take much and would often go undetected as something natural. He flipped over to the obituary after reading local news but opened the entertainment page first and saw a large, color photo of an upcoming horror movie. He was attracted to the large image of a dark figure with fangs overlooking a blonde female with a frightened look on her face. The name of the movie was in large bold letters and he began reading the article. The title, indicating "Large Premier," caught his attention and he read about the show times at the DeLand Drive-In Theater. The writer of the article expected a full capacity for the first three nights of the movie debut and for people to get there early. The soul hunter read the article.

"The horror flick in horrific attraction will attract horror film lovers from all around. Guys, wrap up your gals, and friends, don't travel alone or you'll be frightfully disappointed you missed the movie having your eyes shut by being so scared. Debuting at the DeLand Drive-In this Friday, Saturday, and Sunday, starting at 8:30, the film will play throughout the month of May but be sure to be one of the first ones to watch this instant classic. Bring your friends and load up your cars since you'll definitely not want to be alone… Spaces will fill up quick as we expect the film to be a quick sellout for its first weekend."

He put the newspaper down on his lap and began to think of an area as small as a one screen theater and how people would have difficult times escaping. He went a few doors down to another older woman in their group and sat down for coffee with her in her living room.

"Susan, I have an idea," he said.

"What is it, Fred?" She asked and brought the cup of coffee up to her mouth to take a sip.

"Look at all of us," Fred said, wanting Susan to think about the members of their group. "Look and think of all fifteen of us, what does it look like to you?"

After a moment of thinking, Susan responded, "Looks like we belong in this retirement golf course community."

"Exactly!" Fred spat out, nearly spitting out the coffee he had swallowed. "We are aging and soon will die. We can't feed off the elderly as we have been since its taking way too many deaths for us to regain our youth."

"I agree," Susan said as she looked down at her hand and saw the saggy skin and wrinkles that have taken over her once smooth skin. After looking at her hand she looked back up at Fred and asked, "What is your idea?"

"The drive-in…" he said and paused, waiting for a reaction from Susan.

She sat in her wingback chair and brought her arms up to the armrests and thought for a bit, attempting to think about what Fred had just told her.

"I'm not catching on," she finally admitted.

"There's a big premier, big movie opening this coming weekend on Friday, Saturday and Sunday. I read in the paper that they expect a full, maximum crowd for the movie," he said and paused. Fred continued looking at Susan but she wasn't responding yet so he continued with his idea. "There will be over 150 people there and if we create a good plan, we can trap everyone in the area and find a way to kill them, we can all regain our youth once again."

"Hmm… over 150 people will definitely make us all young again. I'm on board so let's have an emergency meeting tonight to think of a plan. At my house?" Susan asked excitedly.

"Yes, how about at eight o'clock?" Fred asked.

"Sounds good, let's start calling everyone." They went to Susan's kitchen where she had her telephone and started calling each person in the group and had the meeting set up.

CHAPTER 24

The time was nearing eight o'clock and all fifteen members of the soul hunter group were at Susan's house, all wondering and whispering to one another to see if they knew what was going on. Right at eight, Fred stood from the couch and got everyone's attention by clapping his hands and whistling.

"Thank you all for coming," he said. "Are we secure?" He asked Susan, making sure all doors were locked and all the windows shut. He looked over at her and she nodded.

"Great, let's begin. This coming Friday night at the DeLand Drive-In, there will be a large movie opening at eight-thirty. The movie, which is a big debut of a supposed popular film, will lead to a sellout crowd. The newspaper article estimated it will be a fast sellout and over 150 people will be there. Horror movies are usually filled with younger people and college students whereas…fresh souls." A lot of the soul hunters in the group nodded their heads in agreement and made noises to show their approval and hunger for younger souls. "We will all get into our cars and fill about ten cars – enough to be able to block the entrance and exit. We'll wait down the street and once we see the theater is filled to capacity and cars are being turned around, we'll get in line with our cars. Then, once our first car gets to the entrance, we'll all wait in our cars so nobody can leave. Here's where we need some help as to how we can kill the trapped people."

After Fred explained their strategy, everyone in the room looked around at one another for a few quiet seconds, making Fred a bit nervous as the idea might sound too farfetched until someone stood up. A middle aged man looked around before looking at Fred and said, "Fire."

"Yes!" Fred said nearly immediately. Fred began pacing back and forth between the stereo set near Susan's television and the nearby couch until coming up with a solution. "A fire but a combustible fire. That way the fire will spread so quick, nobody would know what was happening until it was too late. We'll all be by the entrance and collect the souls before we speed away as if we're patrons just escaping the fire."

"But, how will we get the fire started?" One of the women said while remaining seated at the dining room table nearby.

"A gas can, maybe even multiple gas cans. I'll be by the entrance and park my truck nearby. I'll keep the gas cans in the back and I'll ignite one and throw it at the entrance. That way, the entrance will catch fire first and nobody would be able to leave. From there on, the first row of cars isn't too far away from what I remember being there a couple of years ago to watch a movie. There are three rows for cars to park and watch the single screen. Once we get the first row, the cars furthest back from the screen to catch fire, then gasoline from other cars and engines will explode and create fire in the small area. The trees will then begin to burn with so much gasoline in the air and once the entrance is engulfed in flames, you all turn your cars around and wait down the street where I'll be so we can collect the souls of those engulfed in the fire."

"We'll be young again!" Susan said out loud. More agreement was seen and heard with noises and head nodding.

"Raise your hands if you are in agreement with the plan," Fred said. Before any major event, they would vote and the majority would win. Even if a majority won and those who didn't agree lost, those people would have to go along with the idea anyway to be part of the group.

Fred counted fourteen hands and was amazed that everyone agreed. He looked around and saw so much gray hair and wrinkled bodies, he knew everyone was clamoring for youth once again.

"Great, we are all in agreement. Those at the movie will be younger people from high school, college, and other varieties so if this idea works, we'll gain many upon many years for our lives and once we become young again, we'll have to look for another place to live though." They would have to move since they would become younger and stand out amongst their neighbors who would notice the change.

"I'm tired of moving so much the last ninety years," one of the older soul hunters asked who had her white hair curled and wore thick glasses.

"It is a burden," Susan said. "But, is it worth moving to gain thirty or forty or so years of life again once we share life from all the souls?"

Barely hesitating, the woman responded, "I see, and will be able to see again without these glasses." The woman then smiled.

CHAPTER 25

The fire happened just as planned and 178 people were killed and all their souls collected. After the fire, the soul hunters all went back to their homes as if nothing happened and planned a meeting the following morning at ten o'clock. Some of them got some rest while a few others weren't able to due to both the thrill and excitement of what they had just done or maybe were actually a bit sad for what had just happened.

The following morning, fourteen of the soul hunters were at Susan's house. Fred looked around and counted and saw one member was missing.

"Harry?" Fred said loudly, wondering where he was. "Has anyone seen or heard from Harry today?" He asked while standing in the middle of the living room. Everyone else in the room looked around and were shaking their heads to say they hadn't.

"Susan, can you please call Harry before we start the meeting?" Fred asked. Susan was near the kitchen. She went into the kitchen to make the phone call and came back less than a minute later.

"No answer," she said.

"Billy, you and I need to go to Harry's house. Everyone else just wait here until we get back," Fred said. He and Billy went to the front door and walked nearby to Fred's truck. Billy was one of Harry's closest friends and Fred wanted to bring him along. They drove a half mile away to where Harry lived and knocked on his door. There was no answer so they knocked louder a second time and Billy put his ear to the door to listen if he could hear any noises.

"I don't hear anything," he said with his ear to the door.

"He keeps a spare key behind a rock by his back porch," Fred said and began walking back. He found the rock immediately and picked up the key and returned and unlocked the door. He cautiously opened the door slowly while Billy looked around the neighborhood to make sure no one was looking at them. Fred took a step inside and yelled,

"Harry?" Upon saying his name, he noticed that the furniture was all gone. He hurried inside and Billy followed behind him.

"What happened?" Billy asked after entering into Harry's home. Fred stood in awe and looked around at the empty house. He then walked to the other rooms in the two-room duplex and saw all the furniture was gone from the other rooms. The carpet was dirty and counters dusty so he knew that Harry had left in a hurry. "Where is Harry?" Billy asked.

"I don't know. I mean, did he tell you anything?" Fred asked.

"No. After the meeting, he shook my hand and said something like, 'Best of luck to us all,' and I figured he was just saying that so we would get through the night at the theater. I saw him sitting in his station wagon last night with a big smile as the fire started but I looked away since I was with Thomas in his car. Then we all started to turn away from the entrance as the fire increased. As we pulled away, I looked at everyone else to make sure we were all doing okay but after we all lined up down the road as the fire took the lives of the people, I don't remember seeing him again."

"So strange but also this can't be good. You cannot abandon a group without us knowing you are leaving," Fred said. It was okay for someone to leave a group as long as loyalty and respect remained in full by letting the group know in advance.

"It's like he disappeared or something. How could he have packed up his stuff so quick last night?" Billy wondered.

"Somehow he did it. Maybe some nearby neighbors know but I don't want to ask them and bring suspicion to us. Let's go back to the group and let them know."

They returned to the truck and went back to Fred's driveway. They parked the truck in the garage and went back to the meeting. As soon as the two of them walked inside, everyone in the group wondered where Harry was.

"Well?" One man in the group asked.

Fred stood in the middle of the room and looked at the ground for a moment.

"Is Harry okay?" Another soul hunter asked.

"We're not sure. His house is empty," Fred began saying.

"Empty?" Susan interrupted.

"Yes, empty, as if he moved last night or early this morning."

"Why would he do such a thing?" Another soul hunter asked.

"No one is sure, yet. Did anyone hear anything strange or suspicious from Harry yesterday?" Fred asked. He looked around the room but nobody said anything.

"Billy, did you hear anything?" Susan asked, knowing they were great friends.

"No," Billy responded since he was also confused. "He didn't tell me anything."

"This isn't good," Susan said and started to shake her head in disapproval as she looked outside from her bay window and wondered where he could have gone.

"What are we going to do now?" Fred heard someone ask.

"This is tough. We are going to slowly decrease in age so we need a new start," Fred said. After a murder, it would take a week, maybe more or less depending on the circumstance, for the soul hunter to become a year younger. There was no guarantee as how many years someone would gain but with fifteen of them last night and they estimated at least 150 people at the theater the previous night, they estimated each of them would become thirty or so years younger. "We have a few weeks before our aging reversal shows so we'll have to begin a new life somewhere," Fred recommended.

"Where are we to go?" Someone else asked.

"What does everyone think? Any suggestions?" Fred asked but began speaking again. "I'm a bit worried about Harry abandoning us and what will happen with him." Fred and the others knew someone wasn't able to leave a soul hunter group without asking. Doing so could lead to definite termination by the master soul hunter or an elder in the society. Fred and a few others also worried that Harry could no longer be trusted and weren't sure if he was going to divulge their secrets and what they had done. Most of the group knew that Harry had to be eliminated but finding him would be difficult but Fred knew who to ask.

The room was silent for a few moments when Fred finally spoke up to break the silence. "I've been thinking, maybe we should split up for a while and go our separate ways," he said. A couple of soul hunters gasped while the others listened closely. "We'll be getting younger soon and can move to more places than a retirement community and be more active once again. We'll be gaining a few extra decades to our lives so go out and enjoy them. Just don't wait too long to kill again where you get to where we are now."

Everyone in the room looked around at one another, saddened that this might be the last time they got together as a group while most of them agreed that once they became younger in a few months, they would need to start a new life somewhere else.

Susan got Fred's attention and motioned her head to join her in the kitchen.

"Fred, this is sad," she said.

"I know, it really is. But, we're finally regaining some youth for the first time in," Fred paused and pointed at the wrinkles and veins sticking out from his arm, "a long time."

"Where will you be going?" Susan asked.

"I have an idea. I can live a quiet life for a while as well as be around vulnerable people that I can take their soul from when needed," Fred said which gained the curiosity of Susan. "You can join me if you'd like," Fred said.

Fred and Susan had known each other for about forty years and met in southern Georgia. They became friends but went their separate ways until about a decade earlier when they met up again in Florida and joined this group together. Soul hunters rarely have an attraction to each other nor feel the need to get married but it does happen from time to time. Usually, when a couple gets married, they will become parents for the adoption of soul hunter youth and raise them. Fred had never felt the need to marry but felt close with Susan and liked having her around and hoped she would join him. Susan felt the same about Fred and was happy when she crossed his path again when meeting up in Florida. She was curious about what his idea was. She grabbed his hand and had hoped he wanted to settle and become foster parents and asked, "What is your idea?"

"I'll tell you later," he said while whispering into her ear and smiled.

CHAPTER 26

Within the next two to three months, most everyone had packed, put their houses up for sale and moved on. Fred and Susan were both packed and ready to start their adventure together. They had their belongings, just the essentials, packed into one moving truck and began their drive.

"I can't believe you got that piece of land. And, so cheap too!" Susan told Fred, whose hair had black highlights once again. She looked at her hand and arm and was happy at how fewer wrinkles there were.

"Me neither but with what happened nearby, the land was pretty much free," Fred said. They drove the few miles after selling their homes and uplifting, just to move a little ways in the same town. They went down a side road and they turned to one another and smiled. Fred put his hand on Susan's thigh as they pulled into a long single-story building that was partially still being built. The majority of the exterior had been completed but construction was still being done inside.

"How much longer until it's ready?" Susan asked.

"Probably about another four months. Our room is ready in the first wing but the second and third wings have a bit more work to go." They both got out of the truck and walked up to the building and Fred looked around at how much construction they had to do yet to finish the twenty room building.

"Do you think the trees will ever grow back?" Susan asked, pointing at the trees behind the building.

"It'll take time, the fire was pretty big," Fred said and smiled.

Fred and Susan acquired the land next to the former DeLand Drive-In Theater and were building an independent living retirement home. There were twenty rooms for residents, including their own larger room and they were going to operate the retirement home and hire a small staff and have ample souls for when needed. The building was single-story with a large kitchen, a porch on most of the rooms where the residents could go outside for fresh air if they were able to. There was an entertainment room with a piano and a small stage for locals to come and entertain the residents for small pay. There were going to be numerous benches outside under a few trees that would be planted to provide shade. Fred and Susan were ready for their new life together and they planned on being together forever. They slowly moved all their furniture into their room. Being younger and stronger since the fires, their furniture was much easier to move now and got settled quickly. Their room had their own kitchen and dining room. There was a separate bedroom and living room.

Susan cooked dinner their first night there and enjoyed the quiet of the area.

"I can't believe how quiet it is here," Susan said.

"Not for long. Once we have residents, there'll be more noise but for now, nobody besides us wants to be around the old drive-in." Retirement and nursing homes were popular and in demand in Florida and nobody needing care would be scared away from going to Fred and Susan's because of what happened next door it seemed. They had already received numerous calls of interest and few future residents already signed up.

Susan brought the food to the table and sat.

"Chicken looks good. Thanks, Susan."

"I'm sure you're as hungry as I am after all the moving," she said. Fred nodded his head while stuffing a bite of garlic baked chicken in his mouth and following it up with a spoonful of mashed potatoes and gravy.

"I hate to ruin the mood, but have you heard anything about Harry yet?" Susan asked.

Fred continued to eat his bite of mashed potatoes and finally looked up to Susan while he swallowed.

"Unfortunately, not as of yet."

"What's going to happen with him?"

"We need to figure that out soon. I'm sure he's settled somewhere else but we cannot trust him and need to dispose of him for the sake of not only us but for our old group."

Fred leaned back in the chair and looked outside through the sliding glass door that led to their backyard. Most residents had a porch to go out on but they had a backyard with a small grassy area. Fred looked at the incoming gray clouds that were on their way to soak the former theater land in rainfall and wondered what he could do next.

"You know," Fred started. "Let me make a call tomorrow," he said before taking another bite of chicken.

"Who will you call?" Susan asked curiously.

"I'll let you know tomorrow if it all goes well," he said and smiled, reassuring Susan.

The following afternoon, Fred sat on the couch in their living room and had the phone nearby him on an end table. Susan sat next to him reading a book – a book about romantic vampires. Fred despised such romance in horror stories. He looked over at the phone and picked up the receiver. He pulled out an old, previously crumpled up piece of paper he had folded in his shirt pocket. He looked at the numbers written on it many years ago and dialed the number. He spoke for nearly thirty minutes with Susan eavesdropping the entire time until he would hang up the phone.

"Yes, that is correct. Harry McClias, born 1798," Fred said on the phone before hanging up.

"What happened? Will he be able to find Harry?" She asked impatiently not knowing who Fred spoke with.

"Well, since we don't know where he is it might take a while but eventually he'll show up somewhere. Then, we'll have a chance to erase him. Until then, my old friend will keep his eyes, ears, and other senses out for him and let me know."

CHAPTER 27

Nearly three decades later…

The day was pleasant in the town of Asheville, North Carolina. A man named Walter returned home to his apartment. The birds were chirping outside on a windless, sunny day but nobody could hear them. There was a group of police officers as well as a group of neighbors all chatting amongst themselves outside of Walter's apartment building. Walter parked at his assigned parking space and walked a few yards over to the building. He proceeded up the steps that led directly up to his apartment, keeping an eye on the situation around him. As he took each step, the rotting wood creaking on the stairwell, he looked down at the caution tape around his neighbor's apartment. *What could have happened to him*, Walter thought as he continued inside.

Shutting off all outside interference in order for quiet and to be able to concentrate on writing a story, he shut the curtains and blinds to block the flashing lights from outside. He got a glass of water and sat down on his chair as his computer booted up. He was ready to work on his idea. The outside chatter increased as more people showed up. He turned on the radio to drown out the noise. An A.M. station, oldies began to play calmly throughout the room as he sat at his desk. He raised his uncomfortable chair as high as it got and began to think. *What have I forgotten?* Looking around, he had forgotten to get the tape recorder from his bedroom. He got up and walked around the bed to get his recorder and he could still hear people talking amongst each other outside. He arrived back to his desk and sat back down as the music drowned out the outside chatter. He set the recorder down on the top of the desk and began to rewind the tape.

Walter wanted to know what had happened to his neighbor but with so much commotion, he figured he would find out later. He also wanted to work on the new idea he thought of the previous night and he was excited to start on it. Walter was an aspiring writer and had written two previous action and adventure novels but was not yet able to find a publisher. He wasn't giving up since, out of nowhere from a dream, he had an idea – but an idea he should not have thought about.

The recorder rewound for nearly five seconds, which should have reached the beginning by then but instead continued to rewind. Noticing it hadn't stopped, Walter picked up the recorder and looked at it. He saw the tape and noticed it was still rewinding. Possibly, he thought, he may have been so tired that he had forgotten to press 'stop' the night before after recording his idea so he let it rewind all the way to the beginning. Nearly thirty seconds went by when the recorder clicked – letting Walter know the tape was now at the beginning.

He pressed 'play' and a few seconds of static went by when he heard his own voice. He closed his eyes and blocked out all the outside noise and focused on his voice on the recording. His recording said… "A man, lost for days…begins to murder…" After he continued listening to the rest of the recording of his idea, his voice ended. He knew that was the end of his idea so he reached up to take hold of the recorder to press stop when he heard a high pitched shriek on the tape. He looked at the recorder and wondered what that noise could have been. Possibly a sneeze, or something from outside, he figured. Not thinking anything else of it, he decided to continue listening in case he had said anything else. Nearly ten seconds went by when he decided nothing else would be on the tape but just in case, he decided to let it continue to play while he began typing. Setting it back on top of his desk, not thinking anything else was on the tape, he began to type the introduction to his new book.

A day like no other, as calming as the weather had been, today is different. The clouds are not white, there is no sunshine, the weather above upsetting the ground below with the blowing winds as treacherous as ever disrupting the peaceful nature…the psychotic violence about to be endured by the townspeople…

As Walter continued to type, what seemed to be a faint cough was heard on the recorder. He stopped typing and looked up when another shriek was heard. This time the shriek was a lot louder than the previous one.

Where did that noise come from? What is it? He thought as leaned back in his chair as the legs creaked. He folded his arms and crossed his ankles as he spread his legs forward. Acting as if the tape recorder were a television, he stared at it to see what would happen next. Twenty seconds went by, Walter, anxious to continue working on the story, began to type again.

Suddenly out of nowhere, "Your neighbor... kill!" was heard from the recorder in a ghostly, gasping voice.

The voice was so deep and so quiet but yet so intimidating and frightening. Goosebumps ran through Walters' body as he immediately stopped typing. In disbelief, his mind too busy thinking about what he had just heard rather than continuing his story, he stopped. Questions ran through his mind.

Whose voice was that? What did I just hear? He stopped the tape to rewind it for a few seconds and listen again to what he thought he heard.

Again he heard, "Your neighbor... kill!" Still, in disbelief, he listened in anticipation of what else was on the tape. There seemed to be no more chatter outside Walter's apartment, not that his mind would suffice to such distraction now, as his focus was on his recording.

The tape continued as Walter picked it up to see how much of the tape was left when he saw it was nearing the end. He stared with curiosity at the tape as it neared the end when suddenly, there was a loud pounding on the door. He was startled as he jumped up from his chair.

"Open the door, it's the police!" A loud voice yelled from outside Walter's door.

He immediately set the recorder down and walked to the door. Grasping the top security lock, he unlocked it when he then reached his right hand down to unlock the door knob. As he opened the door to the sight of the police officer, a deep, louder voice emulating from his recorder demanded, "Kill him... stab the neighbor to death!"

By then, in such a way that this was all a dream, Walter was being apprehended by two police officers as they grabbed him by his arms.

"Face the wall, spread your feet and place your hands behind your back. You are being arrested and charged for the murder of Harry McClias."

Shocked and in panic, Walter blurted out, "Who?"

The officer replied back in a harsh voice, "The man downstairs who was found stabbed to death with a knife, sticking deep inside his chest that we found out belongs to you."

Walter, who was handcuffed and lying limp, face down, had no idea what was happening with all these events occurring so quickly.

The officer turned Walter over and told him, "We found an eyewitness that told us you marched downstairs last night and forced his door open, holding the same large knife we found in the victim's body that you had in your hand."

Sweat poured down his face and burned as it entered into his eyes, he realized everything that was going on around him and that it wasn't just a bad nightmare. He pleaded to the arresting officer, "I did not kill him!"

Reflecting in his mind what he had heard moments ago on his recorder, a demanding statement telling him to kill the neighbor, he had no idea what was happening or what happened to his neighbor.

"I need to speak to a lawyer before I say anything else," Walter said and thought in his mind that a lawyer would be able to get him out of this mess of a nightmare and he was taken in and booked in the county jail.

CHAPTER 28

The following morning his assigned lawyer sat with him and listened to his story. Little did Walter know his lawyer asked for the case. His lawyer, a man who went by his last name of Knots, sat with his legs crossed in his crisp suit and professional slicked comb over covering the slightest bald spot on his head. Re-telling the events to his newly appointed lawyer, he told Knots to go to his apartment and listen to the recorder.

"You'll find the recorder on top of my desk. Rewind the tape and listen to the full side completely. Listening to the tape, you'll hear my voice for a couple of minutes before you hear an eerie voice that is not mine. I was the only one in the apartment that night so I do not know whose voice this is. Please help me." Tears poured down Walter's face as pleaded and tilted his head downward, still in shock.

Following the meeting with Walter, Knots immediately went to Walter's apartment. He carefully walked under the caution tape and proceeded up the stairs, old as they were, creaking with nearly every step. With the apartment key in hand, he entered the apartment. Knowing everything in here was still evidence, he did not disturb anything. Finding the tape recorder right where Walter told him, he picked it up and noticed it was at the end of the tape so he rewound it. He sat on the desk chair and crossed his left leg over his right until he finally heard a click. Quiet surrounded the apartment as there were no longer any police around and the news crew was gone. He took out his notepad and pen and proceeded to press 'play' on the recorder. A few seconds went by when he heard Walters's tired voice begin to play from the recorder. "A man, lost for days…begins to murder…" The entire side of the tape played, the lawyer's notepad filled with empty space as he didn't have the need to write much. Leaving the apartment, blinds still shut, dark as it ever was, he locked the door on the way out and drove back to the jail.

CHAPTER 29

"Hello?" Fred said after rushing from the kitchen while doing dishes to answer the phone. Susan was outside planting a few seeds in the garden. Fred wiped his other hand on his shirt to dry it.

"Frederick, it's Reginald, I have an update for you." Fred listened closely and was surprised to hear from Reginald since it had been thirty years since they've last spoken.

"I located Harry, finally. The good news is he is no longer a threat," Reginald said.

"Where?" Fred said after being caught off guard. "Where was he? How did you do it?"

"My plan is working," Reginald started.

"What plan?" Fred said impatiently. He hadn't heard from Reginald for three decades and was very excited to finally have an update on Harry. He and Susan had pretty much given up on ever finding him. Fred and Susan had aged almost thirty years in the last three decades. They had ample supply of souls at the retirement home and the deaths were as frequent as any other retirement home but the old and weakened souls didn't provide much life to him and Susan. He and Susan, alongside some of their old soul hunter friends, had found life becoming tougher as the years past with it being harder to kill someone. There were new forensics and sciences to solve crimes whereas they had to be more careful and adjust to the changing times. A lot of soul hunters had difficulties committing murders anymore and many were dying off or being captured and imprisoned, where they would eventually die in prison.

"Times are evolving, my dear Frederick," Reginald said. "I remember first meeting you as a young child with your parents at the hospital after you first became possessed. Then, after you reached eighteen and understood the life of a soul hunter, I took you under my wing for a short time. Not soon after you didn't need me anymore and you went on your own. Back then, what was it, 200 or more years ago, give or take, it was so much easier to kill. These days, it's nearly impossible to get away with it. So many of us are faltering and dying. I refuse to be one and have changed with the times."

"I see. Yes, it has become hard. What have you been doing?" A curious Fred asked.

"I've found a way to get into the psyche of my victims. I've tested it on a weak soul who began writing a horror book and allowed his soul to be vulnerable. I made my way into his spirit and showed his weakness."

"Was it Harry?" Fred asked.

"Close. The proximity was perfect for me to work on this idea."

"How so?"

"Well, this vulnerable being was actually Harry's neighbor," Reginald said and Fred sat down on the couch to continue listening. He was surprised anyone was able to find Harry. "Harry lived in an apartment and had just moved there after becoming younger after he recently killed a married couple. I was able to get inside Harry's neighbor, Walter, and his psyche and told him through a recording to kill his neighbor. And, guess what?"

"He did it," Fred answered and snickered, happy Harry was finally gone.

"Correct. He murdered him which keeps my hands clean and I was appointed to be his lawyer. I studied law and became a graduate, working as a public defender. Those in need of public defending are often weak and I thought this would be a good way to find weakened people and Walter, the man I found, is going to be my first test."

"What do you mean?"

"Walter killed a man and has that on his conscious – in his soul. He is weak and paranoid now and in prison. I'll continue creeping into his life and by playing a recording initially, he killed his neighbor."

"What's going to happen to him?" Fred asked curiously.

"I'm not sure but what I want to happen is to kill him. When I kill him, I'll get his soul as well as Harry's. I'll keep you informed if it works. But, to keep with the changing times, we need to change also. We'll chat again soon."

Susan came back into their room and took off her shoes by the sliding glass door. She brought her shoes up to the front door. "Who were you just talking to?"

"You want the good news?"

"Umm, sure," Susan said, unsure who he was speaking with.

"That was Reginald."

"Reginald? It's been such a long time! What did he have to say?"

"He found Harry and had him killed."

"He did? How?" Susan asked as her mouth drooped, anxiously waiting to hear how.

"He has a new technique he's been working on where he tries to get into the minds of people. As you know, it's been harder to kill in today's day and age," Fred said.

"I know. It was good here for a while but we can only lose so many people and we're not as populated as we used to be with so many other retirement homes around the state opening up so frequently."

"We're getting older again, Susan."

"I know. I still enjoy being with you every day, though," Susan said. "What do you think about a change?"

"What kind of change?"

Susan sat down next to Fred and turned and leaned towards him. "I want to become young again and start raising our own children."

"Really?" Fred asked, surprised as this was the first time Susan had mentioned to him wanting to be a parent.

"Yes, I want to raise foster children who are to become soul hunters. You would be a great father and teacher and I would be a great mother to them."

"You really think so?" Frederick asked and turned to his side and found the arm rest to lean his shoulder back on it. He brought his finger to his mouth and began thinking.

"Yes, I've been thinking about that for a while now," Susan said.

"Well, to be honest, after speaking with Reginald just now and with what he told me about the evolving world, I had another idea."

"What's that?" Susan asked, curious about what his new idea was and also a little sad that Fred didn't seem too excited about being a foster parent. She really wanted to raise their own children and help the youth. After being at the retirement home for thirty years, she wanted a change.

"Give me maybe a few more months and you'll see," Fred said and smiled at Susan before kissing her on the cheek.

CHAPTER 30

Walter underwent numerous administered psychological evaluations and upon the results, Knots sat in front of Walter at the prison. He looked deep into Walter's eyes, "There is no voice on the recording other than yours. I listened to it and heard nothing. Walter, there was nothing."

Sweat surrounded Walter's forehead, puzzled that the lawyer heard nothing and unsure what was happening or what he should do next. Knots told him, "Plead guilty, avoid the death penalty and you may be able to be paroled somewhere in the future."

Surprised in thought, Walter responded, "I, I heard a voice! Why can't I fight this in court? Is there no hope of getting off on this charge?" He looked around as his eyes jolted from left to right in the small room, his heart racing and beating with paranoia running through him.

Knots put his head down for a few seconds when he looked back up at Walter and shook his head. The dead emotionless look on his face told Walter all he needed to know.

"There is no hope, Walter. I looked at every angle of this case and the only way to avoid the death penalty is to plead guilty. This way as well, you may only get life with a potential chance for parole in the future. If you fight this in court, in my opinion, since your voice was the only voice on the recorder, you passed all psychological tests, and there was a witness of you holding the knife and murder weapon going into Harry's room, you will be found guilty and either placed to death or life in prison without parole."

Walter followed his lawyer's advice and pleaded guilty to murder and was placed in prison for life with a chance for parole in twenty-five years as said in his plea bargain his lawyer set up with the courts.

A couple of weeks went by as Walter lived in prison. Unbeknownst of his true intensions, Knots continued working a plan on Walter. Walter, on the other hand, had finally come to a realization of his fate and trying to make the best of his life in prison, wanted to begin writing again. With contact through his family in letters, he asked his mom for a tape recorder for him to be able to take note of his ideas. He wanted a new recorder instead of his old one. A couple of weeks went by when he got a package from his mom. Having been inspected by the guards, the package, already opened, included a tape recorder with a couple of blank tapes. Ready again to begin writing but being late in the day, the lights being turned off soon, he went to bed instead.

He awoke early the next morning with an idea already in his mind so he pressed the 'record' button and began speaking into the recorder.

"Write about an idea like that which happened to me. A mysterious voice telling someone to do something and they do it, like an entire nightmare but actually a reality."

Walter stopped speaking and thought he pressed the 'stop' button and even double checked that he had, the recording continued anyway as he drifted back to sleep. The following day, he was in no mood to write, as Walter was depressed most days as he spent his life in prison. He waited a couple of days to play back the recorder and begin writing again. He sat on the side of his bed with a pencil and paper in hand, ready to begin. The setting was much different than being able to sit in his living room on a chair at his desk with a computer, but he was ready to begin a new story. *Even though my old chair was uncomfortable, what I wouldn't give to be there right now,* he thought.

Grasping his recorder, as flashbacks entered through his mind of when he was arrested and the entire ordeal he went through, he put that behind his mind, trying to forget all that happened and put all his focus on his new story. After rewinding the tape, again, the entire side recorded so it took a while longer to rewind but he didn't notice. He pressed the 'play' button and began to write.

After a few seconds of static, Walter's voice was heard on the recorder. "Write about an idea like that which happened to me. A mysterious voice telling someone to do something and they do it, like an entire nightmare but actually a reality."

He heard his voice end and was ready to turn off the recorder but he needed to write down a few more ideas on his notepad so the recorder continued. The pencil tip snapped. Having to sharpen his pencil, nearly thirty seconds went by when he heard a sound on the recorder that caught his attention. It was the same voice as he heard on his previous recorder.

"Walter, how does it feel to lose your life?" the ghostly voice asked.

A couple of deep coughs were then heard in the background of the recording, likely Walter's, but hearing the voice forced him to drop his pencil from his hand onto the floor. The pencil landed on the cold concrete floor, the sharp point snapping off again as it rolled under his bed. Distraught, Walter grabbed the recorder and immediately pressed 'stop'. Not wanting to hear anymore as this nightmare had re-appeared. He wanted to forget the past but also wanted to hear what the voice had to say.

"It's a nightmare, this can't be happening!" He yelled at himself out loud.

Contemplating a few minutes, Walter decided to continue listening to the recorder and pressed 'play' to continue. Another few seconds went by when the mysterious voice asked, "Do you remember my voice? Yes, the same voice as your previous recording, but again, do you remember my voice? I demand you do to yourself what you did to your neighbor. Do it and get your misery over with," the voice said and the recording ended. Walter's eyes were glued to the recorder once again as if it were a television screen.

"I'm sorry, I'm sorry," Walter said quietly at the recording. He punched his hand on his pillow hard, his fist falling into the bed springs of his thin mattress, not feeling any pain.

He continued staring at the recorder numbly, with no emotions or feelings until he finally shut his eyes and fell asleep as his body temperature increased, sweating into his clothes as he slept. He fell gently alongside the wall and slept. Tears crept out of his closed eyes slowly as he woke the following morning, lying on his side on the bed since he had fallen over while sleeping and resting against the wall. His sweat had soaked into his shirt and pants at night and woke up with stiff but dry clothing. He sat up and moved his legs over the edge of the bed. Everything all just felt like a bad dream but really, just a bad reality.

After a long sleepless night, morning peeked through a small window in the cell and Walter, anxious to speak with his lawyer, got out of bed. He reached for his recorder and rewound the tape. A minute went by when it clicked, reaching the beginning of the tape. He contemplated listening to the tape again but did not have the heart to do so.

Muttering to himself, "I'm sorry... I'm sorry... I did not mean for any of this to happen. I don't even know what happened," he said as he began crying again.

Unable to eat breakfast, he remained in silence in his cell when he went to a guard to request a meeting with his lawyer. Later in the day, after the prisoners on his floor got back from dinner, Walter was called up by the guard. Knots was there to speak with him. Transported from his cell down the hall, he wiped the tears from his face in fear that the other prisoners would see his tears, he continued down the hall. Holding the tape in his right hand, he finally reached a room and saw his lawyer.

"Hi, Walter, you don't look so good. What do you wish to speak about?" Knots asked as Walter sat on a steel folding chair. Knots was expecting to only hear from Walter if his plan was working so he was excited that Walter called for him. Knots sat down and wore a suit a little too large for him and his hair not combed over as before. He looked sloppier as if he didn't need to look professional but he acted compassionately. He was careful with his tone of voice and to keep his voice calm and talk in a slow speaking nature.

Speaking with Knots, Walter detailed the night and what happened. He told the story about his neighbor and what he heard on the tape the day he was arrested as well as what he had heard on the tape just the previous day. He handed the tape to his lawyer.

"Okay, Walter, I will go into my office and listen to this entire recording. I'll come back tomorrow and let you know what I heard as well as what will happen next. Get some rest and don't worry, we'll get this figured out."

Giving a slight grin to Walter, hoping to give some assurance, the pleasantness went right through Walter as Knots stood up and went to exit the room. Turning around and looking at Walter, obviously depressed and frail with the way he slouched in his chair, his lawyer once again reassured him, "See you tomorrow, Walter. Everything will work itself out." Giving a slight grin again, Walter remained emotionless with his face down and eyes staring onto the floor.

"I hope so." Walter slowly responded.

The day for Walter continued as he had another lonely day in his cell. He was still contemplating life and what he had done and was still in disbelief.

Knots returned to his office but didn't play the tape. He already knew what was on it. He placed his pencil on the desk near the notepad where he previously wrote down his plan for Walter. He continued writing his next steps.

Walter woke up tired the following day due to another sleepless night. The tired feeling showed on his face with the pale look on his skin, redness in his eyes and the onset of dark bags under his eyes. When he met with Knots around the same time as the previous day, Walter saw the look on his lawyer's face. It was not a look of happiness or relief, but instead, a look of hesitation and hopelessness as Knots looked nearly as tired as Walter with bags also under his eyes. He hadn't gotten any sleep the last couple of nights with him worrying and focusing so much on his plan.

"Walter, let me tell you. I listened to your tape at the office yesterday…"

Interrupting abruptly, Walter asked, "What did you hear, did you hear the voice?"

Answering with a sense of disgust and a harsher tone of voice, his lawyer said, "Yes, Walter, I heard a voice."

Walter's eyes perked up and began to stare at his lawyer without a single blink. A little sense of relief reappeared in Walter's face as he anxiously waited to hear what else his lawyer had to say.

"Walter, let me start from the beginning. Before your murder trial began, I listened to your first tape. I did hear a voice there, too."

Walter, whose head now turned at an angle as if he were questioning Knots and his actions, waited to hear what else he had to say.

Continuing to speak, Knots said, "Yes, I heard a voice. I heard a voice, Walter… I heard your conversation with yourself."

"What? What do you mean?" Walter asked with a higher pitched voice. He had finally realized what Knots had told him and that Knots heard the voice before.

"Do you remember when I told you the only voice I heard on the recording was yours?"

"Yes," Walter answered and nodded.

"Walter, it was your voice I heard on the entire recording. You were having a conversation with yourself."

"But how, how could I have a conversation with myself? How could I talk to myself and not know who it was?"

"I don't know, Walter, I don't know why you were speaking to yourself or how you did not realize it was your voice, but myself and others that I had listen to the old tape knew it was your voice. Then yesterday after leaving you here, I went to my office and listened to the new tape, and…"

"…and what?" Walter interrupted again. "You heard another voice, right? You had to have heard another voice!"

"Yes, Walter, again I heard your voice and you were having another conversation with yourself."

"But… but, why did you not tell me before that you heard my voice on the first recording and told me there was nothing else there?" Walter asked his lawyer, getting angry and leaning forward in his chair grasping each hand on a knee.

Knots uncrossed his legs and stood from his chair. He took a few steps, ran his hand through his slick hair while he thought what to say. "To be honest, if I were to tell you, you wouldn't believe me. Do you remember the psychological tests you went through with the doctors? You passed every test. There would be no way for you to get an insanity plea, especially with such a gruesome murder and the fact you passed every test given to you. I had you plead guilty since this way, you would avoid the death penalty since the jury would have no self-pity for you with such a disgusting act of murder. Sorry it had to be this way and you had to find out this way, but now, hopefully, you can take in the fact that whatever happened, you know happened and you may be able to settle with your past and your other personality."

Walter sat quiet, motionless as if he were sleeping in his chair with his head down, eyes shut, hands crossed on his lap. A quiet appeared in the room for a few seconds when all that could be heard was a slight weeping from Walter.

Knots placed his hand on Walter's back and gave him encouragement. "Walter, did you hear me? If not, listen again to the recording and listen closely," he said while getting Walter's attention. Walter brought up his head and Knots looked deeply into Walter's bloodshot eyes. He wanted Walter to focus on the voice in the recording which was actually Knots' voice and not Walters.

Walter nodded silently as Knots walked away.

Exiting the room, he looked back and saw Walter in the same sobbing position. Returning the next day, he was pulled aside one of the prison guards in Walter's wing.

"Walter was found dead in his room today. He hung himself with his sheets. He left a note addressed to you," the guard said.

Knots read the note, *I died just as I told myself to do.* Knots shook his head as he read the note and acted surprised. He was questioned by prison authorities to see what he knew but said he knew nothing. As soon as he got to his car, the saddened expression on his face disappeared as he smiled and rushed back to his office.

CHAPTER 31

That same evening, Reginald called Frederick. "Hi, Frederick," Reginald said once Fred answered.

"Reginald, what's been going on? Any news?" Fred asked curiously, wanting an update on Walter's situation.

"It worked just as planned," Reginald said.

"That's great. Hey, can you explain your process to me? I would like for you to teach me on your knowledge of getting into the lives of people such as you had with Walter."

"Yes. I mean, it's not for everyone and not everyone would have the strength to do so but since I know you well, you should definitely be strong enough."

"Thank you," Fred said. Susan was out in the dining area mingling with the residents while they ate dinner. "Can we fly out immediately to see you?"

"Sure, that would be awfully nice," Reginald answered, delighted to see such an old friend.

"We'll purchase tickets tonight and I'll let you know when we'll be there. Hopefully in a couple of days if not sooner."

Susan returned after a half an hour and saw Fred making a phone call to an airline, asking about fares and dates. She didn't know what was going on but waited next to him until he hung up the phone.

"Is everything okay?" She asked.

"Everything is perfect," he said and gave Susan a hug.

"Are we going somewhere?"

"Yes, actually we are. Well, I don't have a date yet but need to call a couple of more airlines to find the soonest date. But, we are going to see Reginald. Sorry that I didn't ask you first, but he called and I was hoping to see him again.

"That sounds nice," Susan said. "I have never met him but heard your many stories about him so I look forward to it," Susan was excited to meet one of Fred's old mentors and friends.

"Also, it'll be time to try my idea out."

"Great! I wish you would tell me your idea," Susan said. "Please?"

"I'm sorry, going to have to make you wait just a few more days. Do you trust me?"

"Of course and I hope it works out," Susan said, always being supportive of Fred.

CHAPTER 32

Two days had gone by and Fred and Susan arrived in Asheville, North Carolina. They drove in their rental car and went to the county courthouse where they knew Reginald worked under the name of Knots as a public defendant. They parked in the courthouse parking lot next to the courthouse and walked inside to the front desk. It was the first time Susan was meeting Reginald so she dressed nice with pearl earrings, necklace, and had her hair done the previous day in a perm. She wore a nice dress while Fred wore a freshly dry-cleaned suit with a collared shirt tucked into his slacks.

"Hi, I'm looking for the office of," Fred started to say, nearly saying Reginald but remembered to use the name Knots, "Knots." Fred realized he didn't know if that was a first name or last name so hopefully, the lady at the front desk didn't ask additional questions.

"Yes, Sammie Knots," she said. "Is he expecting you?"

"Yes, he is. We don't have an appointment but he's expecting us."

"What is your name, please?"

"My name is Frederick, and this is my wife, Susan."

"Nice to meet you. Let me call his office and tell his secretary you are here. Please, wait here a moment."

"Your wife?" Susan asked Fred quietly with a smile.

Fred snickered and smiled back, "We'll see later."

They backed away and they saw her pick up the phone and speak for a few seconds before hanging up.

"Sir?" She said and called Frederick back up to the desk. "Please wait here a few minutes and he'll be down to meet with you."

"Thank you," Frederick said. He and Susan went to the front window and looked out at the street. Before they knew it, they heard a deep voice from behind them.

"Frederick?" Fred and Susan turned around and saw Reginald. He had gained weight since they had seen each other many decades prior.

"You're looking younger every time I see you," Fred said to him and they chuckled.

"I'm so happy you both were able to come to visit. What's with the silver hair, though?" Reginald said with sarcasm towards Frederick. It's been way too long and Susan," Reginald said and turned to Susan. "It's nice to finally be able to meet you." He shook Susan's hand before reaching around to hug her.

"It's finally nice to meet you, too. I've heard so many great things about you it feels like I already know you." Susan and Reginald smiled at one another.

"I'm just getting off work, why don't we go out and get a bite to eat for dinner and do some catching up?" Reginald asked.

"That sounds great. We just landed a while back and got the rental car before coming here, so we're pretty hungry," Susan said.

The three of them walked outside as Reginald held the large door open for them while carrying a small briefcase. They walked down the half dozen steps down from the building to the sidewalk.

"We parked next door, where did you park?" Fred asked.

"I parked just down the street here, assigned parking. Got to love it," Reginald said and smiled. They all walked to his car and talked about where to go to dinner. "Just down the street about half a mile, you'll see First Avenue, turn right and about a half block down you'll see a Thai restaurant. It's a great restaurant. Does that sound okay to you both?"

"Perfect," Susan said.

"Sounds good to me," Fred responded back.

"Here we are," Reginald said as they got to his car. "I'll go first and get a table and I'll meet you both there."

"This is your car?" Fred asked surprised. "A nice classic!"

"Sure is, I've loved this Pontiac Firebird Trans-Am since I got it."

"It's a nice one!" Fred said. He peeked inside and saw the sun coming in from the tinted T-tops, reflecting off the freshly moisturized leather seats. "What cassette do you have in your stereo?"

"More of the classics, classic rock," Reginald said. "You know, as we spoke on the phone, I've had to change with the times and for survival, more of us will have to."

"Exactly, that's why I wanted to come and meet with you. Let's go over it more during dinner," Fred said and Reginald nodded his head and smiled. Reginald opened his car door and Fred stood by the door.

"We'll see you at the restaurant in a few minutes. But, hey, do me a favor."

"What's that?" Reginald asked while looking at Fred.

"I never once in a million years, if I make it that long, would have ever thought I would see you in this V-8 monster with classic rock on the radio. Do me a favor, roll your windows down, blare the cassette loud and rev your engine as you drive off."

"Haha, I have to be careful of my new image. But, it's you, Frederick, so I will for a good laugh."

"Thanks," Fred said and smiled as he closed the door for Reginald. Reginald started the car and rolled both automatic windows down. He put on his seatbelt as Fred and Susan stepped back on the sidewalk to watch him drive away. As the engine roared, Reginald looked behind him to see the road was clear and grabbed the shifter to shift into gear. As he was nearly ready to leave the parking space, the classic rock cassette started playing loudly as Fred leaned over to Susan and whispered, "Watch this." He held tightly onto Susan's hand.

Reginald drove out of his parking space onto the road. He sped off with his tires screeching, leaving a few feet of black skid marks on the street as he drove off quickly with the music still playing loudly. As he drove off, glancing at Fred and Susan for a slight second in the rearview mirror, his music stopped but the cassette continued playing when he heard a voice declare, "Kill yourself!"

Instead of stopping at the stop sign two blocks down, he continued increasing his speed and drove straight and crashed into a large brick office building. The collision was heard for blocks as the noise emanated through the buildings downtown. The brick wall collided inwards and bricks from the second floor fells onto Reginald's car. Hundreds upon hundreds of bricks continued to fall as the building slightly collapsed with the portion of the wall being damaged.

"Fred!" Susan yelled and grabbed onto Fred's arm. She looked over at him when he didn't respond and saw him smiling. "Fred?" She asked again.

He finally looked towards her and said, "All part of the idea. I think I'm ready."

"Ready? What do you mean? Ready for what?" She asked frantically after just seeing one of Fred's old friends getting into an accident and likely being killed. "Fred?" She impatiently asked and stomped her foot on the sidewalk.

"Follow me," he said and grabbed her arm as they walked towards the accident. He dragged her shocked body by his side and after a half-block of walking, they walked past a clothing store with large windows on the front of the old mid-century building. There were mannequins dressed in numerous neon fashion trends but Frederick stopped and looked into the reflective glass with the sun setting behind them. He let go of Susan's hand and readjusted his collared shirt and ran his hand through his thick black hair. Susan noticed Fred looking in the window and the first thing she saw was his reflection. She took a quick step back at his youth and then looked at herself and saw her long, black, and wavy hair going beyond her shoulder. She took a step up to the window and looked in her eyes and looked closely at her face. She turned to Fred and asked, "What happened?" She was astonished at how youthful Fred looked as well as her reflection. "Fred, what's going on?" She asked again, beginning to sweat and not knowing what was happening.

"It's okay, Susan. It's okay," he told her. He turned around to her and put his hand on her back. "Soon, I'll be the new master soul hunter."

PART TWO

CHAPTER 33

Susan had no idea that Frederick was going to kill Reginald since he had only told her good things about his old mentor. After he had killed him, she was a little scared and worried but seeing how powerful Frederick could become and how much better their life would be, she decided to stay with him.

"It's been a long time indeed," Frederick said on the steps of Reginald and Clarice's home in Augusta, Georgia. A white picket fence rounded a freshly green mowed grass surrounded their two-story Victorian homestead. Frederick didn't pay much attention to the house primarily because he didn't care nor would he be there long.

"Frederick, it's such a surprise to see you," Clarice said and appeared with a large smile as she opened the door. Frederick stood silent, exchanging a slight smile in return. "So, what brings you here?" Clarice asked. It was a windy day and her gown hung down to her bare feet. It was still early in the morning so she hadn't changed yet. She moved her hand up to her face to bring a large portion of her flowing, curly hair that had come across her face to the back of her head. "If you're here to see Reginald, I'm afraid he's not home but he should be soon. He had to work today. A lawyer now, would you believe that?" She asked and snickered thinking back at all the jobs he had throughout the past two centuries.

"Well, that's why I'm here," Frederick said and lowered his head, showing a sign of concern to Clarice. She moved her hand up again to move her hair back from hitting her in the face.

"What do you mean?" She asked.

"Can I please come in?"

Clarice stepped back from the threshold and held the door open for Frederick. He stepped in after wiping his feet. He stood by the entryway and looked around the room and admired at how much light was coming in from the two large windows on both sides of the living room.

"You might want to have a seat," he said. She sat on her velvet Victorian lounge chair. Keeping her back straight, she placed her hands on her legs and looked at Frederick who remained by the entryway. "The reason I came today is I have some bad news."

"Is it about Reg?" She asked, expecting the worst.

"He's dead," Frederick said as compassionately as he could. He wasn't sure how close Clarice had been working with Reginald on his new plans so he didn't know what to expect of her. He kept his head lowered and stood in a slouched position to emphasize sadness. Clarice immediately cried and lowered her head and brought up her hands to cover her face. She cried loudly while attempting to ask what happened. Frederick couldn't understand her so he walked over and sat beside her. He consoled her by placing his arm around her. She cried for what seemed an eternity for Frederick while he remained by her side, watching people walk by outside the large window as well as the birds floating in the birdbath.

"How did it happen?" She was finally able to ask after calming down slightly. She had been crying in Frederick's arm for a few minutes and raised her head to look at him.

"Sadly, I came to visit and brought Susan. We were to eat at a restaurant downtown when he crashed his car into a building. I have no idea what happened and we were, and are still just as shocked as you. I'm so sorry it's happened," Frederick said and hugged Clarice tighter with his one arm still wrapped around her back.

"What will I do now? I have no reason to continue getting any younger. He was the only reason I wanted to live," Clarice said and used her silky sleeve from her gown to attempt to wipe the tears off of her face but smeared them instead.

"I'm sorry, Clarice. I really am. If there's anything you need, please, don't hesitate to ask," Frederick said with a half-smile. "What will you do next? Do you need help with the burial or anything?" Frederick asked.

"If anything had ever happened to us, we both planned on getting cremated. So, that's what I'll do. I'll find a place to spread his ashes," Clarice said with a smile. They had both been to so many places with so many memories, she was contemplating many peaceful ideas in her head.

"I'm glad to hear that," Frederick said, continuing to smile. "Before I return home to Florida, can I ask you something?"

"Of course."

"Reginald claimed to have been working on something. A new idea, I guess you can say. Do you have any idea what it might be?" Frederick had already known the idea but wanted to see if Clarice knew or if not, if she knew of any textbooks or writing with additional information that Reginald may have had. Wanting to see Reginald's writings was the only reason he came to his house. Otherwise, he would have just let Clarice know about Reginald's death from the police when they would call.

"Yes, he was still in the process. He didn't tell me much since he said he wanted to perfect it before letting me know. Something, though, about getting into the minds of people. He had mentioned a few other names but names I can't remember. That's about all I know. I can show you his office and anything you want, just take it."

"Names?" Frederick asked, wanting to know more of who he had been working with.

"I don't remember. There were two or three. I can't remember. They were bigger names though."

"Thanks," Frederick said while removing his arm from around Clarice, thinking in the back of his mind if he could recall any peculiar names. Clarice also stood and walked him to Reginald's office. She got a key from one of the drawers in the cabinet in the hardwood hallway. As they walked to his office, Frederick looked at all of their photographs hanging in the hallway. There were numerous black and white photographs as well as more recent sepia-colored and crisper photographs of Reginald and Clarice throughout the years. He knew the two lived a long and happy life and for a slight second felt bad for taking his life. He started to feel guilty inside to take away their happiness but once he got to his office, the regret was replaced by excitement. Clarice reached down with the skeleton key and unlocked the door to Reginald's office.

"Take your time," she said and smiled towards Frederick. She left and walked down the hallway and Frederick figured she was probably going to their bedroom.

Frederick looked around Reginald's large office. There was a tall window behind his desk that let in bright light. In front of the window was an old, oak desk with an oak swivel chair. On the desk were a typewriter and numerous papers and writings in neat piles. He walked into the room and began looking at all the books on the left wall before walking over to the right wall and looking at all the books on that side also. Reginald had collected a lot of books throughout his long life. He glanced quickly at all the books, varying between law books to encyclopedias before he walked closer to his desk. He went behind the desk and pulled out the chair from underneath. He sat on the warm chair after the sun had heated it in the late evening. He looked around at the top of the desk and before grabbing the stack of papers, he moved the typewriter to the side of the desk to give him more space. He then grabbed the inch or so stack of papers and moved them to the center. He browed through the first pages, quickly reading portions of the written text on each and setting them aside once realizing they weren't important. He then began reading another page that had an outline when he could hear the sounds of Clarice's feet sliding down the hallway again. The room was too silent to hear anything else so he waited a few seconds as he heard the footsteps appear closer. Finally, after waiting a few seconds, he noticed her peek around the doorframe.

"Sorry to bother you," her quiet voice said as her head peeked around the opened door.

"Are you okay?" Frederick asked.

"I found something that might interest you," she said and began walking into the room. She was holding onto a large book that looked to have an old, leathered cover and binding on it. She carried it with both hands until she reached the front of the desk. She set the book down gently and stepped back and put her hands behind her back. She kept her eye on the book an additional few seconds before looking up to Frederick who stood by the desk chair.

"What is that?" Frederick asked curiously while looking at the cover of the book.

"It's, well, it was one of Reg's most prized possessions. He's had it for as long as I can remember. At least 150 years. He got it from, well, all I can say is an elder – an old friend. Only a few people have this book and people have even tried to kill Reg for it. So, please, be careful and take care of it and the powers inside."

"Wow, what is it about?"

"The history of the soul hunters. The story includes the beginning and many beliefs and philosophies from the elders. It tells the story of how everything began with the Ancient Pharaoh Narmer and the Egyptian deities. In it, though, is a few spells that can be quite damaging so you must be sure this book doesn't fall into the wrong hands."

"Hmm," Frederick mumbled while hearing about the powers inside the book.

"Reading this is how Reg started his new technique of, you know, getting into people's heads. You'll probably find his writings on his desk somewhere and any other details. Remember, the stronger of a soul hunter you get and the more power one gets, the more in danger they become. I often told Reg to be careful but I guess, well, I don't know," Clarice finished saying and brought her head to look at the floor. She shook her head and held back tears.

"Thank you," Frederick said with a caring smile and slowly moved his arms forward towards the book. He turned the book around so the binding would be on his left and held the binding. With his other hand, he gently caressed the cover, feeling the freshly oiled aged leather cover that was black in color. There was no writing on the cover or binding, bringing even more mystique to the soul hunter's texts. "Do you know who else even has a copy of this?" Frederick asked Clarice while he slowly moved the book back across the desk towards him.

"I never did know. Reg knew of a couple but never told me. I do know that Narmer, the Egyptian Pharaoh, had the original scroll. Soul hunter beliefs go as deep as him and through legend, it's been told that he was buried with his original scroll that was signed by the deity Set," Clarice said and walked to the corner to have a seat on a wood chair facing the desk. "I'm not sure how much you know, but the soul hunters began when Narmer attempted to sign an agreement with Anubis, who is also known as Anpu. Instead, he was tricked by the deity of trickery, Set, who signed the agreement on the scroll instead of Anubis. The agreement was that Narmer would be able to align Northern and Southern Egypt and he would rule all. In exchange for powerful rule and powers, he gave his soul to Anubis. Instead, Set tricked both Narmer and Anubis and after Narmer signed the scroll, Narmer's life and soul belonged to Set. Being angered by Set's trickery, Anubis threatened Set to make things straight so he did. After Narmer's death, the soul hunters began with him reining as master soul hunter."

"How can he still have the power? Even after dying?" Frederick asked while remaining standing.

"Legend goes that in exchange for Set letting Narmer to rule the soul hunters after his death, any soul hunters that die are forced to live an eternity under Anubis' rule. I mean, I don't want to go there but without Reginald, why must I keep living?" Clarice said before raising her hand to her face and scratch her eyelid. She was too far from Frederick for him to see if she was crying but he figured she was."

"That's amazing."

"So much is unknown, though," Clarice said after lower her hand from her face. There is so much mystery surrounding soul hunters but this book holds many secrets but also, many unanswered questions that you would probably not even want to find the answers for. Be careful what you do with this and your future actions. I trust you though that it will be in good hands, rather than have someone steal it from me or find it after my death."

A lot of information was running through Frederick's mind and he couldn't wait to be able to go through the book as soon as he could. He was astonished by how much mystery surrounded the texts and wanted to read more. He began thinking quickly of Narmer and what the scroll must say. He wanted to ask Clarice and see if she knew anything in regards to that.

"Clarice, I hate to ask questions at a time like this, but, you mentioned Narmer and the scroll."

Clarice nodded while crossing her legs and adjusting her gown.

"What does the scroll say? Is there any reference to that?" Frederick asked.

"I'm not sure. Reg mentioned it a few times and wished he could see it in real life. There are a few of the lines in the handwritten text in the pages of the book but no one knows what the whole thing says. Word has been passed down that whoever possesses the scroll can access and gain so much power."

What Clarice said is everything Frederick wanted to hear. He wasn't too familiar with Egyptian history but knew of an old friend who was. "Does anyone know where the scroll is now?" Frederick asked.

"Nobody has located Narmer's grave as of yet. I'm sure archaeologists are searching for it as we speak but as far as I know, nobody has found it yet. When someone does, they will have access to the riches in the grave. Most people would want the gold and treasures but soul hunters who know of the true value would do anything for the scroll."

"Unbelievable," Frederick said, even though he believed every word of it. He knew he must contact his friend for more information but what he wanted to do first was bring the book somewhere quiet and read through the pages.

"There is a list of names towards the back of the book. I remember one or two of them are in or around Egypt. I'm not sure if they're still there or even alive anymore, so check them out if you want," Clarice mentioned. There were a few names of prominent soul hunters and elders and their last locations. The book hadn't been updated in many years so Frederick was worried the list might not be updated.

Clarice pressed up on her thighs to help her stand and she smiled towards Frederick before beginning to walk out the room. "If you need anything, just holler. Take your time in here," she said while her back was facing Frederick before she walked out of the room.

Frederick browsed through Reginald's papers on his desk and glanced through the drawers. He stayed an additional hour going through things before leaving. He kept his anticipation in reading the book until he left Reginald and Clarice's house and returned to the hotel he and Susan were staying at that night before flying back home to Florida.

CHAPTER 34

After returning to the hotel where Susan was taking a nap in the bed, she woke up and asked Frederick how the talk with Clarice went. After updating her for a few minutes, Frederick showed Susan the book. He placed it on the messy sheets of the bed and Susan looked at it.

"What is it?" She asked while she looked around the strange looking cover. She couldn't tell what it was since there wasn't a title on it nor author or any other identifiable marks. She moved her hands and gently touched the cover with her fingertips, feeling the smooth leather.

"It's a book that only the most powerful and prominent soul hunters have," Frederick started to say and had a large grin on his face.

"Really?" Susan blurted out. She was still a bit worried about how much power Frederick wanted since she hadn't seen that side of him before and she was still shocked at how he killed his former mentor, Reginald. Knowing Frederick for a couple of decades, she did know how smart he was and how great of a leader he could be. Thinking about what had conspired earlier that day and seeing the grin on Frederick's face, she was curious about what his intentions were. "What do you plan on doing with this book? I mean, what do you want to do?" She asked since she wanted to know what he was going to do next. She also wanted to know what he really meant when he said he wanted to become the most powerful soul hunter after his plan worked to kill Reginald.

"Have a seat," Frederick said, not realizing Susan was still sitting on the bed next to the book. He walked over to the side of the bed next to her and sat. He reached out his hand and placed it on her knee and looked into her eyes. "Look, Dear," he said. Susan was caught off guard by that remark since as long as she's known him and as long as she's liked him, he's never called her anything but Susan. Frederick continued speaking, "my latest idea worked. With the powers that I've come up with, I can become the most powerful soul hunter. With that, I mean, I want to become the leader. I know it sounds crazy," he said once seeing Susan's eyes get larger. "It's crazy, yes, but I know I can be the leader."

"Why? Why do you want to be the leader?" Susan asked and placed her hand on his knee.

"I know I can. I want to have the best life for not only me but for you, too, as well as all soul hunters! I know it sounds crazy, or even greedy, but I have a plan and have some work to do but I know by becoming the leader, the master, that life will be great for us and we can have our own followers and in a way, raise our own children." Frederick knew that Susan wanted to be foster parents to young soul hunter children so he knew the last statement was a way that might get on her board with his idea. She smiled slightly after hearing him say that.

"I don't mind how life is now, with you," Susan then said.

"But, look at us. We've been operating a nursing home for ten or so years. I can't even remember how long now. We're leaving it but where are we going? We don't have any plans yet but I know that I do have a plan that can give us a better life."

Susan interrupted, "But life is great with you now. As long as I'm with you, I'm happy."

"Well, great," Frederick said and stood up in excitement. He was eager to get Susan on board and even though he had a lot of planning to do, he wanted to get her support. Even though they lived together but were unmarried, he cared for her tremendously and didn't want to lose her. "Susan, this would mean a better life for us. We can travel and see the world. We can meet new people. We won't have to worry about getting older. Life will be ample and we'll be so happy and healthy."

"I mean, yes, that would be great. I guess I'm just scared. Seeing you kill your old friend and mentor, well, I thought he was your friend," Susan said before being interrupted by Frederick.

"Yes, he was a friend. An old confidant. As years go by, though, so does life. There must be sacrifices in regards to survival and gaining in our long lives," Frederick said, hiding his true intentions of why he killed Reginald. He saw a blank look on Susan's face as there was no smile and her eyes stared at his. "We've killed numerous people throughout our life. Do you have any regret or feelings with those deaths you've caused? Remember how many people we killed at the drive-in theater years ago?"

Susan nodded and said, "Yes."

"Well, after each death, we forgot about those we killed since it's human nature for us. We move on and enjoy our lives. This deed may seem heartless to most but for us, it's our way of survival. What I did is the same. We've been told through our lives to not kill other soul hunters, nor should we. Instead, we should work as a team but when a powerful soul hunter is there to kill, we can and when we do, our lives improve."

"Well, yes. That's true," Susan started to say.

"Then follow through with me. Stick with me while I, I mean we, we become the most powerful soul hunters as well as leaders of the soul hunters in general.

"Tell me how," a curious Susan finally asked as she leaned back on the wood headboard on the bed.

"I have some ideas while other ideas rest in this book. I have a lot to do but what I want you to do is go back to Florida. Finish packing up and taking care of the residents until the new owners take over in a few weeks. By then, I will have the plan in full force. I need time to find one of my old friends. I'm not sure where he is but last I heard he was in Alabama. I could drive there from here while you fly back to Florida."

"Who is it? What will you do then? Susan asked, wanting to make sure Frederick would be safe.

"Firstly, don't worry. I'll call whenever I have a chance," he said with a smile to reassure her. He took a few steps back to the bed and sat back down on the edge. "My old friend Jerren. I need to ask him questions about Ancient Egypt and some things about the old pharaoh, Narmer. I have to," Frederick started to say but before speaking any more, he knew what he was about to say would sound crazy and impossible. He had to watch what he said since he didn't want Susan to not agree with what he was going to do. Frederick paused a few seconds before continuing. "I have to ask him about some philosophies as well as read this book to find some old ideas and secrecy amongst the soul hunters and their beginning."

Susan nodded and still wasn't totally sure what Frederick had planned but she had come to think that maybe he hadn't come up with a full idea of yet, even though he had but she didn't know. That night,

Susan and Frederick read through the book until they realized night had passed and it was near morning. Susan packed her items to fly out while Frederick, amazed at what the book said and the texts of some of the most prolific and elder of all soul hunters that brought much excitement to him and his plan.

CHAPTER 35

Susan arrived back in DeLand, Florida while Frederick was nearing his way to Western Alabama where he was to meet his friend Jerren Bernstein. He had last seen Bernstein about twenty years earlier. While Frederick drove the highway to Tuscaloosa, he thought of the first, which was also the last time he had met his friend and the time they spent together in Alabama. Even though it had been twenty years, the less than a handful of decades to a soul hunter isn't much time at all. All he hoped was that his friend would still be there or at least be around there somewhere. He had tried to call the University of Alabama the previous day and spoke with a woman who wasn't aware of Professor Bernstein. Frederick needed to drive there to find out for himself.

Having no personal phone number for Bernstein and if he did find him, the time and drive would be worth it. He knew Bernstein was his best hope to get his help when it came to understanding the beginning of the soul hunters with what he heard from Clarice as well as what he read in the texts. Frederick had to withhold his plan from Susan and he planned to go to Egypt and find Narmer's scroll. He knew the feat sounded impossible and daunting and he even thought to himself that it would be impossible. He knew he had to start by learning more before traveling to Egypt to attempt to find the scroll. He had a feeling that the scroll would be what he needs and what he has to have in order to become the leader of the soul hunters.

A bit later in the day as the evening progressed, having traveled just over four hours after dropping Susan off at the airport to travel back home, the first thing he did after arriving in Tuscaloosa was he found a payphone at the corner of a gas station. He called Susan and she answered in a worried, fluttering voice.

"Hello?" She answered with a tremble in her voice, having just arrived home.

"Just calling to let you know I made it. I'm in Tuscaloosa and everything went well during the drive. No problems."

"I'm glad to hear that. Did you find your friend?"

"Not yet. I wanted to call you first so you wouldn't be too worried," Frederick said and smiled thinking that Susan was worried about him after hearing her voice tremble when she answered. She smiled back thinking that Frederick cared about her feelings. She knew he did and she had been thinking since that morning when he called her 'Dear' and she thought what he meant by that. She was hoping his feelings towards her were becoming more serious. She was also excited when he mentioned raising children from their morning conversation since that had been her dream for such a long time.

"You better get some rest, Frederick."

"I better. It's been a long day so I'll find a place to rest and in the morning find Jerren."

They said goodnight to one another and Frederick got some food at that same gas station before retiring for the night at a small motel on the side of the road. He showered and sat on the bed and opened the soul hunter's text. He read through the pages again about the beginning and Narmer's agreement and betrayal. He wrote down numerous questions on a pad of paper that he wanted to ask his friend the next morning. He was worried though that his friend might not even be there anymore. Knowing that twenty years had gone by, Frederick knew that soul hunters rarely stayed in a place so long since they often had to move to hide the fact they're becoming younger. The last he remembered was Bernstein was a professor at the University of Alabama in the History department. That was twenty years ago though and didn't have his phone number to call.

The two met when Frederick was driving from Texas and stopped a night in Tuscaloosa and saw a presentation called "Life and Death" at the University of Alabama. The lecturer was Bernstein and he listened the hour and a half where he spoke of Ancient Egyptian beliefs of life after death and the Underworld. After hearing Bernstein speak, he pulled him aside. Bernstein was a younger man likely in his thirties or so at that time. He figured he would be older now if he was still there. After a lot of people left the auditorium where the lecture was held, Frederick introduced himself.

"Mr. Bernstein, my name is Frederick," he started by saying.

Bernstein was tired after speaking for an hour and a half and it was late in the evening. He had just finished speaking to dozens of people after the lecture and was ready to go home. He was ready to brush past Frederick and make small talk so he could go home and rest.

"Nice to meet you. I hope you enjoyed the lecture," Bernstein said and released his hand from Frederick and smiled while he nodded his head. He lowered his shoulder to begin walking when Frederick leaned into him.

"So really, what happens after death?" Frederick asked quietly. Bernstein stopped walking and turned to Frederick. They looked at one another in the eyes for five or so seconds while Bernstein tried to read Frederick's facial expressions and how to answer. He didn't feel like getting into a long debate so he wanted to find a quick answer.

"Well, what do you think?" Bernstein asked as a rebuttal.

"It depends who you are, I guess," Frederick answered. Bernstein thought what he had meant by that. Again, they looked at one other in the eyes a few seconds. They were standing by the door to leave the auditorium. Bernstein became a little fidgety and stretched each of his wrists as he stood. He had dressed nicely and wore a wool suit and tie. His hair was full of pomade and slicked to its side. Frederick stood a few feet away from him wearing slacks and a white, buttoned shirt tucked into his slacks. His old fashioned style caught Bernstein's attention while his hair was more astray than usual which made him hard to read by looking at him.

"For the Egyptians, life after," he began to say when Frederick interrupted him.

"But, what about for you?"

"Hmm?" Bernstein started by saying. They were the only two left in the auditorium and by this time, he was starting to become worried who Frederick was and if he was going to do something to him. "For me, all I know is death is uncertain. I hold no beliefs religious wise except for what I've read and studied in my life."

"Where are you from?" Frederick asked after trying to understand his accent.

"Poland."

"Is that where you came from most recently?" Frederick then asked. He knew the history and the end of World War II, having ended just about thirty years earlier, he heard the slight accent and wanted to know Bernstein's true past.

Bernstein took a step back and looked at Frederick's body and features. He noticed Frederick's stillness as he stood with both hands in his pockets. He looked at his pockets to make sure there wasn't anything that he might have been hiding. He saw a gold chain wrap around a belt loop that went into one of his pockets, indicating he had a pocket watch. "Yes," he finally answered.

"I'm not here to harm you. Listen," Frederick said since he saw Bernstein becoming very nervous and fidgety. "I'm just traveling through to return to Florida where I live. I was intrigued by your lecture and the Egyptian's vision of death and life in the Underworld." Bernstein tilted his head to the side and folded his arms in front of him and continued to listen. "But, I saw something in your eyes. I see a twinkle now. It's a twinkle I see in so few people I know. To me, it looks like the North Star."

Bernstein stepped immediately in front of Frederick and placed both hands on the sides of his face. Bernstein took his hands and twisted Frederick's face slightly to the left and right and looked deeply into Frederick's eyes. "What do you know about the North Star?" He asked and stepped back after releasing Frederick's face. He placed his hands on his hips and waited anxiously for his answer.

"The North Star is where he lives."

"Narmer?" Bernstein answered immediately.

Frederick smiled and nodded. "I had a feeling when watching you on the stage. Your face told me everything," Frederick said since he didn't sit too far away from the stage in the small but filled up auditorium.

"Are you hungry?" Bernstein asked and after Frederick nodded, he invited him out to dinner at a local restaurant near the University.

CHAPTER 36

"So, where really are you from?" Frederick asked after they sat at a local college hangout that served good food. Bernstein enjoyed the food there and recommended the quesadillas which Frederick ordered.

Bernstein looked around and saw handfuls of college students congregating around a variety of tables and at the bar. They were all talking amongst each other about exams, dating, sports, and other topics. Bernstein continued looking at all sides while he reached his right hand to his left sleeve and unbuttoned the cuff. Slowly, he brought it up halfway up his forearm as he looked around to make sure nobody was watching. Frederick glanced down and saw what looked to be a sloppy tattoo featuring a six-digit number. Once he noticed Frederick had seen it he hurried and brought his sleeve back down.

"Auschwitz?" Frederick whispered to ask.

Bernstein nodded and buttoned his cuff back up. "Originally from Poland. Born in, um, 1922."

"1922?" Frederick asked. "Now, let's be serious and let me know when you were really born," he said and chuckled.

Bernstein gave a slight snicker and grin before answering, "1822."

"That's more like it," Frederick said and smiled and leaned back in the chair. He looked over towards the bar and saw their waitress carrying a tray with two plates that looked like some sort of tortilla shell. He figured it was their food and moved his glass to the side of the table to make space which caught Bernstein's attention and he did the same thing.

"Things were going great and I lived in Poland with my wife whom I married. She was a soul hunter also. We lived there until the German's began bringing the Jews into camps and killed them. When we were brought in on the train, they separated us and I never saw my wife again. There was no way out of the camps and we did what we could to survive. The Nazi war machine was too much and too powerful and the few of us that survived had traits that helped them. You don't know how much it hurt to do work for their success but it was the only way to survive. That's why today I only hunt Germans when I need to gain life. Sort of," Bernstein said and paused.

"An eye for an eye," Frederick finished Bernstein's statement. Bernstein nodded and took a bite of his quesadilla. "Luckily my ancestry is traced back to Hungary," Frederick said before taking a bite himself and chuckled.

After eating their dinner and getting to know one another, they went their separate ways but as usual, soul hunters keep connected in one way or another since they could trust one another and rely on one each other if problems arise, no matter how many years have gone by.

***

Frederick thought back to when he first met Bernstein and even though they hadn't chatted in twenty years, he knew that Bernstein would remember him. He closed the book and set it on the end table and turned off his light to get some sleep. He woke up early as the sun came through the thin sheer cloth the hotel used as a curtain to the room. He sat up from the bed and walked to the foot of the bed and looked at the wall where there was a mirror. He looked at himself and ran his hand through his hair to straighten it. He got dressed and brushed his teeth and shaved before traveling to Auburn University to locate his old friend.

He parked in one of the University's many parking garages and walked down from the second floor. He stood out on the sidewalk under the sunny sky. He looked around at the campus before looking down both directions of the road in front of him. Realizing there weren't any cars coming, he hurried across the road and stopped once getting to the other side. He saw a map nearby and walked over to the sign and located the history building. He walked ten minutes across campus and watched all the students around. Many of them were rushing or even running while carrying backpacks or with a handful of books. Others were congregating amongst each other and talking, taking a break between classes. Frederick admired a lot of the buildings and looked around. Most of the buildings were brick and numerous stories high. He passed the library and wished he had time to go through the books since he loved to learn but he didn't have time. He finally came to what he thought was the history building and saw the building number on the side. He rounded the corner and above the front door, the words "History Building" was in large font. He walked into the building and was immediately in a hallway. A few students hurried around the hallway as they attempted to be as close to on time as possible for their classes.

Frederick noticed a list of professors hanging on the brick wall and room numbers by each of them. He hurried in excitement to find Bernstein but he didn't see his name on the list. He checked a second time but again didn't see it. He saw on the bottom of the sign there was an arrow for the main history department. He started walking the direction and passed numerous closed doors. A few of the rooms he could hear either students or their professor talking since classes were taking place. He rounded the corner and on the left, he could see a room that was open with an older, gray-haired person coming out of it. He figured that might be it and he walked closer. He peeked in and saw a large desk in front with a couple of young ladies working behind it. They noticed Frederick peeking around the corner.

"Hi, can we help you with anything?" One of the ladies asked. To Frederick, they looked to be college students possibly working between classes or even teacher's assistants.

"Yes, please. I'm looking for an old friend. His name is Jerren Bernstein."

The young lady who he initially greeted Frederick turned to her friend next to her. They looked at each other and to Frederick, they look confused. They stood for just a couple of seconds before one turned to holler back in a small cubicle behind them.

"Professor," the first lady asked, getting the attention of a professor in the cubicle.

An older man with curly, gray hair surrounding a bald spot peeked around the cubicle wall. He brought up his glasses and looked past the desk at Frederick. He stood up and walked slowly up to the desk. He placed both hands on the wood top and looked at Frederick. "You looking for Professor Bernstein?" He asked.

"Yes, my name is Frederick and he's an old acquaintance of mine," Frederick said as he remained standing by the door.

"I'm afraid you're too late," the old man said to Frederick. Immediately, Frederick thought the worst. The man continued, "He just left for Egypt last week."

"Oh," Frederick said surprisingly. "He went to Egypt?"

"Yes. He's no longer in the history wing of the University but instead the archaeology department. He left and is helping lead an archaeological dig somewhere outside of Luxor. He'll be gone for a couple of semesters on sabbatical." The old man was friends was Bernstein so he knew where he had gone.

"Do you have any way to contact him?"

"Well," the man started to say before reaching down to one of the drawers in the desk. He looked through the first one before closing it and opening the second. He pulled out a thin binder. He set it on the desk between the two ladies and they watched him go through it. He browsed through a few pages before stopping on one. He ran his finger about halfway down the page and stopped. "Yes, he is there with a team from the University of Memphis in Luxor. The Head of the team is Alexandra Nosdjov. They're working on some tombs and the archaeological dig is being funded primarily by the University of Memphis. Here's a phone number to contact them at," the old man said as he took a piece of scratch paper and wrote down the phone number. He held it out for Frederick to take. Frederick took a few steps closer and grabbed the paper and nodded.

"I thank you for your time, Sir," Frederick said and looked at the paper to make sure the man's writing was legible. He folded it and put it inside his coat pocket. "Thanks again everyone for your time," he said before leaving the room.

Frederick left the college and having everything packed in his car, he was supposed to be going back to Florida but instead, he needed to change his plan and travel to Egypt. It was worth the time and effort since Frederick trusted Bernstein and knew his knowledge would be very beneficial. He stopped to fill the tank of his car up with gas and afterward he called Susan.

"Susan, how many countries have you been to?" Frederick asked while standing near the convenience store wall at the payphone.

"Well, none, I guess. Why do you ask?"

"Would you want to go to Egypt with me?" Frederick asked. He wasn't sure if Susan would want to or not.

"Is this part of your plan?" She asked after there was a slight silence while she thought about his unexpected question.

"It is, Susan. The perfect place to meet an Egyptian scholar who can help me, and help us with the texts, and well, let me tell you my plan when I get back home. Jerren is there too and he can help. I'll be driving home tonight and be back hopefully late tomorrow. Until then, think about it, okay?"

"Okay, Frederick. I will. I miss you," she said, a usual statement to finish up a conversation with him. "Make sure you drive safely."

"I miss you too," Frederick replied back to Susan's surprise, which was an unusual reply. "I'll see you soon," he said before hanging up the payphone. He checked the coin return but it was empty. He went back to his car and left to return to Florida. He knew he had to go home and plan his trip to Egypt including getting flight tickets and to pack, all while figuring out if he would be back in time to finalize the sale of their nursing home. He had no idea how long they would be gone for.

CHAPTER 37

Frederick and Susan boarded the airplane to Luxor. The flight would be seventeen hours including two layovers. Susan was very excited to leave the country for the first time but she was also nervous that Frederick might be in danger with what he was going to attempt to do there. They sat on the airplane and Susan set the neck pillow she had carried around her neck onto her lap. Frederick placed both his and Susan's carryon bag that he had carried under the front of each of their seats. He leaned back and buckled his seatbelt while Susan then did the same. She looked over towards Frederick who was glancing around the plane to see how many people were around. She looked towards him until he noticed her looking at him. He smiled and Susan did also.

"Are you okay?" Frederick asked.

"Yes, I'm just hoping I can sleep for most of the flight."

"Me too," Frederick said and moved his attention past Susan to look out of the small window. She had the window seat while he sat in the middle seat. He saw the blue sky with slight cloud coverage and hoped it would be a smooth flight. He turned his attention back to Susan who was still looking at him and smiling. She turned her head straight and leaned her head back. It was at that time the pilot made their announcement and the airplane readied for takeoff.

***

The airplane finally landed and once the wheels touched the ground surface, the jolt woke up Susan from a deep sleep. Frederick sat awake with his head back on the headrest to be prepared for the landing. He had his hands clenched on his lap with his elbows partially on the armrests. Once Susan awoke, she quickly glanced around her to make sure everything was okay.

They got off the airplane, grabbed their luggage, and found their rental car that Frederick had reserved. Being in a foreign country was overwhelming and they were both worried. Frederick was worried to drive as well as where he would be driving to. He had already printed out directions to the University in hopes of finding more information on the archaeological dig. After he had gotten back home from Alabama, he called the University and confirmed Bernstein was indeed doing an archaeological dig there. They drove and went to the University where after asking a few people there, he found the office of someone he had spoken to on the phone with previously.

"Professor Anwick?" Frederick asked as he stood in front of the doorway to her office. He noticed her sitting behind her desk, holding a pen after she had just written down some information.

"Yes, how can I," she started to say before pausing. "Are you Frederick?"

"Yes, it's nice to meet you," he said back and walked towards her to shake her hand. "This here is Susan." Susan nodded to Anwick and she nodded in return.

"How was your flight?" Anwick asked.

Frederick looked towards Susan to let her answer first. "Not bad, actually. I slept a lot of the flight," she said and smiled.

"Mine was good, too. Thanks for asking," Frederick said.

"I'm glad to hear. Please, follow me," Anwick stood up and moved in front of her desk and said. She directed them down a hallway. Anwick was likely in her sixties but walked very quickly with long strides. She had her silver-colored hair pulled back and in a bun. She wore a conservative dress that covered most of her arms and legs. Wearing flat-soled slip-on dress shoes, her feed slid across the thinly carpeted floors. Frederick and Susan picked up their strides to take longer steps to keep up to her speed. Walking for about twenty seconds, Anwick stopped in front of a doorway and motioned her hand to her left for Frederick and Susan to walk into.

As soon as they walked into the room, Anwick said, "Please, have a seat." There were two vinyl chairs in front of a wooden desk that the two sat at. Frederick looked around and admired the number of certificates that were hanging on the walls. He couldn't read them from where he was sitting but he admired the amount there were. On the desk were numerous papers thrown about that looked to be in no particular order. There were also a few maps that stuck out from underneath the papers. Anwick walked over and sat in her leather chair. "Sorry for the mess," she started. Both Frederick and Susan smiled as if it was no worry. "So, based on your call, you're interested in an archaeological dig that's going on outside of Luxor. Also, Dr. Bernstein is an old acquaintance of yours?"

"That's correct. He and I go back about twenty years. It's funny that the first time I met him was after hearing a lecture on Ancient Egypt and life and death. I visited the University I remembered he worked at in the States but they said he was here. I've always wanted to visit Egypt so I figured, why not?"

Anwick chucked. "Exactly, why not? He is out on the dig now. I can take you there if you'd like to see him. After you had called before and we spoke, I told him the next day that you asked about him and he was excited to have heard your name. He said it's been a long time. I wanted to ask him first if it was fine that I brought you to the site. You see, not just anyone is allowed out there. We need to keep security tight."

"Yes, it has been a long time and I understand. It would be ideal if you could take us to the site. We haven't really cleaned up after the flight but we might as well see him before we head back to the hotel for the night. How long of a drive is it?"

"About an hour so let's go ahead and head out there. If you want to follow behind me I will take you to the site. I have to stay there later but getting back to town is very easy. There's only one main road."

"That would be fine," Frederick answered. "By the way, what's going on at the dig?" Frederick asked and was curious just as much as Susan. They didn't want to ask too much and sound suspicious or anything.

"We've located what we believe is a grave for prosperous citizens near the Valley of the Kings. It's an unheard-of gravesite, especially for the times, since no one was allowed to be buried so close to the Valley. Well, so we thought."

"That sounds interesting," Susan said, truly intrigued.

"Great, let's go check it out," Anwick said and stood from her chair. The three of them proceeded out of the building and Anwick drove them in her car to where they had parked. Frederick and Susan got into their rental car and followed. Anwick drove just as fast as she walked and Frederick struggled to keep up – especially with him being unfamiliar with traffic and the roads in Egypt.

CHAPTER 38

The three of them finally arrived at the archaeological site and Susan finally unclenched her hand from the door handle from the stressful drive to the site. She was glad they had arrived safely. She heard Frederick take a long exhale after putting the car into park. They looked around the desert landscape and the desolate area. They couldn't see anybody anywhere and were a bit worried. Frederick got out the car first and held his hand on his forehead to block the bright sunlight from his eyes to let them adjust. Susan stepped out afterward. The heat from the sun instantly warmed their bodies with the sun on the horizon without a single cloud for coverage. When they stood outside of the car before walking towards Anwick, they could hear noises of metal clanging and slight chatter from the distance.

"Over here," she said and started walking towards the desert. They followed her as she stood and looked down into a valley. They proceeded next to her and looked down into a large area where there were near 100 people scurrying around. A lot of them were digging while others going in and out of some tents that were spread around. "Let's go," she then said and started walking down a pathway. A few high terrain cars were driving around and up some roads in the distance. There were smaller tents further away from the larger tents and where people were digging. Frederick figured that's where many of them stayed and rested during the night and to keep the site secure during darkness. Darkness would be there in less than a handful of hours so Frederick wanted to talk with Bernstein as soon as possible to get his plan in action.

"Wow, this is very impressive," Susan said as they followed Anwick down the narrow and slippery path. Her and Frederick slipped often going down while Anwick never did since she was used to the terrain.

"It's been a few months in the works. Everyone has been working so hard here and we've made quite a deal of progress."

"Very impressive indeed," Frederick said. They walked down the path and continued watching the numerous people working. It was very hot as the sun lit up the grounds and the only shade provided was the tents. Without a breeze, Frederick and Susan both wondered how anyone could work in such heat – especially at such speed they saw everyone working at.

"Here we are," Anwick said when they got to the flat ground after walking five minutes. She went across towards the first group of large tents in the area. She nodded and spoke Egyptian to a few of the people they came across while those she spoke with started momentarily at the strangers that had come into their site. "Bernstein should be around here somewhere," Anwick said after turning towards Frederick and Susan and continued walking.

"Great, this is exciting," Frederick replied. He watched those who walked by them all wearing scarves and headwear attempting to block as much sun as possible. Everyone was wearing what seemed to be a thin cloth covering their arms, body, and mouths while a few were shirtless. They walked in the shade behind a tall tent that had a canvas cover and canvas walls. They enjoyed the few seconds of slight coolness until they rounded the corner back into the full sun. Frederick squinted his eyes immediately and continued to follow behind Anwick.

"Frederick?" A voice behind him yelled which started him. He turned around while Anwick also stopped and turned around. Bernstein had walked out of a nearby tent when he noticed somebody dressed strangely to be in such a dirty and hot area. He saw the man wearing a plaid long sleeve shirt and slacks with a woman wearing a collared dress shirt and teal green pants. He noticed Anwick walking in front of them so he figured it had to be Frederick.

"Jerren?" Frederick said once he saw the surprisingly aged man outside of the tent. He walked over and held out his hand, ready to give Bernstein a handshake.

"Bring it in, old friend," Bernstein said and gave Frederick a big hug. "What were you thinking to wear such thick clothing out here?" He asked and laughed. Frederick had wondered the same thing once he got out of the car. "This must be Susan?"

"Susan, this is my old friend Jerren."

"It's nice to meet you, Jerren. Thanks for welcoming us out to your dig here. It looks very exciting and so much going on here."

"I'm glad you both were able to come out here. I was sure surprised when Anwick told me that you had called and asked about me. Come, come here in the tent. We can talk in there since it's a bit cooler." Bernstein brought up the part of the tent wall in the middle and Susan walked in first. Frederick looked back towards Anwick who had been standing a bit in the back.

"Thanks for your help, Doctor Anwick," Frederick said and smiled. He turned around and went into the tent, followed by Bernstein.

Susan and Frederick stood inside the tent while Bernstein walked around them to a chair in the back of the tent behind a small wooden desk. He sat and said, "Please, have a seat." There were two wooden folding chairs near the desk that each of them sat at.

"Thanks," Frederick said. "So, how is everything been going? I can't say that I'm not surprised you, out here all the way in Egypt helping lead a dig. It's quite amazing."

"Haha, thanks. It's been quite a while since we've seen one another. I see you, well, are you two married?"

Susan immediately showed a smile and looked towards Frederick who stared straight ahead towards Bernstein, blushing slightly as his cheeks turned a dull red. He was caught off guard and was instantly worried about what Susan was thinking. He turned his head slightly to look out of the corner of his eyes and saw Susan looking at him. He knew he had to look at her to make the situation less awkward. He looked at her smiling face and smiled himself. After a quick second, he turned back around to Bernstein.

"No, I'm afraid not. We do live together and operate a nursing home down in Florida. We're looking for a change of scenery, though."

"That sounds nice," Bernstein said. "What do you need my help with?" He then asked.

"How do you know we need help?" Frederick asked and grinned.

"Well, it's been twenty years. Plus, you traveled all the way out here to the Middle East. You wouldn't come out here for vacation or just to see how I was doing," Bernstein said and leaned back slowly in his chair. He was glad that his old friend had come to see him but also wondered what could be so important for him to travel so far and spend so much money just to come out there.

"Twenty years is quite a while and you look, well, twenty years older?" Frederick asked. The last time he saw Bernstein, he remembered a skinny man with stringy black hair and a smooth-skinned complexion. He looked across the desk as a man with the same facial features but more wrinkles and a head of hair that had more gray than brown with a receding hairline. He had grown a thin mustache that had small curls at each end.

Bernstein laughed slightly and shut his eyes while he lowered his head. He looked back at Frederick and nodded. "You know, not many Germans out here," he said which he laughed and so did Frederick. "Well, to be honest, I've come to a realization. Come closer," he said while he leaned halfway across his desk. Frederick leaned in his chair but was still about five feet away. "Even closer, I don't want anyone to hear," he said in more of a whisper. Frederick moved his chair closer to the desk and moved his face towards Bernstein's. Susan remained back in her chair. Once Frederick got closer, Bernstein whispered quietly while looking into one another's eyes. "I haven't killed since our talk."

"Really? Why?" Frederick asked in a slightly louder voice since he was shocked.

"I've come to a realization. I began having many nightmares of the deaths that I saw in Auschwitz. My family and friends and innocent people that I've seen killed. I had so much trouble sleeping and staying asleep. It came to a point where I was even scared to fall asleep since I didn't want to have the nightmares anymore. I realized that when I saw so much death, that I needed to stop killing. I brought pain to so many innocent families that I regretted what I had done and vowed not to kill again. Instead, I've focused on archaeology and having fun while I'm alive."

Frederick was surprised but understood. He had previously known some soul hunters who learned to regret their decisions and moved away from the life. "I, I am very surprised, Jerren," he replied. Bernstein then moved to lean back in his chair, indicating they didn't need to whisper anymore. Frederick sat back in his chair also as they continued to talk. "Well, with your changed life, I hope you'll still be willing to help me out," he said since doubt had raised in him when Bernstein was speaking about his change of lifestyle.

"It depends. Is there killing involved?" Bernstein asked and tilted his head, awaiting a response.

Frederick wasn't sure how to answer since for Bernstein, there wouldn't be any direct killing.

"For you, no. For me, maybe."

"Okay." Bernstein raised his leg to cross is on top of the other. "What do you mean by that?"

"I need to find Narmer's scroll."

Bernstein immediately knew Frederick meant the soul hunters scroll and a burst of laughter escaped from him for a few seconds until he saw the stern look on Frederick's face that told him he was being serious. "Sorry. That, well. That is quite a feat."

"I know. That's why I need your help."

"What can I do for help?"

"You know Egypt and a lot of history. Much more than I do and much more than anyone else I know. I need your help locating it."

"Do you know how impossible that is?" Bernstein asked. He knew that everyone believed the scroll was buried in Narmer's tomb and that nobody knew where his tomb is.

"Yes, I do. I'm sure you know where the scroll is. But finding where it is, is the problem."

"I know. Nobody even knows where Narmer is buried. People have been searching for hundreds of years. There hasn't even been anyone close to finding it."

Frederick noticed after Bernstein had finished speaking that he lowered his head and looked towards the dirt ground. He wondered what he was thinking about and if he had anything to hide. "Jerren?" Frederick asked after ten seconds went by with him staring at the ground. Susan looked over to where he was staring to make sure everything was okay.

"Yes, sorry. I'm okay," he replied in a somber voice. His voice had changed and his mood seemed to change drastically as if he had become sadder. "Let me ask you," he looked back up at Frederick.

"What is it?"

"Why do you want the scroll?"

"I," Frederick started.

"Be honest with me now," Bernstein interrupted.

"In all honestly. I want to," Frederick started to say and leaned forward towards the desk. Bernstein leaned forwards also while Frederick lowered his voice. "I want to lead the soul hunters."

"Hmm," Frederick heard Bernstein say while holding his hands up to his mouth with his elbows on the wobbly desk.

"I'm being serious here. I want to become the leader. There hasn't been a leader even though there are many powerful soul hunters. A lot of people more powerful than me and probably even some remaining elders from the beginning. I want to bring the good of our people and provide resources through our ever-changing society and world. It's so hard to, well, kill anymore. So many of us are dying or being locked up. I've been learning new techniques and need the use of the scroll to gain more power," Frederick said while staring intensely into Bernstein's eyes. Bernstein saw the seriousness in Frederick's bulging eyes.

There was silence in the tent and for the three of them inside, no outside noise would disrupt their quiet instilled within it. Bernstein took the quiet in the tent to listen for any indication that would tell him to not believe Frederick such as tapping feet or the shaking of the table that Frederick was leaning up against which there was none

Bernstein let out a silent sigh as he sat back again in his chair. He continued looking directly in Frederick's eyes as he stared back at his. Frederick held his serious composure but showed a smile once Bernstein did.

"I believe you," Bernstein finally said after a full minute of quiet in the tent. For that moment it had seemed like all life around them had stopped. Frederick felt immediate relief. "Tomorrow morning, meet me at the Egyptian Museum. Be there and be alert. There is much danger in what you are asking for."

"What do you mean?" Frederick asked curiously. He was getting himself in more danger as he expected he would be in his path for power. Susan raised her hand to her mouth in worry but sat quietly. He ran his hand through his hair to remove the sweaty strands from his forehead.

"Well, a lot of people would kill for that scroll," Frederick said.

"A lot of people would kill for it. A lot of people have killed trying to find it. Luckily it's in a safe place."

"You actually know where it is? You know where Narmer's grave is?" Frederick asked quickly. Frederick and Susan both sat up to the edge of their seats awaiting an answer. Susan was just as excited to hear what Bernstein had to say as Frederick.

"I do. But, the scroll is not in Narmer's grave. That was a tale passed down from generation to generation of soul hunters," Bernstein said.

"But, I read it in an old soul hunters text that stated it was in Narmer's grave," Frederick said, referencing the book Claire had given him from Reginald's collection. Bernstein knew of such a text but never had the opportunity to read it.

"You've read the elder's texts? I've heard from others that inside it tells of the scroll being in Narmer's grave. The truth is it is not. Meet me tomorrow and I'll share more information with you."

"Tomorrow, at eight? At the Egyptian Museum in Luxor?" Frederick asked just to be sure.

"Sounds great. Remember, be careful. You never know who will be around or who people truly are," Bernstein said and Frederick nodded. Bernstein stood up from the chair and said, "It truly was nice seeing you again, Frederick." He looked towards Susan who remained seated, "It was nice meeting you. I hope you enjoy your stay in Egypt and are able to see some great sites."

"Thank you. I've always wanted to see Egypt. All I've seen is what's in books and television," Susan said.

"How about tomorrow, Susan. Why don't you take some tours? Would you be able to recommend any to us, Bernstein?"

"I want to go with you tomorrow though," Susan pleaded and stood from the chair.

"I agree with Frederick," Bernstein said. "What we are going to do will be unsafe. It will be better if you were enjoying yourself and seeing some of the historic sites and beautiful areas Egypt has to offer."

"But," Susan interrupted. "I won't be able to enjoy myself knowing Frederick might be in such danger."

"Not to worry," Bernstein said and started walking around the desk and patted Frederick on the back. "Frederick will be safe as long as we're aware of what's going on." Frederick and Bernstein were on the same page that having Susan there might slow things down if something were to happen. Also, having her there would create a larger crowd and they'd have to worry about her. Having her somewhere else would make things easier.

"Okay, just as long as you take care of Frederick for me," Susan said which embarrassed Frederick. He closed his eyes in embarrassment before finally standing up as Bernstein walked past him to the opening of the tent.

"Of course," Bernstein replied while getting to the opening. He opened the flap and leaned his head out. He looked around to make sure nobody was snooping and saw Anwick in the distance looking at a couple of artifacts. "Dr. Anwick," he hollered so she could hear him.

She noticed him and saw him motion her by moving his head back. Bernstein looked back in the tent and brought the flap back to allow Frederick and Susan out. He smiled towards Frederick as he walked through and Susan followed while he patted her lightly on her shoulder to reassure his safety.

CHAPTER 39

Seven-thirty the following morning, Frederick waited outside on a bench by the Egyptian Museum. Anwick had scheduled a day tour for Susan that she knew was safe so she had left for the bus when Frederick left. Frederick waited anxiously outside and watched a variety of people walking around and driving. Many getting on and off busses for work while a lot of tourists used taxis to visit the sites and get ready to go to the museum for when it opened at nine o'clock. Every minute that went by seemed to take forever since he was excited to hear what Bernstein had to say. He spent a lot of the night going through the information regarding Egypt and the formation of the soul hunters in his book. He wanted to familiarize himself with the meaning of the scroll but was worried that finding it might be very hard and take a lot of work. Even though Bernstein said he knew where it was, it still might be buried in a grave or somewhere very difficult to get to – thinking why Bernstein said it would be so dangerous getting it.

While Frederick lost track of time and no longer focused on anyone in particular, he stared straight ahead and zone out, thinking of what it would mean for him to find the scroll. He realized the power he would have once he found the scroll and be able to control and become the leader of the soul hunters.

"You know," a man's voice from beside Frederick startled him. Frederick was still daydreaming and wasn't aware of what was going on around him. "I've known the scroll's location for many upon many years." Frederick looked to his left and noticed Bernstein moving towards him and sat next to him. He looked at him to hear what he wanted to say. "Many people have asked me for help to find it, but look at me," he said and held out his left arm. He brought up his sleeve to reveal his five-digit number that remained tattooed on his arm, even though a bit faded. Wrinkles spread throughout his arm and hand. "These numbers will always remain and bring back memories, even though they're becoming overtaken by wrinkles. These numbers tell me how many people died in the camps in Germany. I've killed a few German's myself afterward. I no longer kill but yet will die. I will die sooner than later," Bernstein said and as he talked, his head moved around to look at the numerous people in the streets and sidewalks.

"You don't have to," Frederick said while watching Bernstein look around. "It's not too late, Jerran."

"It's not and to be honest, it would feel so good to kill again but then, I remember the families of those that I would kill. I don't mind killing but I do feel bad for the child to grow up without a parent, or the parents of those I kill having to bury their child," he said and paused momentarily. "Also, since I will die soon, I want to be sure the scroll is in good hands. I trust you and ever since meeting you, even though we haven't seen each other since I've felt the connection."

"Me too," Frederick said and agreed with Bernstein. Bernstein finally looked towards Frederick and smiled.

"I'm worried if I die without sharing the scroll that it would be lost forever or like I said, fall into the wrong hands. I guess I was surprised to see you come here but hearing why you were here is somewhat a relief for me."

"I'm glad I came. It definitely was nice seeing you again and we have some great things to accomplish to help the greater deed for the soul hunter community."

"That, we do," Bernstein said. "Let's get going then." Bernstein stood, followed by Frederick.

"Where are we going? What do I need to be prepared for?" Frederick asked as he was worried where they might have to go or who they might run into. "How long until we find it? Until we find the scroll?"

Bernstein noticed with so many questions, which was unusual for Frederick, that he actually must be nervous. "No worries, my friend. We're almost there."

"What do you mean? We're that close?"

"Yes, look behind you," Bernstein answered. Frederick turned around from the bench and looked immediately at the large Egyptian Museum.

"It's here and nobody knows about it? I mean, why does nobody know it's here?" Frederick was curious as to why nobody else has gotten the scroll or known about it.

"It's here in the archives. Down in the dark corner, it sits in a box."

"But, how does no one else know about it? No other soul hunters have gotten to it?"

"Luckily no," Bernstein answered. They both stood and looked towards the museum and Bernstein folded his arms. "The scroll was found over a hundred years ago in a site of a temple. How it got there, I have no idea nor any theories. The temple was found underground, covered with sand from hundreds of years of sand storms. It was uncovered along with many artifacts, including some scrolls within a gold plated chest. Once it was dug up, there were a handful of scrolls. None of which really meant anything to those who uncovered them or researched them. A lot of the meaning made no sense except, I guess just to me."

"Really? It's been here all this time?"

"It has. I've read it numerous times and knew to keep it here since no one understood its meaning, that it would be safe here." Bernstein was nervous to finally be revealing the secrets of the scroll's whereabouts but knew it would be in safe hands with Frederick. Bernstein looked down at Frederick and asked, "Are these the only types of clothes you brought?" He laughed looking at another thick suit jacket and slacks worn by Frederick. Bernstein knew and understood the heat and wore a white button-up shirt with jeans.

Frederick laughed which helped him ease a bit from being so nervous. He was dreading having to go into the depths of the desert, dig into graves or fight thieves for the scroll, only to hear it was in the corner of the museum basement made him relieved.

"Are you ready?" Bernstein asked?

"I am, Jerren," Frederick answered confidently.

"No matter how easy this may seem, make sure you are alert and aware of who's around you at all times." Bernstein had heard of tales of soul hunters and some attempting to find the grave of Narmer just to find the scroll. These people didn't care about the gold or riches within the tomb, as many knew there would be some. All they cared about was the scroll. With that scroll, the person would gain instant power.

"I will," Frederick said.

CHAPTER 40

Using his pass and credentials to get past security and another security check to the archives, they walked down the concrete steps. Frederick followed behind Bernstein and held onto the wood handrail going down. After stepping off the first step, they were instantly surrounded by numerous shelves with many boxes and containers on each. As Frederick looked at both directions they could go, both aisles featured metal and wooden shelves with what he figured were boxed artifacts. The lighting was pretty dim as he expected but bright enough to see throughout. The basement didn't seem very large with the shelves reaching as high as the ceiling so it was tough to gauge how large the area actually was. They went towards the right and as they walked, Frederick glanced as many of the boxes. Most of them had numbers and dashes written on them which were for identification purposes. They hadn't walked long and made a few turns around the shelves when Bernstein pointed straight ahead.

"Almost there," he said and continued walking. The anticipation was great for Frederick until he realized that not having seen the book as he had, how Bernstein knew this is the actual scroll and not something else. Dread set in instantly thinking that it may not actually be the right scroll. It was too late to ask him if he was sure so he continued to walk, not being as excited as he previously was. "Over here," Bernstein then said and Frederick looked around. They had just walked past what seemed to be the last of the shelves and were in a dark corner of what was the basement. Frederick looked around at many century-old wooden trunks scattered on top of one another along with many boxes that were stacked. As they got to the corner, Bernstein looked back and told Frederick to stay there for a second. "Let me make sure we're alone," he said quietly. He walked a few steps back towards where they had come from and he peeked through the spaces between the boxes on the shelves and didn't see anybody. He returned after only a few seconds and walked past Frederick. "Keep your ears and eyes open. You never know," he said quietly and Frederick looked behind him to make sure nobody was there. Light barely reached where they were and he watched Bernstein move a couple of smaller cardboard boxes off of a stack of larger cardboard boxes. Finally, after what seemed to be minutes but were actually just seconds, Bernstein pulled out a scroll. Frederick forgot the dread of it being the wrong scroll and became excited and hopeful.

"Is that it?" Frederick asked as Bernstein carefully held the scroll with both hands. He held it out in front of him and Frederick stared at it, amazed that it was there right in front of his eyes. He hoped that it would be the right one and that he didn't need to find Narmer's grave since the more he thought about it, the more impossible it sounded. "May I?" Frederick asked as he walked over and held out both of his hands. He was too focused to even smile. Bernstein walked a few steps towards Frederick as they met halfway and gently placed it in his hands. Frederick froze as he stood, holding the scroll. Bernstein stepped back and watched. He was no longer nervous about sharing the scroll with somebody else but instead felt more of a sense of relief that the whereabouts of the scroll were no longer his responsibility as he aged.

Frederick quickly glanced around where he stood and saw a flat wooden box about waist high that he wanted to go to in order to have somewhere to lay the scroll down to look at it. The lighting was minimum in the corner but he had to see it to stop the anticipation and make sure it's the correct one. Bernstein watched as Frederick walked the scroll to the box but also kept his lookout behind them to make sure they were still alone. He walked towards the shelves to look through the spaces between the boxes again just to be sure.

"This is it," Bernstein heard Frederick say. He looked back at Frederick who had the scroll unrolled on top of the box. He saw Frederick holding the corner of it up at an angle to get more light on it so he could look at it. Bernstein walked towards him and stood behind him. Bernstein nodded after making eye contact with Frederick. "This is it. It's amazing. Just as I read in my book. I can't believe it," Frederick said astonished. "All the symbols are there. This has got to be it."

"It's it. I'm glad you have it, my friend," Bernstein said and put his hand on Frederick's shoulder. Frederick turned around and looked to Bernstein with a large smile on his face. His upper teeth showed how excited he was to have the scroll in his own hands.

"I need this," Frederick stated, wondering how he could keep it if it was in the archives in such a large museum. Stealing it would be difficult.

"Nobody even cares this is down here. Look, it's shoved in a box no one has even gone through in fifty or more years – besides me. Nobody ever takes inventory so take it. I'd rather it be with you than have someone with evil intentions take it," Bernstein said, after knowing Frederick's good intentions.

"I can never repay you," Frederick said to Bernstein as he rolled the scroll back up tightly but carefully, wanting to get out of there as quickly as possible. He had to be cautious handling the thin papyrus scroll since as the years passed, the scroll had become frailer. The paper had browned and become more brittle and rolling it, Frederick knew he had to be careful. Without the scroll, he wouldn't be able to gain power.

"Did you secure it safely?" Bernstein asked after watching Frederick roll the scroll and slide it carefully halfway down into his slacks. He untucked his buttoned undershirt and placed it over top of the scroll. He also buttoned the bottom half of his jacket to attempt to hide the small lump from the scroll. Leaving the museum past security made Frederick nervous but Bernstein said he had nothing to worry about. He said they trusted him.

"You sure I won't be caught?" Frederick whispered.

"I'm sure. Just be aware," he replied and started walking down the aisle between the shelves. "Stay close."

They made it back up the steps and walked through a door and saw members of the staff walking around the main floor quickly, getting ready to open the museum soon. They knew they had to hurry out so they could get through security as well as avoid other people. They went towards the entrance and Bernstein waved and walked over to the two security members standing by the front door. "Find any good research today, Dr. Bernstein?" One of the security members asked while the other watched.

"I always do," he replied and nodded. Bernstein held out his arm to shake the hands of the security guards and to thank them. Everyone who knew Bernstein there respected him. He had stopped by there for additional information while helping with the archaeological dig and had gotten to know most of the people at the museum. He walked back to Frederick who had edged closer to the exit door when the security guards turned their attention to him and saw him by the door. They didn't think anything was peculiar or out of the ordinary so they didn't stop him and let the two of them leave. Once they got outside, Frederick felt relieved and started to breathe normally, not realizing he was holding his breath a lot of the times before exiting. Bernstein walked outside and as the doors closed behind him, he looked and smiled at Frederick.

"So, what's next?" Bernstein asked Frederick.

"This was easier than expected. I figured I would have to be in Egypt longer looking for the scroll but thanks to you, everything is falling in place."

"That's great, but I have been thinking, how does acquiring the scroll automatically give you power? I mean, if it gave its bearer power, why didn't I get anything special or become the leader as you intend to be?" Bernstein asked. Frederick hadn't thought that far in advance thinking how difficult it would be to find the scroll. He did know there would have to be a ceremony of sorts after he had read before how Narmer signed the scroll to gain power. He unbuttoned his jacket to remove the slight pressure from possibly damaging the scroll. The scroll remained tucked in his pants and his shirt and though awkward at a near foot and a half long, he had to keep it safe and secure.

"Well, Jerren, that will be the true test," Frederick answered which made Bernstein want to know even more. The two stopped walking after they reached the sidewalk from the museum. They looked at one another and though Frederick was mentally exhausted with so many emotions of him being able to acquire the scroll as well as getting through security, he needed to refer back to the soul hunters book for more definite information with what to do next. "Let me head back to the hotel and read through the book. I'll rest up and, do you have any plans for tonight?"

"I'll need to head out to the dig today so make sure everything's on track and to see if there have been any significant finds and I'll be there about half the day. Afterward, would you and Susan like to go out somewhere for dinner? I would like to hear about how she liked her tour," Bernstein said, hoping that Susan was having fun. Frederick smiled and nodded before going their separate ways.

CHAPTER 41

"I recommend the falafel," Bernstein said while he, Susan and Frederick all held menus at their round table. The restaurant was busy on a weekend evening and the streets popular with tourists and locals.

"Sounds good to me," Frederick said and folded up his menu and placed it in front of him. He adjusted the bag on his lap that remained hanging around his shoulder. He didn't dare leave the scroll at the hotel since he worried who, if anyone, followed him there. He wanted to be sure the scroll was safe. He looked around at the variety of people in the café. They sat near the window and saw the tables outside near the sidewalk were full of people smoking and drinking. The day was hot and after everyone had a busy day, they preferred sitting inside where it was cooler.

"Did you have fun today, Susan?" Bernstein asked. Frederick and she had already spoken earlier about each other's day when she got back to the hotel and while they were getting ready for dinner with Bernstein.

"I sure did. We traveled to a couple of sites and the temple. I couldn't believe how large Luxor Temple was. I mean, I stood beside the statues at the entrance, and the columns," Susan said in response to Bernstein's question. Her voice was full of excitement and Bernstein smiled and looked over towards Frederick, happy that she had so much fun.

"Great! I'm glad to hear you had fun!" Bernstein said, excited that she liked the tour Anwick had set up for her.

The waiter came over and took their order for drinks and food. He left with their three menus while the café remained busy and a bit noisy but they were able to speak to one another without having to worry about someone listening in.

"Frederick," Bernstein started to say and look towards Susan. "Did you have a chance to tell Susan what you got today? Were you able to find any more information about it?"

"I did," Frederick said while Susan nodded immediately after hearing the question. "I also found more information but yet, I have an issue."

"An issue?" Bernstein asked. He sat up in his stool and folded his arms on the round table and looked curiously at Frederick. He was worried that maybe it was the wrong scroll but if that were the case, he was sure Frederick would have told him that earlier.

"Based on my readings in the soul hunter's texts, many of the symbols and hieroglyphics that are mentioned are on the scroll. Unfortunately, since no one but, well, supposedly Narmer had seen it so there isn't much detail on the remaining text of the scroll."

"Mmhmm," Bernstein acknowledged.

"The issue is, I can't read hieroglyphics."

Bernstein chuckled. "I can read some. Not much. I did read what I could when I first encountered the scroll and based on what I had heard from previous friends, I knew it was the scroll. I do have some close, trusted friends who can read hieroglyphics."

"I had a feeling you would," Frederick said, knowing Bernstein was a great resource. "Not to be too picky, but are any of them a priest?"

"A priest?" Bernstein asked curiously. He didn't know why Frederick preferred a priest. He sat silently while he waited for a response.

Frederick thought of how to answer so he referred to what he read in the soul hunter's text. "Not to be picky, but reading in the texts, that while displaying the truth of the scroll, only a priest can read the scroll aloud. If not a priest, the meanings will be worthless. When a priest reads the writing, since there is the blood of a priest within the scroll, the words of the past come alive." Frederick had a hunch by having a priest read the text with the blood of a former priest within it, that it would anger the master soul hunter or even the spirit of Narmer. Still, no one knew who the true master soul hunter was, whether Narmer or Anubis himself, Frederick knew he had to awaken the master to overthrow him.

"Okay," Bernstein answered and nodded his head while he thought of any priest that he could truly trust with such a meaningful document. As he continued to nod, he said to Frederick, "I do know of one."

"Who is he?" Frederick asked back, excited that Bernstein might know of a priest.

"The museum uses him when our own Egyptologists and scientists can't read certain writing. Since he's also a priest, if you have further questions, he's a great resource for anything in regards to Egypt's life and culture."

"That's great!" Frederick said and once again, looked around to look at the people nearby. Susan sat next to him on a stool and patted him on his thigh and made eye contact. They smiled at one another and Susan was glad to see Frederick so excited. She knew Frederick's initial plan but wasn't completely sure what he was planning to do next. She saw the scroll earlier and was just as excited as Frederick.

"I can set up a meeting with him for you," Bernstein said.

"Perfect," Frederick answered with a wide grin. "Tomorrow, by chance?"

Bernstein readjusted himself in the high stool that was starting to become uncomfortable. Once he got adjusted he looked back across the table at Frederick who awaited his answer. "I'll make the call tonight and see what I can do."

Frederick was thrilled and gave Bernstein his hotel phone number and room extension. Their food came and they ate. It was the first time Susan had eaten a falafel and she enjoyed trying the new food.

"Thanks for dinner, Jerren," Susan said after Bernstein was generous and insistent to pay the bill. "But, we can't let you pay."

"You've been nothing but helpful, we'll pay," Frederick said to agree.

"Well, thanks. I'm just glad you two are enjoying your trip. I'll give you a call later with what I find out – whether a yes or no answer."

"That would be fine, thanks," Frederick said before they separated and went their separate ways for the night.

A couple of hours later, Frederick and Susan were in their room admiring the scroll. The scroll, once unraveled was about eighteen inches in width but about thirty-six inches in length. They looked through at all the hieroglyphs and wondered what each meant. They were careful with the fragile document as it lied on a table next to two turquoise-colored chairs. Susan sat on sinking but once cushioned chair while Frederick stood over the scroll when they heard the phone ring.

"Hello?" Frederick answered.

"It's me, Jerren. Tomorrow, the priest is available any time in the morning. It has to be after eight though since that's when he finishes morning prayers."

"That's great!"

"Also, I didn't tell him what the scroll was but just told him you needed help with a document and that it was very confidential."

"Do you trust this priest?" Frederick asked once he heard Bernstein say the word 'confidential.' He hadn't thought of not being able to trust the priest but was reminded he had to be careful with who he did trust.

"I do. He's been very helpful since I've been here."

"Thanks, have a great night," Frederick said to get Bernstein off the phone. He was worried Bernstein would ask to join but Frederick wanted to be by himself with the priest. When he heard that the priest was a great translator, he figured he spoke English and knew it was a perfect time to continue his plan.

As he hung up the phone and turned around to walk around the bed, Susan asked, "What time?"

"In the morning. Maybe around nine."

"That'll be good," Susan said. "It would be fun to see a modern temple."

Frederick stopped walking and stood at the foot of the bed after hearing what Susan said. "I'm sorry, Susan. I was hoping to be able to see the priest by myself." He saw the look on her face and couldn't tell if she was upset or just saddened. "You see, I don't know how safe it is. I want you to be safe and if I'm with this scroll, who knows who will be around."

"But, you'll be at a temple. Isn't that safe?"

"Yes, it can be. But, it might be dangerous too. I'll be okay but I'll feel better if you were elsewhere just to be sure," Frederick said to reassure Susan and gave a calming smile with his lips shut.

CHAPTER 42

Frederick woke up early in the morning and went through the scroll more while Susan continued to rest after her long tour the day before. He sat on the edge of the chair and had the curtain slightly open – just enough to let light in to see the scroll. He balanced the soul hunter's book on his left leg and the armrest on the chair and read again through the history of Narmer and the scroll. After about an hour, he heard Susan roll over since there was so much quiet in the room. He looked over to see her looking at him.

"Good morning," she said once her eyes met his.

"How are you feeling?" Frederick asked and slowly closed the book. He set it on the chair and he walked over and kneeled on the floor next to Susan.

"I'm excited. I'll leave very soon and go to the priest."

"Okay, Frederick. Will you be safe?" She asked, continuing to be worried. Frederick saw her eyes staring him as strands of her hair lied gently on the side of her face. He took his hand to gently move the hair back and he ran his fingers through her hair. He wanted to attempt to calm her so she wouldn't worry too much even though Frederick himself was becoming a bit worried. He didn't sleep very well that night due to his excitement but also because he was thinking of everyone who had attempted to find the scroll. Also, what the same people would do to get their hands on the scroll. He continued smiling at Susan and then rested his hand on the back of her head.

"I'll be safe. Trust me," he said to reassure her. "Are you going to rest here?"

"Yes. I'll get up soon and get ready. Probably get some breakfast and find a museum to go to. The Egyptian Museum?" She asked in a question form to get Frederick's opinion on if the museum was nice and if she should go there.

"That sounds nice. You'll have fun at that museum," he replied and stood up. He leaned down and kissed Susan on the forehead before turning to the table to roll the scroll up tightly. He placed his book and scroll carefully in a canvas tote he had brought. The bag goes on his shoulder but across his chest so no one would be able to grab it and run. He went to the bathroom to get ready to leave. He showered quickly and stepped out to dry himself off. He put on his clothing including a pair of brown, striped slacks and socks that matched. He then put on a buttoned long sleeve shirt white shirt. It was too hot for him to wear a jacket or anything over the shirt. He stood by the mirror and used his palm to wipe the moisture that had collected on the mirror during his warm shower. He looked at himself in the mirror and stared at his face. He brought his hand up and rubbed under his jawline to feel the short hair coming in on his face. He forgot to shave before showering but he didn't feel it was necessary. He released his hand and stared at himself for a slight moment in the mirror. For the first time since being in Egypt, he had started to feel nervous and a bit scared. He had been there two days and things had been going better than he had expected. He never imagined it would be so easy to find the scroll but knowing the right people tend to work things out for the better. Even though he had the scroll, he was worried about what Bernstein had mentioned in regards to people killing for the scroll. He knew he had to be safe today but after seeing the priest, the rest of his plan should be done. He needed to stay out of harm's way for just a few hours since he was so close to finishing what he wanted to do. He took a deep breath and left the bathroom. He turned the corner and saw Susan still lying on the bed and looking at him. He kneeled to put his brown shoes on and rolled his cuffs slightly up to just before his elbows before he stood from the ground.

He went next to the bed and grabbed the handkerchief he had on it as well as his lip balm. With the dry air, his lips were chapping more than usual. At this time Susan had sat up and was leaning against the curved headboard. She had on her white, cotton nightgown and she adjusted it from being crooked around her neck.

"Do you have everything you need?" Susan asked as she continued to watch. Frederick reached down to re-adjust one of his shoes and stood up. He ran his hand through his hair to push it more sideways after he had put pomade in it. He used his fingers to wrap the end strands of some of his hair behind his ears so it would stay in place.

"I just need to get my bag and I'll be ready," Frederick said but before getting his bag, he walked over to Susan. He sat next to her on the bed and they looked at one another for a few quiet seconds. She was worried and even though Frederick hadn't shown much feelings or attraction towards Susan through the years they knew one another, he did have many emotions towards her but struggled to show it. Seeing how much she worried about him made him feel special and it warmed his heart. Having been living with one another for over ten years, they hadn't been very romantic with one another but had become best friends. Susan had an attraction to Frederick once they decided to build the nursing home together but she was okay with the lack of affection. Her biggest dream was to settle with Frederick and raise foster kids who were young soul hunters. Knowing Frederick was a foster child at a young age, she had a feeling that he would eventually one day want to help other children like the way he was helped.

Frederick, on the other hand, wanted to become the master soul hunter. He was on his quest to make his own goal come true but watching her eyes, he could see the sadness within her as her eyes watered while they sat together. "Bear with me, Susan, and everything will be better for us soon," he said and placed his hand on top of hers on top of the bed.

"Things are great they way they are, as long as we're together," she replied before turning her hand right-side-up and clenched her fingers into his.

He had a wide smile and showed his freshly brushed teeth to Susan. "It won't be long before I'm the new master and we'll have everything we need."

"But, can I ask you a question?" Susan asked and was worried about asking such a question, she leaned a bit to the left to be closer to Frederick. She looked at Frederick who remained looking at her. He never answered but his silence indicated to Susan to ask anyway. "Tell me truly now, why do you want to become the master?" She asked because she was curious but never was worried to ask before since she feared Frederick might leave her. She really wanted to know because she was worried about his safety and thought maybe she could talk him out of it.

Frederick had been surprised she had never asked him before. Even though he had told her his plans, he never mentioned why nor did she ask. He never wanted to bring it up to her since she might think he sounded crazy and that she would leave him. He didn't want to lose

Susan even though he never really showed much affection towards her. "Well, there are certain aspects of soul hunter life I'm tired of."

"Like what?" She asked immediately. She was caught off guard since he never complained of anything to her before except that it was becoming harder to kill since it was getting easier to be caught when someone was murdered.

"I, for one as a soul hunter for well," Frederick said and paused, doing the calculation in his head for how long he had been a soul hunter. "For over 200 years I've walked this earth and you, as well for nearly 100 or more. Over those years, there's been much change and we've grown as a community but to me, not only is it getting harder to kill, but it feels like the master is hanging us out to dry. You know, like he's not supportive as he once was. We've done what we could and what we can to make him happy and satisfied but he isn't changing with the times. Yes, I worry he will intervene with my plans somehow but I don't know how he can. He infected me when I was eight years old when I was told I brought a horror book into my family's home. My soul was weakened and he overtook me. Since a part of him is in me, I don't think he would or can destroy me," Frederick said while Susan sat quietly, listening to every word he said. He continued, "And yes, many kids are still reading and even today, watching horror movies and bringing them into their homes whereas, the chance to build up our community has the utmost potential. I don't know what the soul hunter's numbers are in regards to population, but with many people I know that are tired of living and wanting to die and even passing away, I don't want to see that anymore. I want my friends and even those I don't know to not want to die. I want them to feel that their life is worth it."

"What do you mean?" Susan asked, confused as to why he worries about other soul hunter's lives when he killed one of his old friends and mentors, Reginald.

"Jerren wants to die," Frederick said and paused a few seconds. "So many people I know are dying and soon, I think our population will be depleted so much that we won't be able to survive anymore.

Susan was scared to ask her next question since she didn't want to anger Frederick but she needed to know. "Then, if that's the case, why did you kill Reginald?"

Frederick released his hand off of Susan's which worried her immediately. He took a deep breath and sighed. He moved slightly from the side of the bed closer to Susan since he had begun to slide off. He turned his head before looking back at Susan after thinking for a bit how to answer.

"I guess you can say, a casualty of war?" Frederick finally responded. Susan had to think what he meant by that and stared at him with her eyes squinted. Frederick knew he had to clarify what he meant better. "He had a new technique and I needed to test his technique. He had the resources that I needed and he was becoming too powerful. He was becoming a threat," Frederick said before getting interrupted.

"A threat?" Susan asked instantly since she was confused about what he meant by that.

"Yes. He told me on the phone that he was going to try his technique not only on humans but fellow soul hunters to surely test this new method. I knew he had the soul hunter's text. I tried to find it in his library before Claire.gave it to me unexpectedly. He was trying this new experiment and was going to do other things of harm to the soul hunter population.

"So that's why you went to talk with Claire? Not to tell her Reginald was killed?"

"It is, sorry," Frederick said, knowing he had lied to Susan.

"That's fine. Out of curiosity, if he were doing evil, why didn't you kill her?"

Frederick looked away towards the window at the sunlight coming up and knew he had to leave soon. He turned back to Susan and said, "She seems to not have known. Plus, she is depressed. She told me she is going to live a normal life and die when the time comes. Whether or not she truly didn't know, I'm not sure. It didn't give me the right to kill her since she'll eventually die anyway."

"One more question?"

"Okay, and then I have to get going," Frederick answered, worried what Susan was thinking inside as he answered her questions.

"You said that Reginald was a casualty of war." Frederick nodded to agree. "Well, how do I know that I won't be one?" Susan asked.

Frederick felt speechless and blurted out the first thing that came to his mind and said without thinking, "I love," and then paused. He attempted to hide his smile as Susan looked at him and he looked away, feeling his face begin to blush. He placed his hand back on top of hers and again kissed her on the forehead. "I have to be going. Trust me,

Susan. You mean a lot to me so I need to be sure you stay safe, okay? Do you trust me?"

Susan nodded her head. After hearing Frederick explain himself, she was more reassured and no longer worried about him harming her even though she knew he really wouldn't. The thought had just slightly crossed her mind. She was also very relieved to hear his true reasoning behind all of his actions but still worried about what would happen. She wanted to ask more questions such as what other evil actions Reginald was doing or planning on doing as well as what plans Frederick had if he were to become to master. She knew his plan since he explained it to her before they left Florida to go to Egypt but she wanted to know how he could better help the soul hunters in more detail. She noted Frederick edging more to the side of the bed as if he was ready to leave so she let him.

"We can talk more later, but for now, promise me you'll be safe," Susan demanded and smacked Frederick on his leg and gave him a wide smile.

"I promise. We shouldn't be in Egypt much longer so go have some fun and see some sights while you can. Will you be safe too? Promise?"

"Of course," Susan said before she kneeled up on the bed and leaned over to hug Frederick before he left.

CHAPTER 43

Frederick sat in the back seat of the taxi with his bag around his torso as he looked through both sides of the windows. He turned his head often to see where they were going and would frequently look forward through the windshield. He felt paranoid since the closer he got to the priest, being unfamiliar with the area, he wondered if anyone would attack him for the scroll. When he looked ahead, he kept his eye out on the driver to see if he was looking back at all. He only caught him look back once and they made eye contact for a slight second but not speaking very good English, the drive gave a forced smile and nod before looking back at the street. The temple was in a desolate area and the past few miles until they got there, the only landscape was a sparse with a building or house on the side of the road every so often. Seeing so much sand and desert and feeling the road turn bumpier made him feel that he was in a less populated area. He felt nervous if he was going to the right place. He looked ahead again through the now dirty windshield and saw a large building in front of them. After what was about a forty-five-minute drive to the temple, Frederick looked outside at the large building after the taxi stopped. He was glad to finally be there after the bumpy ride but he wanted to look around first before getting out of the car to be sure everything was safe. When he looked at the temple, there were six large columns in the front that looked like an ancient temple. He wondered the age of the building and knew it must be pretty old. He stepped out of the taxi and paid the driver. He stood and stared at the large building as he heard the taxi drive away.

Frederick was nervous being by himself in an unfamiliar area. Not that he was scared that he couldn't defend himself but because he had such a valuable scroll with him. He looked behind him across the street where there were two shabby buildings. One looked to be a small store and the other a house within inches of the store. There weren't many homes in the area and he only could see a couple of people sitting outside of the store as they watched him back. He turned around and walked up the steps to the temple. There was a large entrance in the courtyard between the columns. The entrance's doors were open out towards the courtyard. Frederick walked up casually and looked around at the murals of pharaohs and other Egyptian symbols carved into the walls in the courtyard. He approached the entrance and looked inside the large area. There were numerous wooden chairs spread throughout where it looks like people gather once and a while for religious ceremonies. There were approximately forty or so chairs but Frederick didn't see anyone around. He looked around the large room that had high ceilings and open windows on both sides of the temples. There was no glass on the windows and as Frederick slowly walked around, the sand that has blown in makes a slight shuffling noise as he takes each step. Finally, he walked by a small room in the corner, and before looking in, he could hear a slight shuffling noise coming from within. He stopped to be sure he didn't startle anyone when he peeked inside and saw a man with a white and tan cloth robe. The man was kneeling in the corner of the room over what looked to be a book and seemed to be praying quietly. Frederick stepped back from the doorway of the small room. There was a chair in the other corner with some drapery hanging from the walls. The drapes were red and yellow but Frederick wasn't sure what their symbolism was or what they were used for. After about fifteen seconds, the man bent up his back straight from crouching over the book and remained still. Frederick noticed long strands of white hair covering the sides of his head with a small bald spot with surrounding thinning hair. The man remained silent until slowly turning his head to look back. Frederick saw the man's light skin full of wrinkles looking at him and tilting his head in curiosity. The man didn't look a bit threatened.

"I'm sorry to interrupt," Frederick started to say.

"Are you here to see me?" The man asked in an accent while continuing to look at Frederick.

"Yes, I think. I was sent here by Jerren. Jerren Bernstein."

"Oh, yes," the man said and quickly nodded a few times before standing up. He was very short after standing mainly due to his slouched back. He walked slowly towards Frederick and crossed through the room's doorway. His feet shuffled with his head down as his slippers scraped slightly across the sandy floor as he approached Frederick. "You need translating?" The man asked.

Frederick noticed the man only had a slight accent and spoke great English. "Yes, if it wouldn't be too much of a bother."

"Not at all. Come, come here," the priest said when he started walking down the side of the room towards the far side of it. They walked slowly to the front, facing all the chairs in the center and they got to a square, marble table. "Sit," the priest said to Frederick as he walked to the opposite side of the table and sat. He looked across the table as Frederick sat and waited to see the scroll.

"I'm not sure how much Jerren told you but, I hope you can help me with this scroll."

"He told me not much. Where does the scroll come from?" The priest asked while Frederick unzipped his bag and carefully took out the scroll with both hands. The priest had translated many religious scrolls before and had seen much Egyptian history so he was always thrilled to see something new that he hadn't come across before.

Frederick stood up and placed the scroll on the table and untied it with the string he had wrapped around the middle of it. "I guess, well, that's why I need your help," Frederick said while he was unraveling the scroll. He looked at it the hieroglyphics as he unrolled it and moved it so the priest could see it better. Immediately as the top of the scroll was visible, the priest edged forward to the table to begin reading it as he was curious about what the scroll was. Frederick watched the priest as he continued to unroll the scroll until it lied flat on the table. The edges barely came up from the corners with the document so old and weakened. Frederick stepped back and stood by the chair on the opposite side of the table. He watched the priest raise his finger towards the first line as he continued to read the hieroglyphics. Through the years, the ink had faded slightly but being wrapped up so long it was pretty well preserved. After mumbling to himself the first line, the priest looked up towards Frederick.

"What is this text?" He asked with a straight face while keeping his finger pointed where he left off at in the scroll.

"No one truly knows. It was supposed to have been buried in Narmer's tomb."

"Narmer?" The priest asked astonished as his voice raised. "But, what's its meaning?"

"That's why I'm here," Frederick asked, even though he knew what the scroll primarily said. All he needed for his plan to work was for the priest to read it out loud. "Can you please, read it out loud as you go through it?"

The priest looked puzzled towards Frederick and lowered his nose to add more wrinkles on his forehead. After reading the first line in a faint whisper, the priest had started wondering who this guy in front of him truly was. He knew Bernstein so he figured he could trust the stranger.

"Please. The scroll has more meaning when read out loud."

"Oh, I see," the priest said and moved his finger back to the beginning of the scroll. It took a few minutes for the priest to say the first few lines of the scroll since hieroglyphics took time to understand. As the priest continued to read, Frederick began sweating more frequently. He was sweating more due to nervousness rather than the heat. He watched the priest's hand move across the top of the scroll as he slowly read the words and sweated more. His adrenaline began rushing the more he heard and while two lines remained in the scroll, the priest's hand began shaking. Frederick noticed while listening to his voice begin to tremble. He said a couple of more words slowly before backing away from the table. His head was lowered and hands down by his side. He avoided eye contact and stared at the ground and said, "I can't read anymore."

"What do you mean?" Frederick said and raised his voice. He was waiting for the most important part of the scroll and needed for the rest to be said by the priest.

"I, I," the priest began to say before stuttering and then he stopped talking.

"You must," Frederick said with a determined and deep voice. Frederick remained watching the priest as he stood and looked helpless with the way he was hunched over and his head facing the ground. He noticed the priest shake his head to the side in a way to say no.

"Read!" Frederick shouted as loud as he could and raised his hand to point at the priest. The priest looked up slightly towards Frederick's face and saw his bulging eyes and a red face full of perspiration staring at him. He noticed his lips tightened and eyes curl down towards his nose as his hand was pointed at him.

"No, I," the priest said before Frederick interrupted what he was going to say.

"Read it, or else!" Frederick clamored and placed both hands on the edge of the table and pushed himself up to make him look more intimidating as his face became even redder. He needed the priest to read the remaining lines in order for everything to work as he planned. He was so close and needed to finish. The priest had continued looking at Frederick before becoming intimidated that he walked a step back towards the table. He slowly raised his hand back up where he had left off. His hand trembled even worse and Frederick watched his hand as it slowly went across the line in the scroll. The priest's voice had become weakened as he stood scared – both at Frederick's intimidation as well as what he was reading. He never liked reading such violence and terror and as he read through the scroll, he wanted to get it over with. He finally got to the last line and read through it until the end. The priest held his head down as a drop of sweat fell onto the scroll. He held his finger next to the last symbol and regretted what he had just read.

"Come on, read the bottom. Read where Narmer signed the document," Frederick demanded.

The priest lowered his hand slowly to the bottom and read the names, "Narmer and Set. Set?" He asked to himself in confusion. Not knowing the gods ever signed paperwork, he was confused about what this document of violence was. He removed his hand from the document and started backing away from the table.

"Stay!" Frederick demanded and looked at the priest while he walked around to the other side of the table. He got to the other side of the table and situated the scroll at an angle and reached into his pant pocket. From behind him the priest waited and watched in suspense, worried that he would do something to him. Frederick pulled out a pen from his pocket. It was a calligraphy pen with a sharp point. He held the pen upside down for a second to let the ink settle so he could use it without any flaws. After a second, he removed the lid and he bent over the top of the table. He leaned on his left side and with his right hand, he used the pen to cross off the name of Narmer. The priest watched but couldn't see what he was doing since Frederick's body blocked the scroll. After crossing off his name, a large gust of wind suddenly came through the windows. As the wind gusts surprised both him and the priest, the priest lowered his head in an attempt to cover his face and eyes while Frederick shut his and used both hands to hold down the scroll from blowing away. While the wind blew in and specks of sand flew throughout the temple from all directions, Frederick attempted to figure out a way to block the wind. Since wind blew from both sides of the walls from the opened windows and strong wind from the front entrance, he picked up the scroll and turned blindly towards the priest. Frederick's eyes remained shut until he opened one slightly. He saw the priest ahead of him a few feet but a thick wall of sand separated them since the wind gusts continued to blow drastically. With what he could see, he saw what looked to be a desk towards the back wall and walked quickly but carefully to that with the scroll wrapped tightly in his hands. With the strong winds, he was careful to roll up the scroll the best he could to prevent damage.

Frederick was nearly blinded as he approached the desk and hit his knee on the corner. He knew he was there and he crouched behind it where there was a rolling chair pushed underneath it. He shoved the chair out of the way as it moved across the floor in the wind after becoming loose from under the desk. He crouched underneath it and could feel just slight gust from coming underneath where the desk sat on the slightly warped floor of the temple. He unraveled the scroll as carefully as he could and with what little light remained in the temple with the surrounding dust, he saw where he had crossed out Narmer's name. He put that portion of the scroll on his knee and as he placed the point of the pen on the parchment paper, the ground began to rumble. He instantly thought about what was happening but knew he had to hurry and sign the document. Through the trembling, Frederick's leg and arm shook but he was able to secure the scroll enough for him to sign his name above where he crossed off Narmer's. He removed the pen from the scroll and as he did, everything felt surreal as the wind stopped blowing and the ground stopped trembling. He dropped the pen where he kneeled and moved from under the desk. He noticed the light was bright coming from the large windows in the temple. After he crawled out, he stood and turned to see the priest crawling on the floor.

"Stop," Frederick yelled when he saw the Priest crawling as fast as he could towards the front of the buildings. Frederick's clothes were dusty and his hair disheveled but he didn't care. He walked quickly towards the priest who had stopped but kept his stance on the ground since he was scared. The priest trembled and arms and wrists became weak while holding himself up off the ground. Frederick approached near the priest's head while the priest kept his face towards the dusty ground. "Stand up," Frederick said in a calmer voice.

The priest moved one hand off the ground and used the other to stabilize himself as he raised his upper torso off the ground. Remaining on his knees, he looked up towards Frederick who glared at him with large eyes. The priest was intimidated by what he had just gone through and worried that he was going to be killed. He wanted to do whatever Frederick said in hopes he would let him live. As he looked at Frederick's face, He moved up one knee and used his hand to press up off his knee to stand upright with a slightly hunched back.

"I need you to seal this scroll. Use a candle. You must have a candle."

"Yes," the priest said back in a quiet voice. "There, I think there's one in the office." He knew there was but was paranoid what Frederick was going to do so he was indecisive with his answers. The priest began slowly walking to the room they had been in earlier. Frederick followed him to the office and watched from the doorway. The priest opened a drawer in a small dresser on the side of the wall and Frederick watched closely to be sure he wasn't getting anything other than a candle. He watched as he pulled out a half-used candle and turned around and was startled seeing Frederick standing in the center of the doorway with both arms hanging down and the scroll in one hand. Frederick backed away as the priest walked towards the doorway as they returned back to the marble table they had initially gone to. Frederick rolled up the scroll nicely while the priest set the candle on the table and used a match he had gotten from the dresser to light it. He lit the wick and he watched Frederick stare at the candle while the wax began to burn. They both stood in silence for nearly two minutes until a small puddle of wax sat inside of the candle where the wick continued to burn.

"Seal it now," Frederick said and held the scroll out with both hands. The priest grabbed the candle with one hand and brought it up to his face. He blew out the flame and a slight smoke rose from the candle. He waited a couple of seconds before he took the scroll with his other hand and set it on the side. He moved the candle overtop the scroll while keeping his hand as still as possible. His arm shook slightly while Frederick stood beside him. He tilted the candle carefully and watched as the wax moved overtop the opening of the candle and watched as a few drops fell towards the center of the scroll. Holding the candle within an inch or two, the priest was careful not to damage the old scroll. As a few more drops fell onto the same section, there was a slight circle around where the scroll ended to seal it. The priest moved the candle back knowing there was enough wax and set the candle back onto the table. He stepped back while Frederick let the wax cool and harden for a few seconds. Frederick grabbed the scroll and held onto it with both hands; one hand on each side.

"Light the candle again," Frederick demanded in a softer voice than before. He kept his eyes on the scroll while he saw out of the corner of his eye the priest walk back up to the table and take ahold the candle. He took another match from the matchbook he had taken from the dresser and sparked the match. As the head of the match lit, he moved it over the warm wick and lit the candle again. The priest held onto the candle with one hand, unsure of what to do with it. "Place it on the corner of the table here," Frederick said and moved away from the corner he was standing to indicate where to put the table. The priest set it down. After waiting a few seconds, Frederick concentrated on the scroll and knew he only had one chance to do what he needed to do the right way. He took a deep breath, worried that one misstep would ruin everything he had worked towards since there was only one scroll, and if he messed up, there was no way of starting over. He moved the scroll closer to the candle and the priest gasped, shocked that it looked like Frederick was going to burn it.

"Why?" The priest whispered while seeing the scroll hover over the candle just far enough not to burn. Frederick was too focused to hear the priest or worry about what he was thinking. Frederick took a deep breath in and looked up to the high ceiling and exhaled loudly while shutting his eyes. As he exhaled and shut his eyes, knowing the scroll was so close to the flame, he lowered his hands just slightly. The old and dry scroll instantly went into a burst of flames. The priest's breathing increased quickly as he was shocked to see Frederick burn such a piece of Egyptian antiquity.

Frederick's hands increased in temperature as the flames surrounded his hands. As the heat increased within seconds, waiting until the point of being unbearable where he wouldn't be able to hold it anymore, he kept his eyes shut while his face was looking up. Finally, he felt the flames caress both palms as the heat became so drastic and painful that he couldn't hold on anymore. He used the strength in both arms to throw the scroll as high up as he could. As he threw the scroll, he opened his eyes to see the tail end of the flames as the scroll vanished.

The priest stood astonished, wondering why there weren't any ashes and after a couple of seconds, after the scroll disappeared, he looked at Frederick who remained looking up towards the ceiling. The priest kept his eyes on Frederick but knew he wouldn't be able to outrun him so he remained standing and obedient if he did need anything else.

Nearly a minute went by as Frederick remained looking up towards the tan-colored ceiling and the priest watching Frederick. Frederick couldn't hear anything since he was too focused while the priest noticed a silence coming from outside. Usually, he would hear a slight chatter from across the street or from the few people that live in the area but everything seemed silent. Suddenly, as he watched Frederick, he saw his face change expressions as his eyes got bigger and his mouth opened. The priest looked over towards the area Frederick was looking and watched as something fell onto the table. As it fell, a slight gust of air hit the candle wick and put out the flame. The priest was amazed himself when he saw what seemed to be the same scroll sitting on the table. He watched Frederick pick it up. As Frederick used both hands to grab the end of the scroll and he brought it up towards him and rotated it, the priest was confused about what had happened but saw the same wax seal that he had put onto it but it was broken in half. How? He thought to himself as Frederick stared at the scroll with and smiled.

Frederick looked at the scroll that looked exactly as the same brownish color as it was before he burned it. He moved a couple of steps to the side of the table and set it down onto it. He unrolled the scroll and seeing his signature on the bottom remaining and Narmer's symbol crossed out, he knew everything had worked as planned. Suddenly, he heard a thump to the side of him which caught him by surprise. He noticed the priest lying on his side on the hard floor after he seemed to have fainted. He left the scroll unraveled on the table and moved quickly towards the priest's head and placed his hand near his neck to feel if there was a pulse. He could feel a slight pulse and knew the priest was still alive. Lying near the side-wall, Frederick took ahold of the priest's shoulders and leaned him up against the wall to make sure he would be safe. He felt for the pulse again as the priest slouched on the wall and he could feel it as well as see his chest moving to indicate breathing. Knowing the priest would be okay, he stood back up and went towards the table and gently rolled it back up. He took ahold of it and was thrilled and excited knowing his signature was still on it after being sent to Set to make the transformation official.

Doing what he could to become the master soul hunter, Frederick focused on the good he could do for the soul hunters but didn't focus on what would happen to him if he died. One of the agreements on the scroll was that Narmer's soul belonged to Anubis after death and now, Frederick's belonged to Anubis. Instead, all Frederick focused on was what good he could do for the soul hunters and to give them better lives which in essence, would upset Anubis even more.

CHAPTER 44

"It's not too scary out here," Clint said as he stood next to a somewhat fallen marble tombstone in a cemetery on the outskirts of Oak Hill, Tennessee. The cemetery was built before two decades before the Civil War for the nearby towns and expanded slightly during the war when some of the soldier's dead bodies were returned to their hometowns. Numerous other cemeteries had been built since the turn of the twentieth century and this particular one had become forgotten and dilapidated. As the decades had gone by, many of the tombstones have fallen or been desecrated by vandals. Trees and brush have started to take back their land. Roots have grown and pushed some of the caskets higher, making it easier for some past grave robbers to take out the bodies in the caskets and throw the bones around after stealing what personal belongings the bodies once had. Not all tombs had been vandalized where most of the damage had been caused by trees and other elements of nature taking over the last hundred years since newer cemeteries had become more used and cared for.

"Yeah, not too bad," Wally said while he hid his slight trembling under the dark sky in the middle of the cemetery. Wally and Clint had been friends ever since they could remember. Being the same age, they were in a lot of the same classes since kindergarten, and now being seniors in high school, they, had been best friends for many years.

"Look at this one," Clint said when he walked near what used to be a large wooden cross. He leaned partially down and took the top of the cross in an attempt to straighten it. The two pieces of wood, attached by an old, rusty nail was too loose and the top of the cross was too weak. He let go of the cross and it fell gently back to where it had been. Wally walked over and saw the cross leaning and looked around at the area. A few oak trees were overshadowing the moonlight, making some of the areas darker than the rest. It was hard to see those areas but where there weren't trees, the half-moon created dark shadows throughout that made Wally feel a bit paranoid. He didn't want to go to the cemetery but Clint did. Often, kids went outside of town to the cemetery to drink and hang out. It was a Friday night but Clint and Wally were the only two out there. They continued walking down what used to be a path through the cemetery but was now covered by leaves, branches, and other natural elements that made it impossible to follow the path correctly. They unknowingly walked over graves since some of the graves had fallen tombstones that were either buried under the sand or had been destroyed. They had been at the cemetery nearly an hour and were rounding back closer to where they parked their car on the side of the street.

"Race you to the car!" Wally yelled and without warning, had already begun running. He was ready to go and the longer they were at the cemetery, the more creeped out he was feeling. As he quickly ran, he grabbed onto his hat that had become loose and nearly flew off. Clint saw Wally running before he even heard what he had said. He immediately bolted after his friend and being on the track team, Wally knew he needed a head start. Running past a couple of graves and not being able to see as he rounded the last grave to go around a large oak tree, the top of his toe dragged slightly across a large root. He stumbled a step before falling harshly on his side. His body hit the dirt ground and his was knocked off his head. Clint saw Wally fall and at first, was worried but when he a few steps away from his, he saw Wally starting to get back up. He knew he was okay. Clint adjusted his jeans and having not worn his belt, the jeans were starting to fall down his lanky torso. After slowing down a bit to make sure Wally was fine and to adjust his jeans, he sprinted again and went to pass by Wally.

"Come on, Wally, run faster!" Clint yelled, still full of breath since he had great running endurance. Wally was nearly out of breath, especially after falling but he hurried and he got back on his knees. As one leg stood, he began running again and chasing Clint. Wally was laughing that he fell while Clint looked back towards him. Clint rounded the last grave that sat on the edge of the former trail. Wally knew he needed to find a shortcut and run as fast as he could when he decided to jump over the large grave. He hurdled using one leg and reached as far across the wide mass of dirt that covered the grave. Even though Wally was a bit chubbier than Clint, he knew he had a chance of making it across the pile of rocky dirt. Clint looked back once he rounded the pathway and saw Wally leaping over the grave to catch him. Within the darkness, as soon as Clint turned around to face forward, his head crashed against a low hanging oak branch and knocked him backward and he landed awkwardly on his left shoulder blade. When Clint finally awoke, he found himself in a strange room.

CHAPTER 45

Clint raised his head from the chair he was sitting in and slowly opened his eyes to look around. He looked and saw shiny, white tiles covering the walls with a mirror on one side while he sat next to a small, metal table. He went to rub his dry eyes and when he attempted to raise his hands, his left hand raised a few inches when he felt it stop and what sounded like a chain hitting metal. He looked down and noticed he was handcuffed to the metal chair. He tried to move it again and using his other hand and all his power, he pulled his wrist away from the chair until his wrist began to hurt. He released his wrist from pulled on the handcuff and started to yell.

"Help!" he yelled while holding the vowel a few seconds. Again, he yelled, "Help!" He began looking around the room and stood up from the chair while his wrist was still attached to the chair. He turned around and saw a door and went to walk towards to but couldn't get close since the chair was handcuffed to the small table that was bolted to the wall. "Get me out of here!" He yelled again when he failed to escape from the chair. He turned back from looking at the table and looked towards the door when he saw it opening. "Help me," he pleaded when he saw the first glimpse of someone coming into the room.

A man wearing slacks, a dark, buttoned shirt with a tie came in holding a small stack of papers. His hair had seemed to not be combed but fallen nicely naturally. His face was clean-shaven and he looked younger than her age. "Please, Sir, you need to calm down," the middle-aged man said while looking at Clint. Behind him, an older and heavier set man entered. The second man was dressed just as nicely as the first man but had silver-colored hair combed back and a thin, silvery mustache. His broad shoulders were more square and intimidating than the first man. The second man was also holding papers in his hands.

"It's about time you woke up," the second man said, walking over and pulling out a metal chair.

"Have a seat," the first detective said. Michael Broder had been a police officer for sixteen years before moving up to detective. After he sat, his fellow detective, Marcus Leggley, who had been a detective in a different town for over two decades before transferring, sat down and leaned back in his metal chair. Clint remained standing. "Sit!" Broder said in a louder, more demanding voice. Clint looked from Broder's face and glanced at his chair beside his leg. He walked gingerly towards the table and straightened his chair. He had no idea what was happening except that he thought he was in a police department when he saw the gold badges on the waistband of each of the men that walked into the room. He moved the chair closer to the table and awkwardly moved his left wrist back since it had become tangled attempting to move the hair. He sat and looked across the table only to see the two men staring at him.

"Why am I here? I want my mom!" Clint said. His voice quivered and was shy in tone since he wasn't sure what he was doing there.

"Bring in his mom," Leggley said and waved at the two-way mirror. Within a few seconds, Clint's mom was let into the room. She went beside her son and her son gave her a hug with one arm.

"Clint, just be honest with the detectives," she said. "Tell them what they need to know. Honesty is very important so please just tell them what happened."

"What are you talking about, Mom?" He asked while looking at her. She stood back up and smiled towards him. An officer who was holding the door shut it and let his mom stay in the room. Even though Clint was considered an adult at age eighteen, they wanted his mom there to bring some sense of trust and comfort to him.

"So, Clint, let's get to the bottom of tonight," Leggley said which gained Clint's attention. He moved his attention away from his mom and looked at the two detectives across from the table. Clint's hair was disorderly and a few strands stuck to his forehead which had begun to perspire. Leggley rolled up both of the sleeves on his arm while Broder got his paper and pen ready to ask questions.

Broder clicked the top of his pen to extract the pen tip and touched the paper by writing the time and date. Leggley began the tape recorder.

"The time is 2148 hours on Friday, May 15, 1998. This is Detective Broder and I'm with Detective Leggley here to question Clint Barklay."

"Question me with what?" Clint barked out and placed his hands on the edge of the armrests of the chair.

"Were you at the cemetery on the outside of town tonight, Oakwood Cemetery?" Broder asked while keeping his pen on the paper but his eyes focused on Clint.

"Yes, but what does that have to do with anything?"

"Ok. What were you doing there?" Broder then asked.

"Just walking around. We weren't doing anything illegal."

The detectives didn't know that Clint was with someone else so they were a bit caught off guard. "Who were you with tonight?" Leggley asked with his hands folded on the table in front of him.

"Just me and Wally."

"Does Wally have a last name?"

"Yes, where is Wally?" Clint asked, wondering where he was. Once he said his name, though, he was hoping he didn't get his best friend in trouble but he was still confused about what was going on. The detectives ignored Clint's last question and Broder continued to write notes on the paper. In the few seconds of silence, Clint looked up at his mom who stood helpless in the corner of the room by the door. She wanted to go to her son and hug him to support him but she had to remain strong as the officers instructed her to do and remain by the door.

"Where is Wally?" Clint asked again after waiting in the quiet too long. His tone of voice was more demanding since he was getting inpatient not knowing what was happening.

"I remember being your age once, Clint," Broder said once he stopped writing. When I was a teenager, my friends and I went to the cemetery once and a while. It was cleaner and in better shape back then but just as scary. Seeing so many of the old tombstones, many from the previous century, made it suspenseful and a fun place to hang out at night. The problem is, we just hung out and never vandalized the cemetery and areas as kids have done these days." Broder looked at Clint and remained looking after telling his short story. He saw confusion in Clint's eyes with the way he looked back and didn't tense up or act in a way that would tell him that he was hiding something.

"I remember last decade when kids had dug up some of the graves which is totally disrespectful to desecrate the bodies of the dead and now in the late 1990s, we haven't had any instances of that until tonight," Broder said, hoping to recollect some emotion from Clint from what happened that night.

"I still don't know what you're talking about," Clint said and leaned back in the chair, keeping his arms on the armrests.

"Come on," Leggley said and leaned back himself. He put both hands behind his head and looked at Clint. "Obviously, you were there. Your body was found there so we know it was you. Just tell us. As your mom said, honesty is very important right now."

"Look. All I know is Wally and I were at the cemetery tonight. Yes. But, the last thing I remember is we were racing to the car when I rounded the final corner and tree and looked back at him, he was jumping over the large grave on the same corner. After that, everything just blacked out. I don't even remember how I got here."

Leggley remained motionless since he didn't believe a word Clint was saying. Clint looked back at his mom who initially had a look of worry on her face but put on a smiling façade when her son looked at her.

"Clint," Broder started to say. "Your story is hard to believe."

"But, it's the truth! I have no idea what happened after that."

"Clint," Broder said again to take back control of the conversation. He let out a large sigh to let Clint know that his patience was running thin. "An officer drove by the cemetery tonight on patrol and as they often do. He said he saw a car parked so he shined his spotlight into the cemetery when he saw your body. He hurried over to you and noticed you were breathing and called for EMT. When EMT arrived, he checked out the area. Near your body, I believe it's the grave you just mentioned on the corner, he saw that the body had been dug up."

"What?" Clint asked curiously and sat up high in the chair.

"He observed the area and saw fresh dirt was thrown about around the grave and where the grave was, there was an old wooden casket with the lid removed. Not a body inside," Broder said.

"No," Clint started to say.

"Where is Wally?" Leggley interrupted Clint and asked.

"Wally? I, I don't know," he answered honestly.

"It looks to me like," Broder began saying. "When EMT came, they put a bandage on your forehead. They said you were bleeding but not enough of a laceration for stitches. They bandaged you up while they cared for you in the ambulance. You were breathing and began coming into consciousness and opened your eyes for a moment. You shut your eyes and rested while they released you and the officer brought you to the station so when you awoke, we could contact your mom and question you what had happened."

"Honestly, I don't remember anything that happened after I saw Wally jump over the grave to try and catch me."

"We were finishing up here after a long day at the station when you were brought in. To me, one of my ancestors is buried at that cemetery. I care for the grave often and I take offense when kids vandalize the area," Leggley said.

"We weren't vandalizing anything!"

"Then where did the body go? And where is Wally?" Leggley asked and smacked his palm on top of the metal table.

"I know where you're getting at that you think Wally took the body. There's no way he would do anything like that. That's not the type of person he is," Clint answered. Clint's mom was shaking her head in agreement since knowing him for most of his life, she knew Wally wouldn't do anything like that. "I mean, is my car still there?"

Each of the detectives looked at each other for a second before turning towards the two-way mirror. The officer who brought in Wally was waiting there and after hearing his question and seeing the detectives waiting for an answer, he peeked inside the room. "Yes, still parked on the side of the road."

"Wouldn't Wally have taken that if he stole the body? This makes no sense!" Clint said loudly. He wanted to leave and make sure Wally was okay.

The two detectives looked at one another, knowing that by not hearing a confession that it would be hard to press charges on Clint and hold him. Even though he was at the scene of the crime, he didn't have the body nor did they know where Wally was.

"Wait here a minute," Leggley said as he and Broder left the room. They shut the door behind them. Clint's mom went over to him to console him and make sure he was okay. She believed her son and was also curious where Wally had gone to.

"We can't hold him," Broder told Leggley as they stood outside the room. He had already realized that. The two of them stood in the room while the officer that brought in Clint stayed sitting in one of the chairs.

"We'll just have to wait until Wally appears again and question him," Leggley responded. Broder nodded and walked back to the door.

They reentered the questioning room and un-handcuffed Clint in silence. Broder unlocked it while Leggley stood back on the other side of the table.

Clint stood up and rubbed his sore write that had turned red and looked up to Broder. "I'm being honest," he said.

Broder replied, "When Wally appears, have him call us immediately. Also, when you see him, you call us and let us know, too. We really need to speak to him."

"Okay," Clint said as Broder handed Clint's mom his card with his office and cell phone number on it.

***

Three days had gone by and no one had heard from or seen Wally. With so much time going by and after being inundated with many phone calls from Wally's family and friends, they officially opened up a missing person case for him. Again, the same two detectives that questioned Clint on the night he was found at the cemetery, questioned him again. Broder and Leggley were assigned to the missing person case and wanted to find Wally not only for his own well-being but also to find out what happened the past Friday night at the cemetery. They asked Clint more questions but not having heard from Wally, he didn't have any answers but they kept him close. He was still one of the suspects since he seemed to be the last person to have seen Wally and been with him at the cemetery. The detectives had to keep all options open until Wally was found.

CHAPTER 46

Frederick walked into his hotel room and cautiously opened the door and noticed everything was still dark inside. During his taxi ride back to the hotel, he didn't feel any different. He wasn't sure how different he would feel after signing the scroll. The only change he felt was an increase in paranoia as if he was being followed. He stood near the entry to his room and turned back around and looked down the hall both directions to make sure no one had followed him. The whole way back, he was still worried someone might have followed him or knew what he was doing. He did continue to think that everything felt the same within him. He didn't feel any strange sensations or anything different but again, he wasn't sure what to expect after becoming the master. He was a little worried that maybe he had messed something up and it didn't work but then thought, if he hadn't done it right, the scroll wouldn't have come back with the seal broken. He walked into the room and with the door still slightly opened, he turned the light on and quickly looked around to make sure it was safe inside.

He closed the door and immediately lied down. He took off his dusty clothes and even though dust covered his skin and hair, he was too exhausted to shower at that time. He set his shoulder bag next to the bed on top of the nightstand. He knew that Susan would likely be back in a few hours, if not sooner, so he wanted to rest up while he could. He lied down and placed a silk sheet over his body to temporarily cool his skin, he rolled over to his side and continued to try and feel inside to see if anything had changed. *Maybe it takes time*, he then thought to himself. Then, again, he began to think and thought, *maybe I did it wrong*. While he began to replay the scene at the temple in his mind, he fell asleep. As he fell asleep, a slightly orange-colored light came through the thin curtain and covered a section of the corner of his room. The rest of the room was dark since he had every light off. He fell into a deep sleep until he awoke by a crashing noise.

Being startled and awakening from a deep sleep, still lying on his side, his eyes opened towards the corner as the light was less since the day had gotten later. He quickly turned his head in the direction he thought he heard the noise but couldn't see anything. He nudged back towards the headboard and reached up to the lamp to turn it on. He turned on the lamp and looked around the room, figuring the noise was likely from the hallway or room next to theirs. He then saw a crease of light coming into the room from the front door. Remembering he had shut the door and locked it, he immediately turned back towards the lamp on the wall above the nightstand and saw his bag was unzipped. He grabbed the back quickly and within a second, realized his scroll had been stolen. He threw the bag in anger across the room as it hit the opposite wall violently. He stood up quickly and put his pants and shirt on and still being barefoot, he swung the door open and quickly looked down each direction in the hallway. He couldn't see anyone so he ran down the thinly carpeted hallway as the balls of his feet thumped with each step. He ran towards the stairs, the only way he knew out, needing to catch who stole the scroll. He reached the steps and opened the door and grabbed the handrail on the side-wall and hurried to the first floor. He opened the door and stepped out and looked around at the small lobby. He noticed the front desk clerk standing behind her desk looking towards the front door.

Frederick stopped in front of the desk, startling the clerk. "Did you see anyone just leave? Someone holding something in their hands?"

The clerk looked at Frederick who looked very sloppy and frantic with messy hair and not wearing shoes. She had no idea what was going on and Frederick became impatient with her. "Did you?" He asked again but louder. He slammed his fist onto her large faux marble counter and moved his face closer to hers in rage. He was upset that his scroll was stolen. Seeing his face, she looked towards the front door and pointed.

"A, a woman just rain out. She was, she held something, I think,?" The clerk said with a quivering voice.

Frederick ran to the front door without saying a word and went outside to the street. He stood on the busy sidewalk and looked in all directions of the hectic street. Cars, taxis, and a couple of busses were driving by near the intersection where the hotel was. He looked around for anyone holding his scroll but being overwhelmed by so many people, he wasn't sure which direction to turn. He took a step in one direction before stopping and turning around to move the other direction. He was so unsure which direction to go when he could hear someone call his name.

"Frederick?" A woman's voice yelled. He turned to where the voice came from and could see someone running towards him. He saw Susan running quickly towards him.

"Susan!" Frederick yelled while remaining by the hotel's front door. She noticed him wearing dirty slacks and shirt which was unusual but even more unusual was he didn't have any shoes.

"Are you okay?" She asked once she got closer to him.

"No!" He yelled, being upset that he lost the scroll and didn't see who took it. He lowered his head and put his hands behind his skull for a second. He released his hands and yelled while moving his face towards the sky.

"Frederick," Susan said calmer in hopes of calming down Frederick. She placed her hand on his bicep.

"I lost it," he said quieter and lowered his head in disappointment.

"Lost what?" Susan asked, not knowing exactly what Frederick meant.

"The scroll?"

"How? Where did it go?"

"I don't know, Susan. Someone took it from our room. Wait, the lady at the desk saw who took it. Let's go ask her," Frederick said before turning around to go back inside the hotel.

He walked up to the counter, calmer than before, and took a deep breath to keep himself calm. "Did you see who ran out of the door that I asked about?" The clerk nodded her head. "Can you describe them for me? You said it was a woman?"

"Yes," the clerk answered. "A woman, maybe in her fifties, or more. She had, I don't know, black or gray hair, or some of both. It was past her shoulder and she wore just a regular looking Tadashi."

"Do you recognize or know who she is?" Frederick asked, already knowing the answer would be no.

The clerk shook her head to indicate she didn't.

"Any other features?" He asked to get any details he could.

The clerk shook her head again and said, "Sorry."

Disappointed, Frederick and Susan returned to their room and Frederick sat on the side of his bed next to his empty bag on the nightstand.

"What are we going to do next?" Susan asked after Frederick told her everything that had happened that day.

"I don't know, Susan. I'm very disappointed and unsure of what will happen. I had it. I mean, I had it!" He said louder.

"It's okay," Susan said and consoled Frederick by giving him a half hug as she sat next to him on the side of the bed.

"Susan, I had it," he said again and turned to look at her. "Everything worked," he then said and lowered his head towards the floor in disappointment. She continued to hug him when out of nowhere, their phone rang.

Frederick didn't flinch while Susan became startled and looked towards the phone on the opposite wall sitting on the dressers.

"Hello?" She said after picking up the receiver. After a few seconds, Frederick heard her say, "Frederick, Doctor Bernstein needs to speak with you." She held up the phone and looked at Frederick who wasn't in the mood but felt like he had to since Susan had already indicated he was there.

"Hello," Frederick said once he picked up the phone.

"Frederick, big trouble."

Frederick already had a lot of trouble going on so he didn't want to be involved with Bernstein's problems.

"What happened?" Frederick reluctantly asked and leaned against the torso and watched as Susan walked to the bathroom.

"Dr. Anwick," Bernstein said and paused.

"What about her, Jerren?"

"She seems to have um," Bernstein started to say and kept Frederick waiting for him to finish. "It's strange, she seems to have vanished. Or, run away."

"What do you mean?"

"I went to the dig today and a couple of people ran up to me and were a bit frantic. I figured they had found something until I saw the shocked look on their faces. Then I immediately thought something bad had happened but after hearing them, they said that Anwick ran away from the site. They said a couple of people yelled for her name and when she didn't answer, they chased after her but weren't able to catch her. I found that strange also since she would have told someone there where she was going so they could contact her if anything happened. So, I called the University where they said they hadn't seen her since that morning. I called her portable phone and her house phone but again, no answer."

"No idea where she went?" Frederick asked.

"Not really. A little later on I heard that, I guess before she took off running, a couple of people in a tent that she ran by heard her say something that sounded like 'scroll'."

"Scroll?" Frederick asked and stood up straight from leaning on the dresser.

"The two in the tent looked out and saw her sprinting away from their tent, constantly muttering the word scroll before she went up the hillside to where she parked. They weren't aware of any scroll and they asked some of the people around at the site and no one was familiar with what they meant. When I heard that, I thought of you and wanted to give you a call."

Frederick paused for a few seconds thinking which made Bernstein wonder if something had happened. Finally, Frederick spoke, "Do you know what she was wearing?"

"Not really. She usually wore a traditional brown Tadashi or similar."

"It was her!" He yelled in the phone, catching the attention of Susan.

Susan walked out of the bathroom and peeked her head out of the door, "It was who?" She asked, not realizing he was still on the phone.

CHAPTER 47

Frederick met Bernstein at a park near the hotel. Susan stayed behind to pack their belongings since Frederick wasn't sure what they would have to do next but Frederick wanted to be prepared for anything.

"Frederick, thanks for meeting me with such short notice. I hope everything is alright," Bernstein said once he saw Frederick walking the sidewalk briskly towards the large rotunda he was waiting at.

"Not really, as you can imagine. Any update on Anwick?" He eagerly asked.

"Yes," Bernstein answered and sat on a concrete ledge. Frederick took a seat after Bernstein had sat. "I got a call out of nowhere from an old friend in a small town in South America. He used to work with us at the University about a half a year ago when he went to a dig in Argentina to find some sort of temple. He called me and wondered what Anwick was doing there."

"In South America?"

Bernstein nodded.

"South America?" Frederick repeated in a soft mumble. He looked around at a few people walking by. The park was on the side of the street between two small buildings. It was kind of out of place but it was a popular spot for people to get away from the city a while. He wondered what she was doing there. "What's in South America?" Frederick asked to see if he knew why she went there.

"Not sure. She was last seen in," Bernstein started to say and brought out a small folded piece of paper in his shirt pocket. He unfolded it and read, "Chacras de Coria."

"I need to go there immediately," Frederick said.

"I'll go with you," Bernstein said instantly, wanting to go and not only help Frederick but see what Anwick was doing.

"No, it's much too dangerous. Plus, you have your archaeological dig here to help watch over."

"They'll be just fine a few days while I'm gone. We have a good team. Let me go notify the University and pack and we'll fly out immediately. Meet me outside your hotel in two hours and we'll go to the airport," Bernstein said.

Frederick was fine going by himself but was glad to have Bernstein accompany him. He went back to the hotel and saw Susan had already packed so he was ready to go. He called the airport and found a flight that took off four hours later that night and booked it by buying two tickets. He then purchased a flight for Susan back to Florida.

"Why can't I go with you?" Susan asked, sad that she couldn't go.

"It's much too dangerous. Please, trust me again, Susan," Frederick said and placed his hand behind her head to run his hand through the back of her hair. He looked directly in her face as she looked to the side of the room, saddened she couldn't go with.

"It's going to be dangerous," he said and placed his hand on the lower of her back and walked her over to the bed. They sat on the foot of the bed and Frederick sat facing her and had her leg folded across the other to be able to face her better. She sat straight ahead facing the dresser on the wall. "Susan, please," he said and she looked towards him.

"I don't understand why?" She asked.

"Argentina is a dangerous place for people like me. Not only because Anwick was seen there, but," Frederick started to say but was worried to finish the sentence. He didn't want Susan to worry about him but he needed to be sure she knew the seriousness of what was happening. Now that someone had stolen the scroll he had just signed, he didn't want the scroll falling back into the wrong hands. "This scroll is very important. Not just to me, but the existence of soul hunters. Remember how much good I wanted to bring to everyone. If it were to fall into the wrong hands, who knows what will happen to everyone." He finished speaking and looked at Susan whose head remained lowered but now she had her eyes shut. She was no longer saddened she couldn't go but saddened instead that Frederick was going back into danger. He continued to look at her and nudged closer towards her. He then wrapped his arm around her and placed his head on her shoulder. She leaned her head closer to the top of his as they sat in silence for a moment. He gently moved his head up so he wouldn't hit hers and leaned over to kiss her on the cheek. She turned towards him and upon opening her eyes and smiling, he saw the redness in her eyes.

"Please, be safe," she said.

CHAPTER 48

"Officer, I know this sounds crazy, but this morning I saw my friend," Clint said upon walking into the local police department. He went in to report he saw his missing friend, Wally.

"Okay, where did you see him?" The police officer asked after they both sat down at a long table in the meeting room. The meeting room is usually where they held community events and city hall meetings but it being a busier day than usual, the detectives had their questioning room occupied. They sat in the quiet room while the officer flipped to a new page in his notebook. He clicked the pen and began writing on the blank sheet.

"He was walking from town. I don't know where he was coming from but I was going to school today when I saw him. I live near main street," Clint began to say.

"Oh yeah, I know where you live," the officer said. Being a small town, most people knew one another.

"So, leaving home, I thought I saw him walking across the street the opposite direction," Clint said while pointing at the wall blankly as he explained his directions." Being a single lane road, it was easy to see across the quiet street.

"Mmhmm," the officer said while looking directly at Clint.

"When I looked and saw the person, I did a double-take once I thought it was Wally. I was like, 'Wally!' when I saw him and quickly looked to my left to make sure there wasn't any traffic coming. Then, I started to jog across the street and took a step off the curb. I looked the other direction and saw it was clear so I ran to meet him across the way."

"Ok. And then what?" The officer said without writing any information yet.

"It's strange," Clint said and stopped talking. He looked puzzled with the way he tilted his head and scrunched his nose.

The officer waited a few seconds before asking, "What happened?"

"It wasn't him. I guess?" Clint said as if it were a question.

"What do you mean?"

"It had to have been him."

The officer sat and brought one leg up to cross it over the other and readjusted his notebook. He looked at Clint and wasn't sure where he was getting at. He had known Clint and his family fairly well and knew he didn't do drugs and was pretty stable. He found his behavior out of the ordinary. The officer waited another few seconds before Clint spoke again.

"I know it's him!" Clint said loudly and brought his head back across the top of the chair and sighed deeply since he was confused himself.

"What did he say?" The officer then asked.

Clint continued looking at nothing towards the ceiling and rethinking what had happened and how he was sure it was Wally.

"I mean, he was only gone one night. He was wearing the same clothes as the night before. He wore the same jeans and the same striped blue and white t-shirt. He looked dirtier but I've known him for years. I know it had to be him."

"But, what did he say when you approached him?"

"Nothing."

"How did he act? What did you do?"

"When I got across the street," Clint said and readjusted himself in the metal chair. "After I called his name, he didn't even look at me. I got closer to him on the sidewalk and he continued to walk. I said his name again, maybe even twice and he kept walking. He was walking very quickly so I followed beside him and tried to get his attention. I found his behavior strange so I ran a couple of steps and stood in front of him. He tried to walk around me so I opened my arms so he couldn't walk on the sidewalk. He tried moving onto the grass but I moved with my open arms until he stopped," Clint said after standing up and moved his arms, emulating what he was doing that morning in front of who he thought was Wally. "Before stopping, his face was strange. It was as if he wasn't even looking at me but look straight ahead. Once he finally stopped, he looked directly in my face. I said, 'Wally? What happened?' I was curious what had happened when we were at the cemetery and you know, where he went," Clint finished saying and sat back down.

By this time, the officer was scribbling very quickly on his notepad. He finished writing and removed the police cap he was wearing.

"How did he respond?" The officer asked after finishing his quick notes and Clint and calmed down a bit. Clint used his hand to wipe the sweat that had appeared on his forehead. He lowered his hand and placed both hands on each knee as he leaned forward.

"He looked at me as if he didn't know who I was. Like a zombie!" Clint said and raised his voice to emphasize a zombie.

"What do you mean, zombie?"

"I, I mean, maybe he has that am," Clint said and tried to think of what to say.

"Amnesia?"

"Yes, that's it!" Clint proclaimed. "Maybe something happened."

"Hmm," the officer replied. "He didn't say anything else to you.

"Well, after I called him Wally, he continued to look at me as if he was staring deep into my soul. Totally not like him at all. Again, I said, 'Wally?' He finally responded, 'It's Jefferson.'"

"Jefferson? Do you know anyone by that name?"

"No!" Clint said in a loud outburst. He wasn't mad at the police officer but instead mad at the situation.

"You can't think of anyone by that name?"

Clint took in a deep breath and motioned his body back to lean into the chair and held his breath for a few seconds. He exhaled loudly and said, "No. No one that I know of."

"What happened next?"

"That was it. I lowered my arms in confusion and stood still as he walked past me. I stood motionless for a moment and I turned around to see where he went and he was gone."

"So, you didn't see where he went?" The officer said and placed the notebook on the table and clicked the pen to close it.

"No. But, I know it had to be him. It looked like him. He wore the same clothes as last night. I know him, I've known him for many years and it was him. It even sounded like him," Clint said and lowered his head and shook it in disappointment.

The officer stood from his chair and grabbed his hat from the top of the table. He put it back on before removing it, motioning his hand back on the sides of his head to move his hair behind his ears. He put the hat back on and picked up his notebook and pen.

"If anything else happens, call me." The officer took a card out of his pant pocket and handed it to Clint. He set his hand on Clint's shoulder to help him out of the room. Clint left the police department, not getting any answers to the many questions and confusion he had gone through earlier thinking and knowing he saw his best friend.

CHAPTER 49

Frederick and Bernstein arrived in Argentina, not knowing what was happening but Frederick knew he needed to get his scroll back. They walked off the airplane and went to the baggage claim. Walking around numerous people, Frederick kept his eyes alert since he wasn't trusting anyone. He placed his hands in his pockets as he had his shoulder bag around his torso. He looked down frequently, in a habit of making sure the scroll was safe until he remembered it was gone. He looked towards Bernstein who seemed excited to be in Argentina with the way he smiled, likely since he had never been there before.

"What do you think we're getting ourselves into?" Frederick asked Bernstein as they walked to the escalator to go down to the baggage claim.

"Another fun adventure, I presume," Bernstein answered and shrugged his shoulders as he looked at Frederick.

"Why did you wear a Hawaiian shirt?" Frederick asked in a jokingly manner but his presence with a lack of a usual smile put off a more serious demeanor. Usually, when asking a joke to be playful, he would give off a slight grin but this time with his frustration, his grin didn't show. Bernstein saw Frederick's serious face and wondered if he was mad at him.

"I don't know, I guess just to be comfortable?" Bernstein answered in a question form since he wasn't sure a good way to answer. After answering, he heard Frederick chuckle slightly so he knew he was just having fun. Inside, though, Frederick actually wondered why he wore such a bright and colorful shirt. Such a bright shirt Frederick thought would get them easily noticed if anyone were watching them but looking around at a lot of the bright shirts at the airport, Frederick felt more at ease.

They both got their luggage that had arrived safely and they left the airport. They planned on going to a hotel that Bernstein was able to book and Frederick wanted to get unpacked and call home to leave a message for Susan that he made it safely. Also, to ask her to call his hotel and leave a message for him that she made it home safe as well. Her flight was longer so she was not yet home.

"So what are we doing first?" Frederick asked Bernstein. He asked him since he was the one that knew where his friend had seen Anwick.

"Well, my friend saw Anwick back in a forest area around, or outside of Chacras de Coria. I'll call my friend and let him know we're here. He said yesterday that he would be able to meet us somewhere tonight and to let him know when we arrive."

"Great, we need to find her," Frederick said as they sat in the backseat of a taxi. He looked around at the streets in the busy area from the Mendoza airport on the way to Chacras de Coria – about a half-hour drive. Frederick wanted to get the scroll and get back to Florida as soon as possible. Even though he didn't feel any difference after signing the scroll and possessing it, he knew that he needed it to also keep it out of the wrong hands. He had only met Anwick that one time from the University but he didn't know her well enough to know why she would take it.

"Why do you think Anwick would take the scroll? And out of all places, come here?" Frederick asked. He wanted to hear Bernstein's opinion since he knew her better and had worked with her for some time at the archaeological dig.

Bernstein wiped his forehead since the weather was a bit more humid than what he was used to in Egypt. The humidity reminded him more of his home in Alabama but it had been a while since he had been there. He turned to Frederick who had turned his attention out to the front of the taxi. Bernstein wasn't sure why she would have taken the scroll and he was very curious also why she did.

"I can only assume but I have no idea her true intentions," Bernstein said which brought Frederick's attention back to him. Frederick looked at Bernstein's reddish face as sweat ran slowly down under his sideburns. He was hot too and was also sweating but he trusted Bernstein and believed what he said.

"By assume, what would you say?"

"The only thing I can think is she heard us talking inside the tent at the dig. I mean, it's not like her to steal artifacts or anything of value. She's one of the most respected people in the department at the university as well as in the archaeology profession."

"Hmm," Frederick said, still contemplating why but knowing they had to get it back. "Do you think she is selling it in the black market?" Frederick asked.

"Possible. I mean, she's found numerous artifacts that were near priceless during her career that she could have sold and had millions. Why the scroll?"

Frederick paused a second to think. "Well, the scroll, if known to someone who understood it, could sell it. Wait," Frederick said and raised his finger in the air. Frederick looked at the driver in the rearview mirror to make sure he wasn't listening. Frederick turned back towards Bernstein and leaned in closer. He used his finger to motion Bernstein closer. Bernstein moved his ear towards Frederick while watching the driver in the mirror. "What if she's a soul hunter. What if she sold it to the wrong group of people?" Frederick asked and moved back to his upright position in the backseat of the taxi. Bernstein remained leaning for a second to think. He had never thought she might be a soul hunter nor did he expect it. He remembered seeing photographs of her at museums as a child and knew that she couldn't be one since her age seems to match up from the time of her photographs she showed him.

"I don't think so. She grew up going to museums and historical sites and has pictures to prove it. I've seen it. I've even met her mother when I first arrived in Egypt. I just don't think she could be."

"Hmm," Frederick said again, attempting to think of anything else. He looked around at all the palm trees overcrowding the lush, green areas between buildings. He watched as people walked around on sidewalks and ran across streets, rushing to go somewhere. They both sat silently in the car and watched out each of their own windows at the countryside. Before they knew it they had gotten to their hotel. Frederick was impressed as it was much more ornate with carvings and multi-colored paints covering the outside. There were several tourists walking around and street vendors selling food and touristy shirts and accessories. The taxi driver helped them with their luggage and they went inside to check in. Frederick called and left a message for Susan while Bernstein called his friend that had seen Anwick.

"What did your friend say?" Frederick asked while he unpacked his bag when Bernstein walked back into the room.

Bernstein shut the door gently behind him and stopped to look at Frederick. "Well, a bit odd," he started.

Frederick was impatient and wanting to know what happened. He set down the shirt that he had just brought out of his bag. "What happened?"

Bernstein walked over and leaned up against the wall beside his bed. Frederick's bed was beside his with a window on the adjacent wall. The curtains were open, letting in the bright sunlight. Just outside their window was a nice view of numerous buildings with a beautiful landscape of trees and numerous flowers and flora.

"He said he's scared." He brought up his arms and folded them in front of him and looked blankly down at his bed.

"Scared?"

"Yes," Bernstein said and was occupied why he would be so scared and didn't understand what had happened to his friend.

Frederick wanted to know more and stood up from the bed and placed his hands on his hips. He needed to know what happened so he would know what to do next.

Finally, Bernstein told him more. "He said he was scared. That he didn't want to get involved." Bernstein was worried by what he had said and wondered what was really going on. He had asked his friend what he meant but he was scared to go in more detail before saying, 'that's all I want to say about it. Be safe.' His friend hung up immediately, leaving a deathly feeling ringtone in Bernstein's ears.

"Involved in what? Is Anwick still here?" Frederick asked since he was now worried that she had gone somewhere else.

"He said she was. That she was involved with something that he didn't want to be around. That's all he said. When I asked for more information, all he told us was to be safe."

Frederick sat back down on the edge of the bed and sat on the shirt he had just placed there. He leaned forward and picked up the shirt from underneath him and looked at it. He raised it in the air and threw it on the comforter of the bed. "Well, did he at least say where she was?"

"No, just from before that she was in the forest.

"But, how do we know she's still here."

"I know she has to be with what he said yesterday that she was here. And, on the phone just now, which he didn't want to get involved tells me that she is here. Possibly dealing with dangerous people. Maybe she is trying to sell it on the black market?"

"Maybe," Frederick answered and shut his eyes and faced down towards the floor. Bernstein walked over to his suitcase and unzipped it. He resituated the clothes he brought inside to prevent even more creases and wrinkles.

While going through his clothes, Bernstein heard Frederick ask, "What next?"

Bernstein reached up to the zipper on top of his suitcase and pulled out a small stack of papers he had inside. He took his finger to quickly browse through them and pulled out three pages. "I brought a few maps of the area and I think we should go and base our search on what Nik, my friend told me."

"What clues?" Frederick asked and stood up to check out the maps. Bernstein turned around to set them on the table that had a small television on it. There was a tray with a large ice bucket and a few plastic cups. He moved that over next to the television to make more space. He set the three pages next to each other and they both looked over them. Frederick used his finger to look closer at the first page. He moved it slightly towards him and bent over to look at an overall satellite image of an area. He saw a large forest and a small village near the northern side of the forest. There didn't seem to be anything else or any other sign of life near the small village tucked inside, near the edge of the forest. While touching the page, he quickly glanced at the other two and saw an overlay of the town as well as a large-area map. He looked back at the page with his finger pressed on it and asked, "What is this?"

Bernstein looked at where Frederick's finger was pointing and saw what looked to be a small area or even a few collective buildings. It was hard to see on the blurry, black and white image. "I'm not sure. It looks to be some buildings."

"Do you know what else is around it?" Frederick asked.

"No, I don't. By the looks of it," Bernstein began to say while looking around the rest of the page of the map, "I don't think there's anything but land and forest. "Do you think we should go there in the morning?"

"No, we need to go now," Frederick said, knowing they needed to act quickly before they lost Anwick as well as the scroll. A slight chill came across him as he removed his finger from the map. He shut his eyes temporarily while he felt a bit of discomfort run through him and he reopened his eyes. He pushed through the discomfort of not knowing where they were going and what was going to happen since he needed to get the scroll back and keep it safe.

"Ok, it looks like the forest might be a, well, maybe an hour ride. Just up outside of Mendoza, near the border of Chacras de Coria to the West."

CHAPTER 50

Frederick and Bernstein rented a high clearance SUV from a car rental business in town. They needed high clearance since they weren't sure how far into the forest they would need to go but they needed to be prepared for the worst. Frederick drove while Bernstein carried the map while sitting in the passenger seat.

"It's beautiful out here," Frederick said as he turned one of the corners that Bernstein told him to.

"Sure is," Bernstein replied after he picked his head up from looking at the map to look around. They were moving away from the touristy area of town where people worked, lived, and visited. They then turned down another road a few miles further and the pavement ended. Before they knew it, the road was bumpy as dust flew up from the tires behind them. Bernstein reached up to buckle his seat belt since he hadn't yet done that. "Pretty bumpy."

"Yes," Frederick said as their vehicle hit a bump and caused him to stop speaking. "That one hurt a bit."

Bernstein struggled to focus on the map with all the bumps on the road in the suddenly desolate area. He grabbed each side of the paper and pulled it gently to be able to get rid of the creases in the paper. Frederick looked around and reached out to push the driver's side mirror back into place since one of the bumps caused it to move. He was sure to be observant of not only the road and the condition of the dusty path but to make sure no one was following them or around them. He saw some more bumps in the road up ahead that looked like a small gulley where water would cross during storms. He slowed down which caused dust to come back from behind the vehicle and enter through their windows that were down. Bernstein looked up to see why Frederick had slowed so much and saw the gulley. He held onto the map with one hand and reached up to grab the handle on the top of the ceiling of the car with his other. Frederick eased off the gas pedal and waited until the vehicle slowly gained speed going down the slight hill and once he nearly reached the narrow but deep gulley, not sure of how soft the sand would be, he pressed hard on the acceleration and they hit the edge and bounced up from their car seats. Moving up the hill from speeding up, they made it back to where the road was more level and continued like normal.

"I think about another two, or one or so miles ahead we need to turn left."

"The road is getting narrower," Frederick said while keeping his eyes on everything around him. He looked straight ahead to try and notice the turn but could not yet see it. He did notice there were more trees than before that encroached onto the roadway. When they first started down the dirt road, there was enough space for two cars but now, just enough for one. "I hope we don't come across anyone else out here, the road is so narrow now."

"Yeah, nor do I want to know who else would even be out here," Bernstein replied and turned around to look behind them in the back window. He didn't see anyone else and turned back to face the front. He looked around at all the large, old trees that provided a lot of shade. They could barely know the sun was above them if it wasn't for a small patch here and there where the sun appeared out of. "Up ahead," Bernstein said while sitting up in his seat and pointing. Frederick looked ahead and saw where he was pointing. There was what seemed to be a turn while the main road continued to go straight. He wasn't sure where the main road kept going but followed Bernstein's direction since he had the map. As they approached the turn, Frederick saw a large rock on the corner of the turn and wondered if that was some sort of marking to let people know where to turn – whoever was out there.

"I wonder who all is out here. We need to keep our eyes out," Frederick said while he straightened the steering wheel.

"If Anwick is out here, I don't know who else would be. I still don't know why she would be out here. I mean, unless there's some sort of archaeological dig in the forest. But, why would she steal the scroll?"

"That's why I'm worried. Maybe she's dealing with a bad crowd out here so we need to be sure we're careful and aware."

"Or, how many there are out here. Being this far in the forest, they might be armed and dangerous," Bernstein said and adjusted himself in his seat and looked to the left and right. He looked back down at the map after seeing the area was clear, for what he could see anyway since it was hard to see through all the trees and brush.

They drove slowly for another twenty or so minutes until Bernstein said, "Up here, to the right about a half-mile is the structure on the map. Drive slow."

Frederick moved to the edge of his seat and grabbed the steering tight with both hands on each side. He moved closer to the now dirty windshield that had been smudged since there was no windshield cleaner when he used the windshield wipers in an attempt to clean it. He found a cleaner spot and leaned down to look through it. He looked straight ahead and saw something large up near the road. He came to a quiet stop. "Can I see the map?" He asked.

Bernstein handed him the map and Frederick looked at it. Bernstein looked around and all they could hear in the forest were random birds quailing and wind rustling the branches and leaves. Frederick looked close to the map and realized what he saw was the structure on the map. In a whisper, he told Bernstein, "Here. Up ahead," he said and pointed. Once Bernstein looked the direction he was pointing, he moved his finger to the map at the structure. Bernstein followed his finger down towards the map. He took out a handkerchief and wiped the sweat from his forehead and put it back into his pocket.

"What should we do next?" Bernstein asked.

"I'm not sure. I do know we need to keep alert at all times."

Bernstein nodded and reached into the backseat to take ahold of one of the bottles of water they brought with them. He took a swig and moved the slightly cold bottle up to his forehead to cool down his face and skin.

After a moment thinking and coming up with a strategy, Frederick finally said, "We're here. We need to find out what's going on. I don't want Anwick to get away and if she sees us here, she's bound to run." Then Frederick also reached behind for a bottle of water. He couldn't find it so he set the map on the center console and looked behind him to find one. He grabbed it and brought it up to take a drink. He took the keys from the ignition and placed them in his lap. "We need to quietly look around and see who all is here and where we even are. We can park here."

"Ok, I'll bring the map," Bernstein responded and slowly opened his door. He kept the bottle of water in hand and map in the other. He used his elbow to close the door as quietly as he could. He didn't quite close it all the way and he was worried the car battery might die so he put the water under his arm. He used his fingers to open the door and keeping the handle pulled, he shut the door and released the handle to make sure the door was shut. Frederick stepped out and shut his door quietly, bringing his water also. He put the bottle into his pocket and it made him a bit uncomfortable but it was secure in his pants pocket. He walked to the front of the car and Bernstein walked up to meet him. Bernstein looked at the map and noticed the road that they were on went straight a little further before gearing to the right. The building was on the left side and what seemed to be a small, even narrower path went in front of it. "There's a narrow road in front of the structure," Bernstein said and Frederick looked straight ahead. He used his hands to take the bottom of his cotton t-shirt and moved it around to bring air onto his hot and sticky skin. He regretted wearing jeans but that's all he had brought that weren't slacks. Bernstein wore baggier jeans and a cotton polo that was a bit thicker than Frederick's. He did bring a hat with a large rim around it that helped block the sun from his face and neck. Frederick squinted his eyes and tried to see the building the best he could to see which way they could go to it and not be noticed.

CHAPTER 51

They could see a large portion of the building but a lot of the walls and roof had trees and other limbs and vines growing up around it, helping to camouflage it. The building seemed to be a compound of sorts with grayish colored, almost to a black hue, built out of concrete. It seemed to be single-story but both Frederick and Bernstein wondered if any of it went underground. Looking around the side that they could see, they didn't notice any windows or any doors for access.

"Let's go through the trees over here," Frederick said and pointed to the right near where Bernstein was standing. There was no path but it seemed to be the best route to go to avoid being seen. There was space between the trees that they could walk but they had to be careful as they approached, not to step on any limbs or make much noise. Being in the forest, some of the slightest noises would flow through the area loudly. They could hear tree branches snapping as squirrels and other animals crawled and jumped throughout so they had to watch their steps.

Bernstein began walking, watching his steps as he began to slowly tread through the trees. He folded up the map nicely and placed it in his pocket to prevent him from losing or damaging it. Holding onto the water, he used his arm to push away the branches that hung in front of him. Frederick followed closely behind him and was aware of the branches and limbs that Bernstein was pushing aside so they didn't come back to hit him. They walked carefully for a few minutes and stopped. Frederick looked back to be sure they weren't being followed and could still slightly see their vehicle still parked on the street. They both looked towards the building and only saw bits of it through where no branches and leaves were blocking their views.

Frederick touched Bernstein on his upper back to gain his attention. He raised his arm and with his finger, he motioned Bernstein to walk ahead a bit more but to angle to their left to approach the building closer. Bernstein looked at Frederick and nodded in agreement. He began walking slowly again and after an additional few moments, they could see the building closer to them. Once the building was in better sight, they stopped. Frederick used his hand again and pointed to the ground in order to motion Bernstein to kneel down. As he was motioning him, he kneeled and Bernstein followed. They both kneeled and used the large brush in front of them to block and cover them in case anyone else was out there. Frederick reached ahead and pulled down a branch on the brush so they could see better. They leaned forward and looked straight ahead and carefully observed the area. They were at what they thought was the front of the buildings since they saw a door. Along the flat front that looked similar to the side, there was a large, wooden door in the middle. The door was shut but there were no other windows or anything else that could be used for an entrance. They looked around the building and the trees and area surrounding it and after a moment, Frederick released the branch.

In a whisper, he told Bernstein, "Maybe there's no one out here. Might this be abandoned?"

Bernstein curled up his bottom lip and shrugged his shoulders, indicating he wasn't sure. He turned back around to look at the building once more. He turned towards Frederick and whispered, "But, why would Anwick be out here?"

It was now Frederick's turn to shrug his shoulders since he couldn't figure out why she would be. "Let's go around some more and see if there's anything else," he said quietly to Bernstein. They both carefully stood up and looked around to make sure they were alone. Frederick looked behind them to check and they proceeded to walk more. They walked for an additional few more moments through the trees, stepping gently on the fallen twigs when suddenly, they could hear a man's voice yell in the distance. Bernstein froze while leading, scared, and caught off guard while Frederick immediately fell onto one knee. He reached ahead of him and pulled on Bernstein's shirt. He looked back and saw Frederick crouched so he knelt down also. They both looked around frantically, peeking their head up slightly over the brush that surrounded them but couldn't see or hear anyone in the forest around them. After a few seconds of looking around, they heard someone yell again. They both looked up towards the left where they heard the voice come from. Frederick patted Bernstein on the shoulder and pointed ahead and moved his head up to motion him to continue towards the voice.

Remaining crouched, Bernstein moved ahead and went in between the trees to where he thought he heard the voice. Again, more yelling was heard but this time it sounded like two or more voices. Frederick followed behind Bernstein closely and continued to look behind him to make sure there was no one behind them. Suddenly, Bernstein noticed they were nearing an open area in the forest. He stopped suddenly and Frederick stopped also. Frederick moved up next to Bernstein and they both looked in the open area where they noticed a group of people standing. The open area was small but followed the narrow path that went in front of the structure. Bernstein brought out his map and pointed to where he thought they were. Beyond the open area was more forest and it seemed the only way to get out if they had to rush was back where they came from. As Bernstein pointed on the map, Frederick nodded and looked up towards the group of two men standing with their backs towards them. They couldn't see who the men were talking to since the men seemed quite large with tan overcoats on. They each wore what seemed to be a military hat of sorts and both Frederick and Bernstein thought they might be militants or guerillas. Frederick started to move slowly to the right of Bernstein and through the forest to better see what was going on. Bernstein followed behind him.

Frederick continued to walk for thirty seconds as the voices continued to yell loudly but they couldn't quite comprehend what was being said. The group of people in the open area were speaking English but with a thick accent. Frederick couldn't tell what the accent was but thought maybe Spanish or something local to Argentina. Upon hearing the accent more closely, Bernstein stopped approaching and paused. He became instantly worried and froze. Frederick took two more steps when he suddenly heard a female's voice.

"Anwick," he whispered to himself, not knowing that Bernstein had stopped a few steps behind him. After realizing it was Anwick's voice, he stood up and rustled a few branches and twigs where the two men heard him and immediately turned around. The two men saw him and the one closest to him pointed his hand at him.

"You!" The first man yelled. Frederick didn't know what to do so to show himself and not being a threat to the men he didn't know, he raised both of his hands. He looked to the right of the men and saw Anwick there. She stood, wearing a robe that covered her arms and head while her face stared at Frederick. The second man turned his attention back to Anwick while the first man walked towards Frederick. He continued keeping his arms up in the air.

"I mean no harm," Frederick finally said, unsure how he should respond as the man approached closer.

As the man walked closer, his overcoat moved to the side and Frederick noticed a gun in a holster in his side and a knife on the opposite side. He wore greenish colored pants and a shirt with a matching hat – the same uniform the other man was wearing. The man had a light skin tone on his face with a thin mustache above his lip. His eyes squinted and remained attentive at Frederick while, with his hands remaining up, the man felt around Frederick's pants and pockets when he realized there were no weapons. At that time, he noticed Bernstein a bit further in the forest who remained crouched.

"Hey! Come here!" He yelled towards Bernstein. The second man quickly turned his attention to his friend to make sure he was safe and what was happening before he looked back and watched Anwick. Anwick continued to stare at Frederick the entire time. Bernstein stood up slowly, his arms shaking and sweat falling from the pores in his face at a quick rate. He also raised his hands but was only to raise them halfway with all the shaking he was enduring. He walked towards Frederick as Frederick watched him. He had never seen Bernstein so scared and trembling so much. Bernstein moved his eyes for a slight second from the strange man and looked at Frederick. Frederick saw a hollowness in his pupils as the white of his eyes overwhelmed the majority of his face with his eyes opened so large.

The man took a couple of steps backward while facing Frederick and Bernstein. "You two, come here," he said while continuing to walk back towards his friend.

Bernstein looked past the two men and saw Dr. Anwick. "Dr. Anwick?" He said loudly while slightly lowering his hands even more. "Dr. Anwick, what are you doing here? Why did you," Bernstein started to say as they approached her more closely.

"I don't know you," she said. Bernstein was unaware that she was no longer Anwick but instead, her soul had been taken over by Narmer.

"Why did you steal the scroll?" Frederick asked while the two men stood towards the middle of the three of them.

"You stole it from me," she answered which caught Frederick off guard.

"No, it's mine!" He said and walked towards her, lowering his arms but instead clenching his fists tight in anger. His right shoulder lowered and his head tilted while he stared at her in anger. He looked around her but didn't see the scroll in her possession. "Where is it? Did you sell it to these," he started to say and looked towards the two men.

"Sell what?" The first man asked. Frederick looked back towards Anwick.

"Now's not the time to argue or fight," Anwick finally said.

At this time, Bernstein lowered his arms and a thin, silver bracelet he wore fell back down from his forearm to the bone on his wrist. The glare caught the attention of one of the men as he looked down at the bracelet. He nudged the man beside him with his elbow. The man turned towards him and while continuing to look at Bernstein's wrist, the other man looked also. He turned back around to look at his friend and tilted his head.

"Look, gentlemen," the first man said to both Frederick and Bernstein. I think we're off on the wrong foot. My name is Josef M," he said but stopped before finishing his last name. "This gentleman here is my protégé, you can say," he said and smiled, holding out his hand for a handshake.

"I'm Frederick," Frederick said and shook his hand, wanting to be brave in front of them and not show he was intimidated in any way. "My friend, Jerren," Frederick said and reached to his side to pat Bernstein on his lower back. Bernstein didn't move forward so Frederick looked back towards him and noticed him looking at the two men as sweat continued to fall from his face – more than Frederick had seen him sweat before. He wondered what had happened to Bernstein and pushed him with more strength in the back to more him forwards a step.

Finally, Bernstein reached out his hand unwillingly and said, "Jerry." Frederick wondered why he had introduced himself as Jerry.

As the two men shook hands, the first man, while holding Bernstein's hand, he leaned in closer to look at the numbers on Bernstein's forearm without being noticed. Bernstein knew though what he was looking at. He pulled away his hand and stepped back. At that time, from behind where Anwick stood, three additional men walked towards them. Two of them wore the same type of greenish uniform without overcoats while the other wore regular clothing. He had on a striped shirt with regular tan slacks.

"Who do we have here?" The younger man wearing regular clothes asked. Frederick noticed he didn't have any accent but instead, sounded American.

"I'm Frederick, and this is," he hesitated before looking at Bernstein and said, "Jerry." As the man came towards them, Frederick found it strange that Anwick moved and stood beside him. Rather than being worried he was here for the scroll, he wondered why she was more intimidated by the men coming towards them.

As Anwick slowly stepped to stand beside Frederick, again she said but this time whispered, "Now isn't the time." Frederick had no idea what she meant by that but all he wanted to know was where the scroll was. He no longer cared as much as to why she stole it but just wanted to get the scroll back and get back home.

"Frederick, is that what you said?" The same man walking towards them asked.

"Yes, that is correct. And, you are?" Frederick asked while the three men got to the group and stopped. The young man looked around at everyone and with a fake smile, attempted to make everyone there feel at ease and to earn his trust. Anwick already knew what was happening but Frederick and Bernstein were confused.

"My name is Jefferson," the man formerly known as Wally responded as he did a slight courtesy.

"It's nice to meet you," Frederick said in response.

"Is it?" Jefferson said in return and immediately hid his smile while looking at Frederick. "I know who you are," he then said, raising further suspicion in Frederick as well as Bernstein who was paying attention to what was happening.

"I'm sorry?" Frederick said, wanting more answers. He was beginning to sweat more as well as a bit of worry rushed through his body since this strange man seemed to know who he was. He then thought maybe this was the man Anwick sold the scroll too which is why he knew his name and who he was.

"You murdered my son," Jefferson then said.

Frederick paused and a moment of silence surrounded the group. Finally, shocked by such a statement, Frederick asked, "Your son?"

Jefferson remained standing and started laughing which caused the men around him to laugh also until after a few seconds, the laughing stopped once Jefferson raised his hand. Jefferson took a few steps towards Frederick and stared deep into his face. With his upper teeth biting his lower teeth to hold back the rage, Jefferson answered, "Reginald."

"Reginald?" Frederick said surprisingly as his voice raised. He took two steps back and moved his hands up slightly since he was caught off guard. After waiting a few seconds, he followed up by saying, "No."

Jefferson nodded his head with the same deep stare.

Frederick responded and said, "Reginald said his father was dead."

"I was. While I was dead I saw what you did. Upon coming back, I'm going to finish what my son started."

"No!" Frederick immediately yelled, knowing the evil that Reginald had been planning which is why he wanted to eliminate him in the first place. He then realized who the military men were that were around him and fear instantly rushed through his body, creating goosebumps on his sweaty skin. Upon dreading what was happening, he was unsure what Jefferson had meant when he said he used to be dead. Frederick then looked at the four men that stood beside Jefferson and saw them all staring at him, Bernstein and Anwick.

"How, how did you come back?" Frederick asked, wanting to know what happened.

Jefferson chuckled. "Because of you," he said with a large smile.

"Me?" Frederick asked and pointed to himself.

"Yes. You signed the scroll, angering Set, right?" Jefferson asked, not expecting an answer. "Well, afterward, Set was so angered and wanted to get his scroll back. Since you signed overtop Narmer, his soul was free to escape the afterlife," Jefferson started to say and took one step closer until Anwick started to speak.

"And while being set free," Anwick started by saying, getting the attention of Frederick and Bernstein. "Set told me to rescue the scroll and keep it from Anubis," she said while raising her hand and pointing at Jefferson, the first time she had had interaction with him. Frederick lowered one shoulder and his head tilted in confusion. Bernstein stood behind him and watched and listened and everything felt so unreal. She continued, "He told me to get the scroll and to stop the killing of soul hunters. Anubis wants soul hunters to die – to make his army in the Underworld stronger. The only way for us to get me back onto earth was to place a curse on which Set did. Whoever walked over a soul hunter's grave, the soul hunter would be placed into that person's body. This curse worked for both good and bad," she said and looked again towards Jefferson. Jefferson remained standing with one foot forward until he finally moved his foot back to meet the other. The four men alongside Jefferson stood and faced Bernstein, Frederick and Anwick. They stood a few feet apart from one another surrounded by trees deep in the forest.

After a minute of silence went by, Anwick took her left hand and moved it in front of Frederick and placed it on his stomach. She began to push back, putting pressure on him and at the same time, she began stepping backward. Bernstein saw the two of them start walking backward so he joined them. They stared cautiously at the four men and Jefferson while backing away. Frederick and Bernstein were unsure of what was happening and who Anwick truly was. It was hard to believe that she could be Narmer but then again, Frederick was surprised that the young man claimed to be Jefferson – Reginald's father.

Continuing to walk backward, they finally reached the tree line and Bernstein was the first to turn around to walk through the trees. His heartbeat finally began to calm as they got further away from the group and he began walking down a similar path that they had originally walked to get there. Anwick was the second to turn around and followed Bernstein while Frederick was more cautious and watched for an additional few seconds. Finally, he turned around and shouted just loud enough for Bernstein to hear, "Run!"

Bernstein began running, ducking in and out of limbs and trees while Anwick continued after. Frederick ran in the back, looking back every few steps to be sure they weren't being followed but didn't see anyone behind them. He worried they might be taking the narrow path in front of the structure in the forest and try to cut them off.

"Keep running," he said, this time louder.

They continued to run until they could see their car ahead. Bernstein and Frederick were relieved the car was still there and Frederick grabbed the keys from his pocket and ran around to the driver's side to unlock it. He reached across and unlocked the passenger side and back to the back door to unlock the back door. Bernstein went into the backseat, letting Anwick sit in the front.

As the three of them got in the car and Frederick started the ignition, Bernstein shouted out from the back seat, "They're Germans!"

"I know," Frederick replied, clenching tightly onto the steering wheel as adrenaline rushed throughout his body. His skin had a chill from the sense of relief that they made it back safely to the car. "They're Nazis," he continued, awaiting a response from Bernstein.

"How did you know?" Bernstein asked since all the men wore were greenish uniforms with no insignias or symbols anywhere.

"Part of the reason I wanted the scroll," Frederick said and looked towards Anwick who sat in the passenger seat, staring straight ahead through the dirty windshield, "was to stop Reginald. Reginald was my, well, my mentor. When I found out he was going to try and get into the heads of soul hunters and force them to kill themselves, I wanted to stop him. I found out he was working with Germans who were soul hunters themselves, I had even heard some of them were former Nazis.

"They killed my family," Bernstein murmured heavily stating the words from his throat.

"Indeed. I wasn't sure where they were but now that Jefferson has appeared, continuing where Reginald left off at, we need to stop them," Frederick said.

"Frederick, remember when I said I didn't want to kill anymore?"

Frederick turned his head back towards Bernstein for a second and nodded while Anwick continued looking around through the trees. Frederick replied, "Yes, Jerren."

"Who did I only kill before?" He then asked Frederick.

While looking up ahead and seeing the road was getting wider, Frederick answered, "Germans."

"I'm game," Bernstein leaned up towards the middle console and replied immediately. He then looked towards Anwick and saw her looking blankly through the windshield. He was confused about who she really was and wanted to know more.

Suddenly, Anwick turned towards Bernstein and said, "I'm willing to help." Frederick looked at her direction for a second before continuing to focus on the road and drive as fast as he could. She continued, "Being sent back onto Earth, I have and need to keep the scroll in safekeeping, out of harm's way. It is very dangerous to sign it since if you die, you'll suffer the same fate as I had but also, it could fall into the wrong hands. I'll need to transfer it back over to me once we're done."

Frederick wanted to ask more questions but the first thing he asked after hearing what Anwick said was, "Done with what?"

Bernstein turned his attention from Frederick and looked toward Anwick. A gust of breeze blew in the window while Frederick turned the vehicle as they got closer to town.

"Killing the Nazis."

"The only soul hunters that need to die," Frederick quickly replied.

"Yes," Anwick said while turning her attention back to look straight ahead. In a deepened voice, she said, "They deserve to suffer with Anubis in his darkened hell." A sensation of chills ran through Frederick and Bernstein's bodies when Anwick then said, "Even though I'm the true master soul hunter, he controls the army of dead soul hunters and what he wants is more power. The more soul hunters that die, the more power he has. He is working with the Nazis and formerly Reginald, but now that his father has come back which was by no means meant to happen, they want to kill soul hunters."

"But, then why was Jefferson sent back?"

"Accident. The only way to get me back here to get the scroll was to place the curse that Set did, not thinking who else might conjure up from the dead. He figured the more dead soul hunters that rise, the lesser Anubis' army in the Underworld would be."

They all sat silently momentarily, taking in what was going on and thinking what would happen next.

CHAPTER 52

About a quarter-mile from the paved road that would lead the three of them back to Chacras de Coria when suddenly, there was an explosion. Unknown to them, the Nazi compound had set traps around the area for their safety. They watched from a distance through binoculars and once Frederick drove near the bomb, they detonated it. The loud explosion caught them off guard when the vehicle flipped from the front right tire and twisted violently backward. The back left bumper hit the dirt road, forcing the rest of the vehicle to flip around where the driver side windshield smashed and landed primarily on the driver's side. The wheels spun as the car slowly settled and rested on a strange angle. Sitting upside down, Anwick unbuckled her seatbelt and held up one hand to catch herself. Her weight was too much where she landed awkwardly on her shoulder. She looked towards Frederick and could see glass shards surrounding his body and blood on his face as he seemed unconscious. Trying to regain composure herself, she heard Bernstein from the back, lying on his side since he wasn't wearing his seatbelt. Most of the vehicle was crushed where Frederick was seated so Anwick kicked the remaining glass in her door and crawled out feet first. She was careful to watch out for the remaining glass. Once she got out she went to the backseat and was able to open the back seat from the passenger side. Bernstein looked up towards her while she pulled him out and he landed on his knees.

Bernstein caught his breath as he remained resting on his hands and knees on the ground, coughing and trying to bring his breathing back to normal to regain his focus. He rose his head and looked around and his sight was blurry. Anwick had rushed around to the driver's side and saw the door jammed and smashed where only half the window was accessible with no glass remaining. She knelt and bent down to look at Frederick who seemed unconscious or, even worse, dead. She reached her arm in and placed her hand on his neck and felt a slight pulse.

"Jerren!" Anwick yelled. Bernstein got up from his hands and brought up one knee. He placed his hands on his knee and stood up the rest of the way. He stumbled a step back before hitting the car and stabilizing himself. He turned to where he thought he heard Anwick yell and his eyesight came back to him. He rushed and saw her reaching into the car to get Frederick. He rushed over and knelt beside her. He looked down and saw Frederick, still bucked in the car seat with blood dripping from cuts on his head and face. With Frederick's eyes shut, Bernstein looked over to Anwick to see what to do next. "Hold him stable and I'll unbuckle his belt. Make sure he doesn't land on his head," she said while reaching into the car to find his seatbelt buckle. Bernstein reached in through the broken windshield and grabbed each of Frederick's shoulders so when Frederick would fall, he could pull him forward and instead of landing on his head, he would land on his shoulders and upper back. "On the count of three. One, two, three," Anwick shouted and a slight click was heard. Bernstein quickly pulled after the count of three and Frederick landed on his upper back.

Anwick moved away from the driver's side window to go over where Bernstein was and grabbed half of Frederick's upper body. Bernstein used both hands to grab the arm and shoulder of his other side.

"Pull," Bernstein said as they both pulled. Pulling Frederick slightly, as the top of his head reached out from the windshield. "Pull," he said again as they both exhaled strongly and pulled once again, The rest of Frederick's head came out from the windshield. "Pull," Bernstein said once again after they regained their composure quickly but Frederick didn't move. "He's stuck," he said to Anwick.

She bent inward and saw the plastic dashboard had collapsed and trapped Frederick's lower body. He tried her hardest to push up the large plastic piece but it didn't budge. At that time, Bernstein heard a vehicle coming from the direction behind them. He quickly looked and saw a green utility vehicle coming down from the road.

"Anwick, we need to run!" Bernstein said when he saw the German's coming towards them. The vehicle was down the road about a half-mile away. Anwick looked up and moved her heard from around the front of the car and saw the car in the distance as well.

"Frederick," Anwick said while leaning to the unconscious Frederick. "We'll be right back," she said before standing up. She and Bernstein began running up the road towards the main road about a tenth of a mile away. They would quickly glance behind them and saw the vehicle slowly coming up the road. They reached the road after running as fast as they could and ran towards a warehouse nearby and was directly across the street. The warehouse was the closest building in sight. They ran across the pavement and looked back while the Germans stopped at their flipped vehicle. They walked at a quick speed and hid behind a storage building to the side of the warehouse. They both peeked around and saw one German get out of the passenger seat first, and then another from the driver's. They couldn't see close enough which one each was but saw they both walked around the flipped vehicle. Suddenly, the two men stopped when one noticed Frederick's body slightly coming out of the front windshield. All of a sudden, as they continued watching from behind the small concrete storage building, they saw one guy bring something out his pocket and they could hear two gunshots. The man who shot Frederick stood while the other knelt to do something. After a few seconds he stood up, nodded and they went back to their car. As they got back to the car, the man who was driving stopped before getting back into the car. He turned and looked around the area before looking straight ahead at the warehouse. Seeing the man and thinking they were possibly noticed, Bernstein and Anwick moved their faces behind the building and turned to look somewhere to hide. They ran behind the large warehouse building and saw a metal ladder going up to the roof.

Bernstein put his hands on the ladder and tugged it to make sure it was sturdy. The ladder didn't budge so he began climbing up it. Finally, he reached the top of the two-story building and bringing his head up to see the roof, he saw there was nothing up there so he climbed the rest of the way and turned to look at Anwick. He motioned her by waving his hand for her to come up. She climbed up and getting to the top, she saw Bernstein on the opposite side, crouched and looking the direction of where their vehicle and Frederick was. Anwick made it to the top and rushed over the roof to look that direction also. They both silently crouched behind the rooftop, peeking over the top of a two-foot-high wall that surrounded the rooftop. They watched for nearly thirty seconds while both German's stood outside their utility vehicle and moved their heads, looking in all directions. A sense of relief was felt when they both got back into their vehicle and backed up to turn around.

CHAPTER 53

At the compound in the forest, Jefferson stood outside the front door with a radio and got the message from the German's that Frederick was killed. They made no mention of the others but as long as Frederick was dead, his revenge was complete. The man who killed his son was dead himself and he was thrilled.

While the German's drove back to the compound, waiting until their car was out of sight, Anwick and Bernstein stood up from the rooftop when they heard someone yell at them.

"Hola!" A man's voice came from below them. They were startled and weren't sure where to look. They looked back at the direction they had been facing and noticed down below them by the building was a man.

"Hola!" Bernstein yelled back. The unfamiliar man then yelled a few other words but they couldn't understand him as they didn't speak Spanish. They turned back around to go towards the ladder. Stepping down first, Bernstein placed his feet down on the pavement and turned to see the man. He was startled seeing the large man who had quietly approached the bottom of the ladder. The young man, likely in his mid-twenties and over six feet tall, had large muscles and was well built. He wore a regular baseball style hat that had one time been white but now a yellowish color due to sweat.

"Hola," Bernstein said seeing the young man. He wasn't sure what to do but did know the man wasn't German so he figured he likely worked there. At that time, Anwick had made it down and saw Bernstein and the man standing from one another. She walked towards them and wasn't sure what to do.

"Help, help," Anwick said and pointed down towards the storage shed and road they had originally come down. Knowing the German's were gone, they wanted to rush to see if Frederick was alright and what to do. The young man looked where Anwick was pointing but wasn't sure what she said.

Thinking back to what little Spanish he did know, Bernstein said, "Ayudar, ayudar. Help." The young man opened his mouth as a sign that he understood and nodded.

Anwick began running and passed the young man and began going back towards the road. She turned to the young man as she passed him and waved him to come with her. Bernstein followed immediately after. The three of them rushed quickly to the vehicle a little ways away and the young man could see the vehicle upside down and wanted to help. Anwick began running faster as they got closer and the other two followed and they quickly approached the vehicle. She reached down and saw even more blood had come down from Frederick's head but the bleeding had stopped. She reached down again and checked his pulse and held her hand still for a few seconds. She removed her hand and looked up towards Bernstein as she was crouched and shook her head side to side. Bernstein didn't know what to do or say and was shocked that he was dead. Anwick slowly stood up and took a couple of steps back. The young man looked down at the body and was aghast since he had never seen anyone around so much blood.

Anwick looked over towards Bernstein and then up to the young man next to him. "Nombre?" She asked him.

The young man took off his hat as a sign of respect as his long, neck length hair stayed in place as the sweat made his hair sticky. He looked towards Anwick and said, "Matias."

"Matias," Anwick said back and smiled partially and nodded. "Um," she then said and looked back towards Frederick. After a short bit of thinking, attempting to come up with an idea, Anwick had settled her thought. She looked back up at Matias and used her hands to make a motion as if she was digging. After making a few movements of her hands going up and down in a digging form, she pointed at Frederick's body and made the motion again. Matias understood and knew she meant to bury the body. Bernstein wasn't sure they had time to bury the body and knew they had to leave soon before the German's came back since he knew they were outnumbered. Anwick knelt down while Matias put his hat back on and knelt beside her. He looked into the front and saw the dashboard and was able to push it away. Anwick slightly began pulling Frederick out so Bernstein rushed behind Matias and reached in to grab the other side of Frederick's body. After his torso was almost out, Matias let go of the dashboard and helped pull him out. Anwick stood and turned and walked a short distance into the trees. Right off the road, she found a spot where there wasn't much overgrowth and would be easiest to dig a small hole.

"We need to hurry," Bernstein said towards Anwick as he walked behind her to the area she was standing.

"I know," she said but was interrupted by Bernstein.

"What if the German's come back? We're not ready and we're outnumbered."

She looked over to him and said in a deep voice, "I know." She then looked over to Matias standing by Frederick and pointed to Frederick's body and used both her hands and curl up her elbows to her biceps to indicate picking him up and carrying him over to where they were.

Anwick heard Bernstein sigh and turned back to him and said, "Start digging. The faster we dig, the faster we get out of here and plan our next step."

At that moment, Bernstein found a rock nearby and got on his hands and knees to begin digging. Anwick did the same thing and Matias had come over and gently placed Frederick's lifeless body down onto the ground. He got on his hands and knees also and with his dense hands, he began digging. After about a half an hour, the hold was big enough to cram Frederick's body into it.

"That's enough," Anwick said and stood up. Bernstein and Matias stopped digging and Anwick walked over towards Frederick. She grabbed each of his legs and Bernstein and Matias each grabbed a side of his upper torso and walked a few feet to the hold that was about four feet wide and a foot and a half deep. The whole wasn't anywhere near big enough but Anwick knew it would be enough. They placed him into the hole while one leg and arm remained outside of the grave and Anwick bent his body up so all his extremities were inside. They each took handfuls of dirt that had been piled up to throw overtop Frederick's body. As they piled the dirt on, taking longer than Bernstein would like, they kept grabbing surrounding dirt until just enough covered the body. Each of them were on different sides of the body and Anwick stood up and walked over to Bernstein once the body was covered. She leaned over to him as he remained on his knees and said, "Whatever happens, don't move." He looked down at her and wondered what she meant.

Suddenly, as Bernstein looked at her, he saw her shut her eyes and fall to her side. She fell onto the dirt and collapsed, landing on her hand to help the fall as she pretended to lie unconscious. Matias saw her fall and land on her side, with her head resting on its side in the dirt. He quickly stood and rushed over towards her, running over Frederick's body. As soon as he got to Anwick's body, he collapsed on his stomach and face. Hearing the commotion, Anwick sat up and looked towards Matias while Bernstein walked over.

"What happened?" Bernstein asked, wondering why Anwick fell and then Matias.

"Give it a minute," she said and remained kneeling beside Matias. Bernstein stood behind her, wiping his dirty hands on his pants and beginning to lick his lips since he was getting dehydrated. As he moistened his lips, Matias finally began to move. He rolled over to his side and both Anwick and Bernstein looked at his face. His eyes were shut but slowly opened, squinting once again once he saw the bright sunlight from above. After narrowing his eyes, he slowly began to open them again and looked up towards Anwick and then Bernstein standing behind her. He used one of his hands and arms to push up from the ground and remained sitting. He looked down at one hand and then the other. He looked at what part of the body he could see and noticed his muscular legs and big forearms resting on his legs.

"Frederick?" Anwick said while looking at Matias' face. Matias raised his face and eyes towards Anwick and smiled.

EPILOGUE

Preston sat up quickly after awakening abruptly. His sheets were scattered around the bed and were halfway covering his lower body. He removed the sheets off of his legs away from his sticky skin as he looked around his bedroom. The sun lit up a portion of the corner since he hadn't closed his curtains completely the night before. He looked around from the light to the remaining darkness within his room and gained his composure from the nightmare he just had. He reached over to the nightstand that was angled from the corner of his room and he grabbed his wristwatch. He picked it up and squinted, seeing the time was just past ten in the morning. It was a weekend and he had studied a little the night before for his upcoming finals and had stayed up late to do so. He set his watch back down and moved his legs over the side of the bed to stand up. He adjusted his baggy basketball style shorts and walked quickly out from his room to the small hallway that led past the bathroom to his kitchen. He went towards the wall by his cabinets where his telephone hung on the wall and immediately called Jackie.

The phone rang nearly five times when finally, Jackie answered. "Hello?" She answered, not knowing who was calling her.

"Jackie! It's Preston," Preston said with a disheveled and somewhat frantic voice.

"Preston, what's wrong?" Jackie worriedly asked after hearing the bit of excitement in his voice.

"Put your books down. We need to go to the old drive-in theater. Remember the one in DeLand? The one that burnt down?"

"Yes. But, why?" Jackie curiously asked.

"Be ready. I'll be there to pick you up in a half an hour. Something is wrong there."

ABOUT THE AUTHOR

Benjamin Mollenhour lives with his wife, Vy, in Washington State. He is the author of the horror novels *Carnival Ride* and *Murders of the Prophecy* as well as a western horror titled, *The Lure of the Traveling Man.* He has also published a memoir, *Letters from Fort Lyon Sanatorium, 1929-1930.* During free time, he likes to go hiking, camping, take road trips and learn history and visit historical areas. He has written and published numerous historical articles in publications such as the *Tombstone Epitaph.*